Becoming The Wealthy Woman

"An entertaining and painless way for women to learn about money management."

Monica Townson, economist and author, Chairperson of The Ontario Fair Tax Commission

"I read the book over the weekend and loved it! I plan to give it to my daughter. This book gives a straight forward account of RRSPs, mortgages, divorce settlements, life insurance and wills. There is also a little gem called 'Money Management Tips for Women' which is worth the price of the book. This is a great book—clear, interesting and timely!"

Judith A. Alexander, Copyright Board of Canada

"This is a good primer for women who know they must take charge of their own finances, but don't know where to start. Women can no longer afford to let someone else balance their cheque books."

Gillian Shaw, The Vancouver Sun

"Important, easy-to-read advice for any woman seeking financial self-reliance."

Gillian Steward, award-winning business writer

"A readable, commonsense guide for any woman seeking to improve her financial future—and who isn't?"

Catherine Swift, Canadian Federation of Independent Business

"Women who know little about the subject of financial planning will welcome the non-threatening language and relate to the personal experiences of the three main characters."

Shirley White, President, Canadian Federation of Business and Professional Women's Clubs

"Reading 'Becoming the Wealthy Woman' is like sitting down for a good heart-to-heart chat with your best friend. It's warm, it's personal and above all, it's helpful. In a very natural way, you learn how to make your money work for YOU—and by doing so, ensure a future that is both comfortable and secure."

Elaine McCoy, QC, former Alberta Minister of Labour, responsible for Women's Issues

le, self-employed professional accountant, has some
inions on the role of women in contemporary society—
 common sense advice for her clients. When she makes
w friends following her psychologist's funeral, it's not
ore these women, too, are turning to her for financial
ling and support. Francie, less well-known as Frances
Systems Analyst, is a victim of insecurity and a smoker
even worse addiction to credit cards. Marlene Henderson,
and the comfortably-placed wife of a banker, leaves the
ement of financial matters to her husband. Though she
ses not to be concerned over her lack of independence,
comes aware of her vulnerability when her husband asks
for a divorce. Angela Larocca ("Please call me Angie") is a weary
wife and mother, trying to balance an advertising career with a
traditional Italian home life.

Mary decides to compile her advice to these women and
their families in the form of a book, as a present to her daughter
on her twenty-first birthday. For her, as for any mother, it's the
ideal gift; all the hard-won expertise of her lifetime passed on
for her child's benefit.

With this act, our fictional author mirrors the intention of
real-life co-authors Susan Blanchard and Henry Cimmer, who
have used the experiences of Mary and her companion characters
to pass on a wealth of experience to those seeking personal and
financial independence.

Becoming The Wealthy Woman explores the options open to
women of almost every age and financial circumstance and
challenges them to realize their true potential.

Becoming THE WEALTHY WOMAN

A STORY OF FINANCIAL PLANNING
FOR WOMEN OF ALL AGES

HENRY B. CIMMER
WITH SUSAN F. BLANCHARD

SPRINGBANK PUBLISHING

Published in 1994 by
Springbank Publishing
5425 Elbow Drive SW
Calgary, Alberta
T2V 1H7

First printing June 1994

Canadian Cataloguing in Publication Data
Cimmer, Henry B., 1943-
Becoming the wealthy woman

ISBN 1-895653-11-8

1. Finance, Personal–Fiction.   I. Blanchard, Susan F.,
1951-   II. Title.
PS8555.145B4 1994   C813'.54   C94-910500-7
PR9199.3C55B4 1994

Design: Catherine Garden Design
Production: DaSilva Graphics Ltd.

Printed and bound in Canada

Acknowledgements

In creating a book intended to help women achieve financial security, we quickly discovered the special obstacles faced by single women, working wives, stay-at-home mothers, divorced women, single parents, and women returning to the workforce. It became clear that, in addressing a group of such varied personal and financial circumstances, there could be no single, pat formula for success. It made sense then, that we research the experiences of a number of women and adapt proven wealth-building techniques to reflect their individual ideas and concerns.

The book began as a series of conversations with a variety of women and women's organizations, most of whom continued to provide advice and consultation as the work progressed. Particular acknowledgement is made to those who read drafts of the book and improved them with their personal observations, especially Kathy Arkell, Janice Beaton, Kathy Blood, Janet Eby, Melanie Guenther, Cathy MacLeod, Myra Ripley, Helene Hladun, Pat Trottier, Tammy Herringshaw, Doris Herringshaw, and Patti Newton.

Many others provided valuable help by reading and commenting on parts of our drafts, providing examples from their own professions and generously sharing their thoughts. We gratefully acknowledge the assistance of Maureen McVey with Financial Concept Group, Dell Stephens, Gail Kingwell, Donna Shea, Trina Marriott-Vandermeer and Faye Huggins—the last two representing the Women in Business Network Directory and the Women's Financial Planning Centre respectively. Although space demands that we list them together, each person's contribution is individually appreciated.

Particular thanks are extended to designer Catherine Garden for her obvious design skills, to graphic artist Jill DaSilva, to keyboard specialist Brenda Bodmann, to photographer Rick Boden, to copy editor Linda Jarrett, and to the multi-talented John Newton for promotional writing.

CONTENTS

BECOMING
THE WEALTHY
WOMAN

A STORY OF FINANCIAL PLANNING
FOR WOMEN OF ALL AGES

CHAPTER ONE
WOMEN: THE WORLD'S
MOST WASTED ASSET

WHERE DO I BEGIN? My name is Mary Poole, I'm forty-four years old and I'm a chartered accountant. Doesn't *that* make you want to go on reading? Here we are, with the 21st century just around the corner and accountants are still stereotyped as boring, uncommunicative people. Remember T.V.'s L.A. Law series? Somehow Hollywood just never got around to Kansas City Accountant, or even the Canadian version, Accountants From Athabasca.

Maybe some accountants' images do lack a bit of "excitement" but my background has helped me avoid the "staid" accountant stereotype.

I grew up in Montreal in the '60s and '70s. I was a pretty good student, though I didn't excel in any particular subject area. Like so many of my female peers, I thought I might be interested in a teaching career and I went to McGill University, where I majored in English. I did well, but by the time I was in my last year I was frustrated with the overly-analytical way in which the academics dissected literature. After all, does it *really* matter why old Will Shakespeare used the word 'the' in a particular context? Either you enjoy his work or you don't.

In the spring of my final year, I received a form letter from the Institute of Chartered Accountants of Quebec. They had decided that the accounting profession needed to entice graduates from faculties other than business into their program. I didn't know it at the time, but they were really looking for engineers! They were offering a special three year crash course after which time the student would be allowed to write the qualifying examination. It sounded interesting and besides, I needed a summer job. I had the option to return to McGill in the fall to pursue a Master's degree in English, but I really wasn't particularly enthusiastic.

Around the same time, I met Jack. Handsome, charming Jack—the life of the party, the perfect counter-foil to my own more retiring and subdued persona. Jack was an engineer, but he was far removed from the bookish slide-rule and pocket protector kind of guy. He worked in the Alberta oil fields and spent weeks at a time in relative isolation (as I later found out) with nothing more than a case or nine of beer and a few decks of cards to keep him and his cronies amused. Of course, he had a lot of time off, and I met him while he was in Montreal visiting his family. We met at a bar where my friends had dragged me to celebrate my "coming of age"...and there was Jack!

The rest, as they say, is history. I took a job at an accounting firm, entered the CA program and rented the upper half of a down-town duplex with a friend. Jack stayed with me whenever he was in town. I took to number-crunching faster than anyone expected, although my prowess in adding columns (those were the pre-computer pre-calculator days) didn't endear me to my male co-slaves at the firm.

I didn't care though; I had Jack. His visits were a welcome interlude from the grind of working all day in stuffy offices while at the same time attending school three nights a week for the required courses. With assignments, exams, and some overtime, especially during the tax season, I didn't have a lot of free time.

At the beginning, it seemed perfectly acceptable to hit the bars three or four nights in a row when Jack was in town, knowing that when he left, I could quickly revert back to my somewhat straight-laced existence.

I became quite a master at nursing one or two drinks for an entire evening, and I remember all too clearly the many mornings when I kissed Jack's sleeping brow and trundled off to work.

He was a charmer, Jack was. I suppose I was too young and naive at the time to know that something was seriously wrong.

2

Jack probably earned four or five times my meager salary in those days and yet that didn't stop him from asking me for money from time to time. "Just a small loan till payday. Come on, Babe, it's no big deal."

I didn't know back then that when a woman makes a loan to a loved one, or for that matter, to virtually any friend or relative, the word loan is spelled g-i-f-t!

The summer after I finished my second year in the accounting program, we got married, and actually spent three whole weeks together in Florida. Florida in the summertime...thank God for air conditioning!

I had BIG plans back then. I was going to *change* Jack. I knew he had talent, and I pictured him dressed in a tailored suit holding down a high-powered executive position in the oil company where he worked. How was I supposed to know that *you don't marry someone expecting to change them?* After the honeymoon, I went back to work and Jack returned to the Wilds of Alberta.

Our separation was only supposed to last for a year or so. By then, I'd have my C.A. and I agreed that I'd move to Alberta.

The next year wasn't much different from the days when we were "stepping out", as my grandmother would have said. Jack visited infrequently. When he did, we spent a lot of time cruising up and down Crescent Street and Jack managed to relieve me of my meager savings with alarming regularity. It finally dawned on me that we were in trouble about eighteen months into the marriage when he phoned from Calgary and said he had decided to spend his leave there with a couple of his buddies, instead of coming home to be with me. "I'm beat, Babe," he said. "And I just didn't feel like getting on a plane. Besides, I figured out a way to get the company to give me the airfare anyway and I'll send it to you, so you can buy something nice." Needless to say, the cheque never came. So, I flew out to rendevous with him in Calgary for a month.

Then I made the big mistake. (In retrospect, it was the best thing I ever did, but I sure didn't know it until a few years later.) I thought if we had a baby, Jack would settle down and become the responsible man I always *knew* he could be. It took a bit of convincing before he agreed. I suppose he'd gone along with it more out of a sense of guilt than from any form of commitment. I told him that I'd only stay home for a year or two and then go back to work.

"On our combined incomes, we'll be able to afford to buy a house, and hire a live-in nanny. Besides," I said, "once you're a father you're bound to get a promotion to head office. I'm sure your talents can better serve the company here than some remote place in Northern Alberta."

Whatever the motivation, Jack finally shrugged his shoulders, we stayed in that night, and, nine months later, along came Jennifer. Sweet, wonderful Jennifer (although I didn't always think so). That was almost twenty-one years ago!

Jack saw his daughter exactly once. He didn't quite make it back to Montreal for the "unveiling" as it were, but he did manage to shuffle about for a week or so after we came home from the hospital. He seemed so uncomfortable around us, it was almost a relief the two or three nights that he asked for "permission" to go out for a few beers with the boys.

Two months later, it was over. Jack called, this time from Edmonton, to say he wasn't coming home. I vaguely remember some enthusiastic babbling about an Edmonton Oiler home-stand, and the chance of a lifetime to see young Wayne Gretzky play hockey two or three times that week. That was it. I filed for divorce and became another statistic—a single parent receiving no support from a former spouse.

Fortunately, my Mom and Dad were supportive (I didn't say support*ing*). I moved into an apartment a few blocks away from my parents' modest home, and Mom agreed to look after Jennifer while I was at work. I stayed with the accounting firm where I had apprenticed for two more years before striking out on my own. (For the record, I passed the finals on my first attempt.) By that time, there was almost an equal number of men and women entering the profession as articling students. But by the time we would have risen to the manager level, four or five years after graduation, the number of women to men was only one in ten, and at the partner level, *there were no women at all*. The prevailing

4

attitude was, "Yes, you can have maternity leave," (how generous!) "but we're not going to let you work on this challenging client because it involves travel" (i.e., we don't want a problem when the V.P.-Finance makes a pass at you). After all, it was still the '70s.

Besides, to make manager or partner, you also had to develop your own client list, and a woman wasn't seen as being able to develop a client portfolio as readily as her male counterparts. Female accountants weren't encouraged to socialize, attend luncheon meetings, or do any other kind of client-producing networking. It wasn't that there was a gap in knowledge or skill. Quite the contrary, when it came to exams, the women quite handily out-performed the men, and we rarely made careless mistakes in putting our files together. But the 'Old Boys' Network' was alive and well, and I, for one, didn't see much point in trying to buck the system.

So, as I said, I struck out on my own. I suppose, in my own small way, I was a visionary in two respects. First, I could see that, with the advent of the computer age, a self-employed professional accountant could do quite well preparing financial statements for small and medium-sized businesses. (The computer takes away the drudgery of crunching numbers and eliminates a great deal of human error. With the computer, accountants are rarely out of balance!) The second trend I was able to foresee was the growth in the number of independent businesses owned by women and I figured I could get my share of clients. I recently read that, in 1973, women only owned 5 per cent of businesses in the United States. By 1992, the percentage was 41 per cent and now, as we approach the year 2000, *a full 50 per cent* of businesses are owned by women. I don't think the Canadian statistics are all that different. I suppose that's not surprising, because business ownership offers many advantages compared with being an employee. For me, one of the major benefits was the opportunity to spend more time with Jenny as she was growing up.

There is one issue I did confront from the very beginning. When I was setting up my practice, I counted on getting new clients from the growing number of women-owned businesses. But this did not work out as smoothly as I expected. It's been

5

my experience that there seem to be two kinds of women in the business world. Towards one end is a group which *embraces* the idea of women networking with and supporting other women. In an extreme case, the credo of "it's us against them" is the rallying cry. Towards the other end, there are many women who are dead set against women's business groups, or the concept of relying almost solely on other women to provide most of their physical, mental and financial needs (i.e., making sure you only deal with a female physician, lawyer, accountant, stockbroker, etc.). This group argues against compartmentalizing people by gender.

In my view, there is really no right or wrong approach and I hope I'll be able to convince you of that as you read through this book.

The trend in our society is moving towards an 'amalgamation' of the sexes—if I can borrow an accounting term—in schools, the workplace, and, for that matter, in the home. In classrooms across Canada, teachers have moved away from referring to "boys and girls" and are even required by edict to address their charges as "students". So, in many respects I think it's counter-productive to take the "us against them" approach.

On the other hand, as any professional will probably tell you, when you come to pick someone to be your accountant, lawyer, doctor, stockbroker, or even your family butcher, you should choose someone to whom you can easily relate. To function, you need a sense of trust and a good rapport. The fact is, women often relate better to other women than they do to men. In the financial field, I've found that women can be less hesitant to ask questions of other women than they are of men. Men and women really do seem to have different methods of communicating. There is a growing number of books and courses that try to teach men how to communicate effectively with women and vice-versa. (I'm not aware of *anyone* who tries to teach *men* how to communicate with *men* and *women* with *women*. That just seems to happen naturally.)

So, when I decided to strike out on my own, my expectation was for my clientele to be predominantly female. As of today, about 70 per cent of my clients are women. That isn't to say that I don't enjoy the other 30 per cent just as much—or even more. It's been my experience that when men and women *are* able to communicate with each other effectively, 'tis a wondrous thing! (Although a Good Man, like in 'permanent relationship', is *still* hard to find).

My practice grew and prospered through the '80s. I blissfully ignored all the threats of Quebec's possible separation and, as Tom Peters put it in his book, *In Search of Excellence,* I "stuck to the knitting". I was busier than the proverbial one-armed paper hanger. I had my daughter and my clients to keep me going. I took several conversational French courses, and, by the middle of the decade, had become sufficiently interested in financial planning as an adjunct to my practice that I enrolled in the Chartered Financial Planners' program. I received my CFP designation in 1988 (with honours, I might add). Although I'm sure I don't possess nearly as many live brain cells today as I did when I was an undergraduate, or even during the years I spent in the CA program, I think I'm a better communicator *now* than I was then. I seem to be able to better pinpoint the questions that are likely to appear on an exam paper. I'm better prepared and with age have gained more confidence (not that I want to make a *career* out of taking exams).

Ironically, my somewhat eclectic background as an English major with CA and CFP designations has served me well. I'm that rare breed of accountant who can communicate with pen or voice as the medium. And that's why I'm sitting here, dictaphone in hand, telling you my story.

As you'll learn shortly, this book is not only about me; it's also about Marlene, Angela, Francie, and yes, my dear Jennifer too. It's about what I taught *them* and what they taught *me*. It's also about what I hope *you* can learn from all of *us*. The underlying theme is effective financial planning. *It's no sin to be rich and it's no crime to plan for your own financial security.*

If you're reading this book, you probably already know some of the grim details:

- Over 50 per cent of marriages end in divorce;

- A full 25 per cent of working women can expect to be poor in their old age; and
- Only 10 per cent of working women will receive pensions from their employment.

In addition, 65 per cent of people who now live below the poverty line in their twilight years are women.

There are almost *two million* adult women in Canada who are separated, divorced or widowed compared to only 800,000 men, and yet, because women tend to outlive men, most of the money (including stocks in publicly traded companies) winds up with women.

But I'm not trying to scare you. *The 21st century is ours for the asking.* Do you remember that old Virginia Slims cigarette commercial, "You've Come a Long Way Baby"? Perhaps the up-to-date caption (if cigarette smoking were still in vogue) should be "You Ain't Seen Nothin' Yet".

A few years ago, Patricia Aburdene and John Naisbitt wrote a book called *Megatrends for Women*. They refer to the concept of 'The Wisewoman'. The Wisewoman is traditionally represented as a crone or witch associated with knowledge of herbs and health. She is depicted as being past the child-bearing years and possesses the experience and spiritual depth younger women lack. Aburdene and Naisbitt state,

> "The leadership to which women now aspire—in politics, the arts, business—*requires* the age, experience and maturity of the Wisewoman."

Their thesis is that the new generation of baby-boom women will revitalize the image of the Wisewoman. She will initiate revolutionary change, according to the authors.

> "Women—whose ex-husbands put them down for incompetence—run multi-million-dollar businesses. Better health care and physical fitness will also help women over 45

enjoy 25 more years of business and political leadership, grandparenthood, travel, (second and third) careers and meaningful contributions to society. A new generation of active women will be freer than ever to heartily embrace their middle and later years...Busy with career and community, less fearful of menopause, women will embrace the stage beyond motherhood with great enthusiasm. Out of the empty nest, where women of earlier generations clung to an old, familiar role, an exuberant young crone will fly, eager for the next adventurous stage of life." (And, catch this) "The status of the Wisewoman can come only through validating one's self and/*or from other women.*"

So, in my own small way, I'd like to try to make a contribution (although I'd prefer it if you didn't picture me as an "exuberant young crone"). I've always wanted to write a book. Haven't you? I'm sure everyone says at one time or another, "I'd love to write a book." Almost everybody, no matter what their walk in life, has *something* to share, but very few actually do. (Remember the old Nike commercial, "Just Do It"?)

Someone once asked the prolific horror story writer Stephen King how *he* wrote his horror books. His response was, "One page at a time."

So, here's *my* book. I present it to you, one page at a time! In April 1992, the United Nations Population Fund annual report stated that "women are the world's wasted asset". That's a pretty strong statement, but maybe it will help remind us that *conservation begins at home.* Only *YOU* can prevent...

CHAPTER TWO

BREAKING THROUGH THE GLASS CEILING

I GUESS I NEVER TOLD YOU WHY I'M WRITING THIS BOOK *NOW*, not last year or next. Well, it's going to be Jennifer's 21st birthday gift. You see, over the last five years or so my friends and I have learned so much from each other, that if I can only get my recollections down accurately, I'm sure Jennifer will get a lot out of it. Much of what this book is going to be about revolves around money, because, if truth be told, it *is* hard to enjoy life if one doesn't have enough money to get by—comfortably— now and in the future. No one should live in fear of a poverty-stricken old age.

But it's about much more than money. This book is also about relationships, prevailing business and economic conditions, and yes, it's even a 'wish list' for changes. So, I'm dedicating this to Jennifer—may she never have to re-invent the wheel. (I guess most authors write their dedications before they even start, and here we are already in Chapter Two, but after all, what difference does it really make?)

So, where shall I begin? Most of the seeds for this book were sown a little more than five years ago. While my career had been progressing quite smoothly and Jennifer, at that time age 16, was doing well in school and giving me far less grief than most of her peers were giving their parents, there was still a void in my life. From the time of my divorce, I had never been able to sustain anything remotely approaching a long-term relationship.

For the first couple of years, I rarely went out at all, telling myself I had too much responsibility towards Jenny to run the risk of matching up with someone unsuitable. And then, as time went on, it seemed all the eligible men were either married or involved, and those who weren't didn't seem to know anything about having a meaningful relationship (sounds trite, doesn't it?). Many men didn't (and still don't) understand that times change. I read in a book once something about the "archaic model", where men plowed the Back 40, hunted and tended to the livestock, while their women were expected to cook, clean and raise the kids. Today the lawn needs mowing only once a week and the oil has to be checked every 3,000 kilometers while women are still expected to cook, clean and raise the kids! To say the least, I wasn't comfortable with the traditional male viewpoint. Between Jenny and my practice, I had enough to worry about without trying to run someone else's household. But, at the same time, I missed the companionship, intimacy, and good conversation that a few (*very* few) of my friends enjoyed with *their* mates.

Eventually, I decided to seek counselling. Initially, I had my mind set on finding a woman psychologist to whom I could relate. I spoke to my family doctor and, surprisingly, she suggested that I might want to talk to a *male!* "After all, Mary," she said, "if you're having trouble meeting the 'right person' of the opposite sex, maybe if you talked with someone who shares that gender, you might gain a few insights!"

I had to admit that what Cynthia told me made sense, and I asked her for a recommendation. She suggested Dr. Michael Frost, and that afternoon I made my first appointment.

We enjoyed a great rapport from day one because Dr. Frost seemed to grasp immediately what the problem was. Instead of belittling me, he surprised the heck out of me by candidly conceding that I was perfectly right in virtually everything I said. In fact, he even backed up some of my *own* views with statistics to support them. For example, he told me that in 72 per cent of families where both partners work full-time and raise children, the wives take the primary responsibility for cooking. Moreover, only 31 per cent of husbands help clean up. An astonishing 79 per cent of women clean house and do laundry, although that same percentage of husbands do most of the repairs and the occasional yard work (Yippee!)

Dr. Frost told me how men, as mates, can be divided into three groups: traditional, transitional, and non-traditional. In one sense, I suppose I was born too soon. There are still not a whole lot of non-traditional men out there who are willing to take a 50/50 role in *all* the work involved in just day-to-day living. On the other hand, I suppose I should be glad I wasn't born a hundred years (or even 30 or 40 years) earlier! I have a friend, Susan, whose mother used to work as a secretary for the railway. Susan's Mom once told me she had to keep her marriage secret for two years because the company's policy at that time in the early 1950s did not allow for married female employees.

Dr. Frost explained how my financial success as a professional accountant probably impeded the establishment of a long-term relationship. "It's the subconscious power struggle that revolves around money," he said. And it makes sense. A number of the men I dated over the years had great difficulty with the fact that I actually earned more money than they did, and in other cases, even if their earnings exceeded mine, I had a larger net worth.

Unfortunately, though, while Dr. Frost increased my awareness, I didn't come any closer towards solving the problem which was (is) to find the right guy! But at $80 an hour, he was also pretty good at counselling "patience".

Then, one day, about six months after my bi-weekly sessions had begun, I received a phone call at the office from Margie, Dr. Frost's secretary, who told me, between sobs, that he had passed away suddenly the night before. I was in total shock. I had never asked him his age, but I assumed he was in his late 40s. (When I read his obituary the next day it mentioned he was actually 52.) It was a brain embolism—sudden, swift, unpredictable and deadly. I must admit, I shed a few tears as well, and the rest of the day I got absolutely nothing done. The notice in The Gazette didn't say anything about a private funeral and I decided to take a couple of hours off to pay my respects. (To be honest, I was pleased Dr. Frost had chosen cremation because I felt it would be hard enough for me to attend the service without also having to make the trek up Mount Royal to the cemetery.)

I was a bit surprised to find the funeral was not well attended. I later found out Dr. Frost was an only child whose parents had both predeceased him. It seems he had been married once but had no children. There were a number of people, though, whom I easily identified as friends and professional associates and there was one other group of three women standing close to each other eyeing one another furtively without speaking. "They must have been patients like myself," I thought as I approached them. Just then, the hushed conversation was abruptly stilled by the sound of somber music and everybody rushed to seat themselves in the closest available pews. Somehow, the three women and I found ourselves sitting side by side, and we smiled tentatively at each other between sniffles.

I don't remember much of the service or the eulogy that followed, but I have a clear recollection of walking outside into the cold, crisp February sunlight, taking a deep breath and telling myself it was good to be alive. I looked around and saw my three companions standing around uncomfortably in silence. It was clear that each one was hesitant to make the first move.

"Excuse me," I said turning to them, "if you've got a few minutes, there's a very nice tea house in the little shopping centre across the street..." I pointed in the vague direction of the small strip mall on the other side on the road. "It's about lunchtime," I continued, "and you're all welcome to join me. Maybe a little companionship would help..."

One of the three, a petite oriental woman in a black tailored suit covered somewhat incongruously by an open mauve ski jacket, stuck out her hand and said, "I think that's a great idea. My name is Francie Chow."

I have to confess I was a bit taken aback. With all the immigration into Canada at that time, I fully expected her to speak, at best, in a heavily accented English. However, her command of the language was every bit as good as my own. I later found out she was third generation Chinese-Canadian, and worked as a systems analyst with Quebec Power. Not only was her English faultless, but I soon discovered she was also fluently bilingual. (In Quebec, this means she also spoke French!)

I introduced myself to Francie and we brought the other two women into our group. The first was a tired-looking woman who appeared to be in her mid-40s. (I later found out she was only 39.) I could see she had once been very attractive, but had obviously put on a few pounds over the years and didn't take nearly enough time with her hair and makeup. She had an olive complexion and her hair, although untidy, was a rich black—clearly her best feature. I guessed she was either of Jewish or Italian extraction, and when she identified herself as Angela Larocca ("Please call me Angie"), I momentarily congratulated myself on my intuition.

The final member of our little group huddled together on the stairs of the funeral parlour that morning was Marlene Henderson, an elegant woman, perhaps in her early 50s with stylishly coiffed, greying hair, and a face suspiciously devoid of wrinkles. I could see that both Marlene and Angie wore wedding bands, although Marlene was the only one among us who was wearing any other jewellery. I looked surreptitiously at her left hand and saw she was wearing an exquisite emerald and diamond ring. Her diamond stud earrings must have been just under a carat each. Her appearance was certainly tasteful, and I assumed there was no shortage of money in her household.

Our little convoy made its way across the street and we entered the restaurant.

"Smoking or non-smoking?" asked the hostess. I looked around with an inquisitive air.

"Non-smoking," said Marlene and Angie simultaneously. I nodded my head affirmatively and turned to Francie.

"Non-smoking will be okay with me," she said. "I've got to get used to being the only smoker." She laughed self-consciously.

We were led to our table, hung up our coats, and sat down to eat. Conversation lagged as we perused our menus. I guess we all suddenly realized we had just met for the first time and not under the most pleasant of circumstances. After bringing us some water and taking our orders, our waiter disappeared, nevermore to return.

15

After a few moments, Angie looked around impatiently and started drumming her fingers on the table.

"I wish he'd hurry up," she said. "I've got to go back to work. When the *guys* take an afternoon off to play golf, it's okay. But if *I'm* an hour late because of a funeral..."

Francie nodded emphatically. "Yes, it's that old double-standard."

"Most of the time," Angie continued, "my boss is reasonably understanding, but he automatically assumes that, because I'm married, I'm just *choosing* to work, while he *has* to work. I can't get him to understand that women work for the same reasons as men. In my family, we need the two incomes, and besides, I enjoy working. Staying home and looking after my daughter was okay for a while when she was little, but dammit, I've got a brain. I also want to use it in a career."

"What do you do, Angie?" asked Marlene.

"I work for an advertising agency. My department does print media. We do layouts for newspaper and magazine advertisements."

"Do you write slogans too?" I asked.

"That's part of it," nodded Angie, "but, unfortunately, most of what I do is technical. You see, all too often the client wants to say too much and space is limited. My job is to try and fit it all in. I'd love to do more creative work," she continued, "but it's difficult. I mean, balancing my family with my work. I'm lucky if I can get by on a 14 hour day. I'm Italian and so is my husband Joey. He expects dinner on the table by the time he gets home.

"And then there's my daughter Marcie. I mean, last week her gym teacher called me at work to say Marcie couldn't find one of her runners. What did he expect me to do? Come down to the school and root through her locker? *I'm* the one who always gets hell if she doesn't do her homework." She shook her head. "I'm always tired..."

"I know how you feel," said Francie, "and I don't even have kids to support. I'm a systems analyst with Quebec Power, and because I'm single they seem to expect me to work 60 hours a week. Frankly, I know I could be a much better administrator than my boss and have more technical knowledge, but promotions are hard to come by. I think I'm probably paid about $2,000 a year less than any of my male co-workers."

"Welcome to the planet with the 'glass ceiling'," I interjected sarcastically.

"Glass ceiling?" asked Marlene. "That must be a business term I'm not familiar with. But, then again, I guess I'm lucky. I *don't* choose to work. My husband..."

"The glass ceiling," I interjected before Marlene got herself in any deeper, "is a term that reflects how difficult it is for women to get ahead in the traditionally male-dominated business world. A woman can *see* her way up to the top of the corporate ladder, but once she gets part way up she runs into this invisible barrier that she can't penetrate. The goals and rewards are there...they're so tantalizingly close and yet she can't break through."

"You sound like you've had some experience with this glass ceiling," said Angie.

I shrugged my shoulders. "Actually, I'm a chartered accountant," I said. "Like most bean-counters, I started out with a large accounting firm. But I learned pretty quickly there was no way I would ever make partner, especially with my responsibilities for Jennifer—she's my daughter—I've been a single mom since she was six months old."

"So what did you do, Mary?" asked Marlene.

"I went out on my own," I replied. "I suppose, it's the best thing I ever did. I don't have to worry about pay equity, the old boys' network and playing the game. I put in many a 14 hour day, but at least if I want to take some time off, I don't have anybody to answer to. If Jenny is sick, for example, I don't have to feel guilty about taking an afternoon off to be with her. Besides, today, with computers I can do a lot at home.

"More recently, I invested some time in becoming a Chartered Financial Planner. I expanded my practice and now I even do some public speaking and seminars."

"Why do you think it's so difficult to get respect in a male-dominated world?" asked Francie. "I used to think it was because I'm Chinese. Often, when I meet Caucasians for the first time,

17

and they start to talk to me, they speak so slowly and distinctly...
loud too...figuring I have trouble understanding the language.
But I'm actually third generation Canadian. They seem surprised
when *my* command of the language is as good as theirs, if not
better. And yet, I don't think it's only because I'm Chinese. It
seems that women in general get a raw deal all around."

I felt a twinge of guilt as I realized that *my* first presumption
had been that Francie was a recent immigrant and that her English
would be heavily accented. Lesson learned! I wondered how these
stereotypical assumptions affected Francie and others in their
day-to-day business and personal lives. Food for thought.

"You're right," I said. "It all starts when we're little. You're
a systems analyst. That means you must be good in math. Weren't
you made to feel uncomfortable back in high school?"

"You're not kidding," Francie replied with a chuckle. "There
were only four of us girls in my Grade 12 advanced math class.
I remember, back in Grade 10, I had a friend Heather, who was
really attractive, and she was bright, too. In fact, we used to study
math together and she grasped the concepts a lot faster than I
did. But the guys started to make fun of her. I guess they didn't
make fun of me because lots of people think *all* Chinese are
instant mathematicial genuises! You should meet my brother—
he's a wonderful artist—but adding and subtracting, forget it!
Anyway, instead of being one of the most popular girls in the
class, Heather started to find herself staying at home Saturday
nights. Would you believe she dropped math in Grade 11 and
switched into home economics? All of a sudden her social life
picked up, but it was such a tragedy. She sold herself down the
river just for popularity."

"I read a book recently called *Hardball For Women,* by a
psychologist named Pat Heim," I said. "It's subtitled *Winning at
the Game of Business.* Dr. Heim says that women's problems in the
workforce stem from their very early years. She talks about how
children's books depict girls as 'homemakers, witches, dancers,
singers, musicians, queens and fairies'. That doesn't exactly reflect
career opportunities in *our* neighbourhoods, does it?"

A wave of laughter echoed around the table.

"When kids are little," I continued, "girls are carried by their fathers while boys are told to walk. The boys get more criticism in school, and they learn to cope with it better, while *we* learn to become more *agreeable*. Business is carried on in accordance with the rules of sports. Look at all the terminology. You've got to 'carry the ball', I can't 'get to first base' with that client and so on. Even the language of the stock market...Do you think it was a woman who invented the terms 'bull and bear markets'?"

I was rewarded with a chuckle.

"Most girls play with dolls when they're little," I went on. "They play house. And that's not exactly a competitive sport, is it? Girls learn to compromise. For example, if Marlene over here wants to play house and I want to play doctor, we'd probably agree that she'd be the mom, her doll would become the sick baby, and she'd bring her doll to me to make it better. Women learn to be fragile, compliant and co-operative, while boys learn to be active, assertive and unemotional. You don't have to *win* at house, dolls or doctor."

"So, what do women like myself and Francie have to do to get ahead?" asked Angie.

"Well," I continued, "if you want to follow the suggestions made by Dr. Heim, you can learn to adapt. You learn *not* to accommodate, and you try *not* to compromise. You don't run away from conflict. Do you ever notice how difficult it is to do something when you're ordered to by your boss, especially when you're not given a reason why?" Angie and Francie nodded. "Do you find when you tend to question your boss he gets angry?"

"I didn't know you worked for Quebec Power," said Francie ruefully.

"Or the Matheson Agency," added Angie.

"Again, according to Dr. Heim, it all stems from sports. When boys play organized sports, they learn to do what the coach says. If they argue, they sit on the bench. They also learn that it's winning that matters. How many times have you heard of that American football coach—Lombardi something-or-other,—who said 'Winning isn't everything, it's the only thing'? Or that baseball manager, Leo Dupont."

"It was actually Durocher," Marlene interjected. "My brother was a big baseball fan."

"Whatever," I continued, "he's the guy who said 'nice guys finish last'."

"This is really interesting," said Francie. "Maybe I just don't understand how the game is played."

"It sure *is* a game," I echoed. "Here's another point you may never have considered. Did you ever notice when two guys get into an argument at the office, they can yell and scream at each other, but at the end of the day they go off together for a few beers? It's because they learn at a very young age that *when the game is over, it's over.* There are no hard feelings."

"You're right," said Angie. "The rare time I have a disagreement with a female co-worker, we avoid each other for days. I guess that's counterproductive."

"But is it really worth it?" asked Francie.

"Good question," I answered. "Dr. Heim's book was really interesting. Her thesis is *you can't* **become** *one of the guys, but you can learn to* **understand** *them.* You can also take advantage of the fact that women have better communication skills to achieve more success in the corporate world."

"But can we break the glass ceiling?" asked Angie.

"That's another good question. One interesting statistic Dr. Heim points out is that only 30 per cent of top male executives acknowledge having had a mentor on their way up, while 100 per cent of top executive women can refer to at least one or two people, generally males, who have helped them in their ascent."

"But, Mary, is it all worthwhile?" asked Francie in exasperation.

"I suppose that's up to you. Times are changing. The school system is waking up, albeit slowly, to the idea that women need the same training as men and shouldn't be shunted off into the traditional female careers of teaching, nursing and so on. Believe it or not, and this might surprise you, I think *the educational system would be a lot better off if girls and boys were taught in separate classes.*"

I could see the shocked looks around the table. "I don't

mean the schools need to be segregated, or that boys and girls shouldn't be taught relationship skills, but I think if *certain* classes were segregated, girls could be encouraged to live up to their potential in maths, sciences, computer technology and so on without fearing that the boys will consider them less feminine."

"You've got a point there," said Francie. "I remember my friend Heather..."

"That's right. There was no reason for her to give up mathematics in favour of home economics."

"I guess your idea isn't as backward as I first thought," said Angie. "I was thinking of the traditional convent schools. I actually went to one until Grade 9 and boy, was I ever socially inept when I got into high school!"

"I find this all very interesting," interjected Marlene, "even though I'm not in the same position as you all seem to be. I guess I'm lucky. I don't choose to work nor do I have to. My husband believes in handling all of our financial affairs. In fact," she added, as she shrugged her shoulders, "I guess my husband is one of the 'good old boys' you referred to. He'd probably sooner kill himself than report to a female boss. In fact, in his company, he once told me there's a quota for women junior executives. A couple of years ago, he got a confidential directive from the president stating that, by the year 2000, 15 per cent of those people earning $60,000 or more would have to be women. In my husband's group that would represent only three out of the 20 top people."

"How old is your husband?" I asked.

"He's 52," answered Marlene. "Why?"

"Well, that's exactly my point. You see," I said, turning to Angie and Francie, "one choice that women have is to simply *wait until the old boys retire.* Over the next 20 years, they'll all be gone! The *new* male executives coming up the ranks are being conditioned to be far more understanding and accepting of women as their equals."

"But I don't have 20 years," wailed Angie.

"Nor I," added Francie.

"I'm afraid you've got a point," I said. "You know, this whole issue of women's equality in the workforce reminds me of free trade."

"Free trade?" Angie and Francie chorused together.

"Exactly," I said. "Here's what I mean. The Americans have a serious problem with illegal immigration from Mexico into their country. Right?" The others nodded in unison. "So, somebody came up with what sounds like a good idea. If something could be done to equalize the standard of living in both the U.S. and Mexico, then there would be no reason for illegal Mexicans to flock into the U.S."

"Makes sense to me," said Francie.

"So, what the Americans did," I continued, "was they brought in free trade and as kind of an after-thought, they decided to include Canada as well. Over the next 20 years, the whole idea is for the average Mexican to earn more money while the average Canadian or American earns less..."

"So that eventually everyone's in the same boat," interrupted Francie.

"That's right," I nodded triumphantly.

"But in the meantime," asked Angie, "doesn't that mean we're going to lose a lot of jobs?"

"That's the problem," I answered. "In the short run, the United States will lose jobs to Mexico and Canada will lose jobs to both the U.S. and Mexico. It'll take a while for the proverbial water to seek its own level. It's the concept of short-term pain for long-term gain."

"So that's why unemployment is so high today," mused Marlene. "I never really paid much attention."

"That's part of it," I answered, "and I haven't even begun to talk about how we've lost jobs to Japan, Korea, Taiwan and so on. But that's beside the point."

"Wait a minute," interrupted Francie. "I can see how in 20 years the North American economy might be buoyant, but what happens in the meantime? I mean, we all have to eat three meals a day now."

"That's the problem!" I crowed. "You see, as a country, the United States or Canada can afford to invest 20 years in the quest for a stronger more stable economy, but, *as individuals, we don't have 20 years*. And it's the same thing in business. *If you're prepared to wait 20 years until all the old boys retire, you may achieve total pay equity, recognition and advancement in business. But if you haven't got the patience to wait—in other words, if you're 40 years old today instead of 20—then maybe you have to look at other alternatives.* There's no law that says you have to play that particular game."

"What choices do we have?" asked Angie.

"There are several. First, many women find it's easier to compete in a commission-based industry. If you're good at selling, you make money."

"I suppose that's why so many of the top realtors are female," said Marlene.

I nodded my head emphatically as my initial impression of Marlene as a pampered, unthinking rich woman started to dissipate.

"I've got a friend," continued Marlene, "who sells Avon products and she earns close to $100,000 a year including perks and a company car."

"Interesting," said Francie, "a commission-based industry... I've never given that much thought. What other alternatives are there?"

"Well, there's entrepreneurship," I answered. "There are over four million businesses owned by women in the United States. This comprises more than 30 per cent of all the businesses there are. Now, I'm not suggesting that becoming an entrepreneur is easy. You've got to have a product or service to sell. You've got to have a strong sense of self. *I am a woman; I am capable.* There's a lot of risk and you may have to be prepared to work 80 hour weeks. But if you're successful, the rewards will be there."

"What if you don't want to start your own business? What other choices are there? I've got a daughter who's only 12 years old," said Angie, "but I don't think it's too early for me to start giving *her* some good advice."

"Another interesting book I read a little while ago," I said, "is called *Megatrends for Women*. It's by Patricia Aburdene and John Naisbitt..."

"They wrote the original *Megatrends* book, didn't they?" asked Francie. "I saw it in the library a few weeks ago."

I nodded.

"In *Megatrends For Women*, they point out how health care and the environment are now key issues that are likely to stay in the forefront of our concern as a society. They explain how the military is becoming more devoted toward humanitarian causes, such as cleaning up natural disasters, rather than making war. They talk about how progressive technology increasingly allows people to work at home. Women, they say, tend to have good language skills which present great opportunities in a global economy.

"So there you have it. Health care, the environment, technology. Technology, by the way, provides tremendous latitude for flexibility. I expect most women would choose a career path with flexible full-time hours and more family time but slower career advancement than a fast-track career with inflexible hours and hardly any family time. You see," I continued, "we shouldn't forget that we've come a long way in the last generation or so. And the good news is that even male society is beginning to recognize the concept of equality. Remember, in 20 years the 'good old boys' will be out of the picture."

"Mary, if you had a wish list," asked Angie, "what would you prescribe in order to accelerate the advancement of women?"

"Ha," I said. "There are a couple of things I'd love to see. First of all, better child care tax breaks within the income tax system. Under the present tax rules, the most any mother can claim as a deduction is $5,000 for each child. If *I* were running the show, there wouldn't be any limits. If, for example, I wanted to pay out *half* my income to someone who would look after my kids, prepare meals, keep house and so on, why shouldn't I be able to deduct it? After all, the person who receives the money will pay taxes on it. I think if women were encouraged to hire housekeepers, this would do a great deal to alleviate unemployment. Also, if women could deduct the full amount they pay, the recipients would have to declare the corresponding income and this would help flush out part of the underground economy."

"But wouldn't you be encouraging women to become housekeepers and nannies instead of scientists and entrepreneurs?"

asked Marlene. (No, she certainly wasn't anybody's fool!)

"I don't think so," I added slowly. "There are many women who are very happy to do work that fosters their nurturing instincts. Government talks a good game about re-educating people in the workforce and gearing up for new technologies. The truth of the matter, though, is that *not everybody has the ability or the interest to evolve into something completely foreign to their natures.* For example, I don't think you can turn every Newfoundland fisherman with a Grade 5 education into an instant computer whiz, so why should we try to force someone who's truly happy as a homemaker into a different role without nearly the same comfort level?"

"What else would you recommend?" asked Francie.

"Beyond better child care tax breaks?"

"Yes."

"I'd also like to see daycare centres become a standard feature in large buildings."

"What do you mean?" asked Marlene.

"Well, you know how all buildings are designed these days to accommodate handicapped workers?"

Marlene nodded.

"If you stop to think about it, how many workers with physical disabilities are there in an average large office building, or in fact, how many physically disabled people visit the average shopping centre during the course of a day, compared to people without handicaps?"

"I don't know," said Angie. "I suspect the percentage is rather small."

"Of course it is," I continued. "And yet, what percentage of workers in large office complexes have young children?"

"I see what you mean," said Francie. "If there were daycare centres in large office buildings...parents would be able to visit with their children during the course of the working day."

"Even *fathers* would be able to have lunch with their kids," said Angie excitedly. "That would be a terrific concept."

"That's right," I said.

"But who would pay for all this?" asked Marlene.

25

"The tenants in the buildings would pay for it as 'common area costs', in the same way that the tenants of shopping centres pay for the open area waterfalls and gardens that are aesthetically pleasing but serve no functional purpose. And the same way as tenants pay for handicapped-equipped washrooms."

"I guess users with children could also pay some of the freight," said Francie.

"They could, indeed," I agreed.

"I guess my daughter is a little too old now," said Angie, "but I sure would have liked to have seen her during the course of the working day...I always felt so guilty...Well, maybe someday we'll have government and corporations that are enlightened enough to implement daycare facilities in large office complexes. In fact, maybe I'll even write a letter to my MP and MLA."

"My husband has a friend who sits as an Alderperson on City Council. I'll bounce the idea off him," said Marlene.

"Hey, let's eat," said Angie. "Our food's finally here. Since I'm going to be late for work anyway, I may as well be *really* late. After all, Mr. Fleming can only shoot me once!"

CHAPTER THREE

THERE IS NO MALE FINANCIAL GENE!

WE ATTACKED OUR MEALS IN RELATIVE SILENCE, and I suppose we all had thoughts of poor Dr. Frost. I couldn't help but wonder what personal problems had brought my new acquaintances to consult with him in the first place, and I suspect they were wondering the same thing about me. But I guess we were each too polite to ask. After all, we had just met.

When we finished eating, we ordered coffee (none of us asked for the dessert menu) and our waiter brought us the bill. Angie picked it up and handed it to me.

"Here, Mary," she said, "you're the accountant. How much does each of us owe?" I glanced at the bill and did some quick mental arithmetic.

"Well, we all ate about the same amount, so I think $13.00 each will cover it, including tip."

We began to reach into our respective purses, fumbling for our wallets. Angie and I pulled out an assortment of crumpled bills and change, while Marlene slapped a shiny gold American Express card on the table. We all waited expectantly for Francie. At last, she emerged from the depths of her purse clutching her wallet. I couldn't help noticing as she opened it that all she appeared to have was a $2 bill and a $5 bill. She sighed deeply.

"I guess I'll have to use plastic too," she said as she pulled out a worn Visa card. "I don't know how I'll ever get out from under," she muttered looking down at the table dejectedly. Suddenly, she looked up at me and her face lit up.

"Mary, you seem to know a lot about finances. I could sure

use some advice if you're willing. I know you've got some answers. Probably even more than Dr. Frost..."

"I can try," I said. "What kind of advice do you need?"

"It's my darned credit card bills," Francie wailed, "I can't seem to save a penny. I always owe at least $2,000 on either MasterCard or Visa. I make up my mind to pay off one of them and by the time I get the balance down to a few hundred, my other credit card gets maxed out to the limit. I can't save any money..."

"Because you're always frustrated by your debt load," I concluded for her.

"How did you know?" She asked incredulously.

"It's a common problem," I replied. "Many people find it especially difficult to save money because they're burdened by credit card debts. A sense of futility overcomes them and they get so frustrated by the whole thing that their only enjoyment is to spend even *more* money and they get deeper and deeper into the glue."

"Boy, did you ever hit the nail on the head," said Angie. "I pay all the bills at home, but in our family it's Joey who's a bigger spendaholic than I am. Fortunately, with our two incomes we get by, but I sure get frustrated when I write the cheques."

"*You* pay the bills?" asked Marlene. "That's interesting. I *never* have to do that. Tom takes care of everything. Is it common for young, married women to pay the bills?"

"As a matter of fact," I said, "I read a statistic recently that says 56 per cent of married women pay the household bills. But I also noted, however, that only 17 per cent of married women make life insurance decisions and only 12 per cent are involved in making investment choices."

"I wouldn't know where to begin," said Marlene. "Fortunately, I don't have to."

"There is no special male financial gene, Marlene," I said, perhaps a little sharply. "Many women today are experiencing the need to eliminate ignorance and dependency. Sometimes death or a spouse's long-term disability forces this issue. The old stereotyped sex roles may be comfortable for some, but they stunt our growth as human beings."

"I can see your point," said Marlene, "but Tom's health is great and I'm really quite comfortable with his managing our finances."

"Well, Marlene, if it works for you, well and good."

"Mary, what advice would you give," asked Angie, "for those of us who have the same problem as Francie?"

I shrugged my shoulders and waded in.

"Francie, the first thing to do is *get rid of your credit cards.* Credit cards are a wonderful convenience for people who know how to use them properly. In other words, if you can charge the things you need and pay your bill promptly at the end of each month, then they're much handier than carrying lots of cash or having to make frequent stops at the banking machine. But not everybody is capable of using credit cards properly. It's not a sin to admit you have a problem because, believe me, you're not alone. In a sense, having credit cards is like being constantly exposed to alcohol or even tasty desserts. Most people would agree that having a glass of wine with dinner is a pleasant experience, just like enjoying a rich dessert once or twice a week is pleasurable. But we all know that if we drink two bottles of wine each night with dinner or have dessert following every meal, we're going to get into BIG trouble. So, if you find yourself in a position where it's difficult for you to avoid excessive indulgence in alcohol, desserts, or spending on credit, you're best off..."

"I know," interrupted Francie, "staying away completely. You're right. But if I start concentrating on paying off my credit cards, where am I going to get money for my everyday expenses?"

"In your case," I replied, "the answer is really quite simple." I reached across the table and pointed to Francie's cigarettes which had fallen out of her purse. "How old are you?" I asked.

"Thirty-four. Why? Actually, I'll be thirty-five next Tuesday."

"How much do you smoke?" I asked.

"Well...If you really want to know the truth, it's about a pack a day and I've been craving one for the last hour."

I chuckled.

"What's so funny?" she snapped, now on the defensive.

"Oh, Francie, I don't mean to laugh at you," I said, "but at your age, quitting smoking is the key to your long-term financial security. And, besides, many people believe smoking ages the skin faster and hastens the onset of wrinkles."

"I've heard something about that and I've thought about quitting," Francie said. "But you can't tell me that a pack a day—what is it, $5.50?—is the key to my financial security."

I smiled at her and gently nodded my head.

"You've got to be joking," she retorted. "I'm sure there's a lot more to it than quitting smoking."

"Of course there is," I replied, "but you have to start somewhere, by deciding what's of value. You see, achieving financial security is like putting together a jigsaw puzzle. You have to put the pieces in their proper places and then, at the end, the meaningless fragments become a beautiful picture."

"And here I thought you were an accountant, not an artist," she exclaimed. "You lost me on the meaningless fragments, but, then again, most business publications and financial advisors also lose me because they hand out fragments without a simple manual and I don't understand what they're talking about. And I'm supposed to be a clever systems analyst."

"Listen, Francie," I said. "If you just slow down for a moment and give me a chance, I'll show you how simple it really is. You just told me you smoke a pack a day at a cost of what, $5.50?"

She nodded.

"Okay," I continued, "over the next 30 years, if you don't quit, can we assume conservatively that you would be spending, on average, $200 a month on cigarettes? Oh, and *what I'm going to show you applies equally to the woman who stops every day for a drink or two at the bar before going home, or even a junk food addict.*" I reached into my purse and pulled out my little hand-held calculator. I divided $200 by 30 days in an average month. "I think I'm being conservative," I said. "It works out to $6.67 a day."

"I suppose you're right," said Francie. "With inflation and taxes it might even cost more."

"Okay," I said, "now, let's assume, instead of smoking, you took $200 this month and invested it at 7 per cent and then you added $200 each and every month for 30 years. What do you think you'd have?"

"I have no idea," replied Francie. "It's been a long time since I've taken the mathematics of finance and I don't remember the formulas."

"Well, here, I'll show you," I said. I reached back into my purse and pulled out a book, *Henry B. Cimmer's The Money Manager for Canadians.*

"I don't believe it," said Angela. "You really *are* an accountant, aren't you?" We all laughed.

"It's amazing what I carry around with me," I said. "In fact, I don't usually travel around with more than one book at any time, but I also carry a notebook where I jot down ideas and interesting stuff from articles and books that I've read. It's funny," I said as I pulled out my notebook, "not that long ago, Dr. Frost recommended a book to me called *Men, Women and Relationships* by a fellow named John Gray. Remember before lunch we were talking about some of the differences between men and women? Dr. Gray had a whole page on how you can contrast males and females by the differences between wallets and purses. I found what he had to say so thought-provoking that I made a copy and inserted it into my notebook. Let me read it to you." I flipped through the pages. "Here we are…"

WALLETS AND PURSES

Contrasts in how males and females confront the world are most visually apparent when we compare a woman's purse with a man's wallet. Women carry large, heavy bags with beautiful decorations and shiny colours, while men carry lightweight, plain black or brown wallets that are designed to carry only the bare essentials: a driver's licence, major credit cards, and paper money. One can never be too sure what one will find when looking into a woman's purse. Even she may not know. But one thing is for sure, she will be carrying everything she could possibly need, along with whatever others may need too.

When looking in a woman's purse the first thing you find is a collection of other, littler purses and containers. It's as though she carries her own private drugstore and office combined. You may find a wallet, a coin purse, a makeup kit, a mirror, an organizer and calendar, a chequebook, a small calculator, another smaller makeup kit with a little mirror, a hair brush and comb, an address book, an older address book for really old friends, an eyeglass container, sunglasses in another container, a package of tissue, several partially used tissues, tampons, a condom package or diaphragm, a set of keys, an extra set of keys, her husband's keys, a toothbrush, toothpaste, breath spray, plain floss, flavoured floss (her children like mint), a little container of aspirin, another container of vitamins and pills, two or three nail files, four or five pens and pencils, several little pads of paper, a roll of film in its container and an empty film container, a package of business cards from friends and experts in all fields, a miniature picture album of her loved ones, lip balm, tea bags, another package of pain-relief pills, an envelope filled with receipts, various letters and cards from loved ones, stamps, a small package of bills to be paid, and a host of other miscellaneous items like paper clips, rubber bands, safety pins, barrettes, bobby pins, fingernail clippers, stationery and matching envelopes, gum, trail mix, assorted discount coupons, breath mints, and bits of garbage to be thrown away (next spring). In short, she has everything she could need and carries it with her wherever she goes.

To a woman, her purse is her security blanket, a trusted friend, an important part of herself. You can tell how expanded a woman's awareness is by the size of her purse. She is prepared for every emergency, wherever she may find herself.

Ironically, when she is being escorted to a grand ball she will leave this purse at home and bring a little shiny purse with the bare essentials. In this case, she feels, this night is for her. She is being taken care of by her man and she doesn't have to feel responsible for anybody. She feels so special and so supported that she doesn't need the security of her purse.

When I finished reading, I could hear the chuckles around the table. Sometimes it's good to lighten up a financially-oriented discussion!

"That's neat. Maybe that part about being taken care of is a bit condescending..." said Francie, "but do you mind if we get back to the question of how kicking the smoking habit is going to make me rich? Do you have all those formulas written out in that notebook of yours?"

"No," I said, "knowing formulas isn't necessary. All you really need is this book here." I pointed to my battered copy of *The Money Manager.* "It was written by a chartered accountant, Henry Cimmer. He's a Calgarian, tax expert, and former lecturer at McGill and the University of Calgary. He was the first person to explain how math tables work in a financial sense without worrying about the formulas." I handed the book to Francie. "You don't have to read this now," I continued. "In fact, you really don't have to read it at all if you don't want to. Just flip towards the end of the book and you'll find several pages of tables. It's easy to pick out which table you need, and once you know the right table to use you can make any financial calculations you want. It works somewhat like the mortgage tables you've probably seen. It's a great little reference book, although, of course, the drawback is that, by itself, it really doesn't give anybody a *plan.*"

"Wait a minute," said Francie, "I'm confused. You just told me all I need to do is *plan* to quit smoking. Is there anything else?"

"Of course," I said, "there's lots more, but let's take it one step at a time. The whole key is the concept of compounding."

"Compounding?" asked Marlene.

"Yes," I answered. "If you invest $100 at 7 per cent at the end of one year you'll have $107. Right?"

"I suppose," said Marlene.

"So, what would you then have at the end of two years?"

Marlene thought for a moment. "$114."

"No, that's not right," interjected Angie, "you'd have more than $114 because, in the second year, you'd be earning 7 per cent on the $7 that you earned in the first year."

"Yes," said Francie, "you'd actually have $114.49."

"So, what's the big deal?" said Marlene crossly. "I can't really believe that an extra 49 cents is going to make any difference."

"Not in the short term," I said, putting my hand gently on her arm, "but over a long-term period, earning compound income *does* make a significant difference in what you wind up with. Now, the example I just used talked about investing $100 *one time only*. I'm sure it's easy to understand if you put aside $100 *a month* and you earn compound earnings, the difference between earning income *on your income and your deposits* instead of earning income only on your deposits will be significant."

"Does it really matter that much?" asked Marlene.

"Well, take a guess," I said, "what if Francie quits smoking and puts aside $200 a month for the next 30 years? What do you think she'd have at the end?"

"Well, let's see," said Marlene as she reached into her purse, pulling out a beautiful burgundy Mont Blanc pen, "I suppose I can use this napkin here. I'm not totally ignorant when it comes to arithmetic, you know. Let's see," she said, "$200 a month times thirty years is $200 a month times 360 months...So 360 months times 200 is $72,000...7 per cent interest, oh, figure another $20,000...That's just..."

"Just under $100,000," said Angie.

"Hey, that's not bad!" Francie whistled. "You mean, I'd be burning up $100,000 over the next 30 years?"

I laughed. "Well, I must admit Marlene's made a good attempt at calculating the result, but I'm afraid to say—or I guess pleased to say would be better—that she's way off. Let's look at the table." I picked up Cimmer's *Money Manager* and flipped through the pages at the back. I showed the group a table entitled **The Future Value of One Dollar Invested at the End of Each Period.** "Here we are," I said, "at 7 per cent return with deposits made monthly, one dollar a month would amount to $1,219.97 after 30 years. Now you figure out what $200 a month comes to." I handed Francie the calculator.

"Well, let's see. If one dollar a month becomes $1,219.97, then $200 is 200 times…what is that again?—$1,219.97…that's," she looked stunned, "you're kidding me!" She shook the calculator. "That's not possible. $243,994! That's a small fortune."

"That's nothing," I said. "Look over here at the future value of one dollar invested at the end of each month at 10 per cent."

"Um, $2,260.49," Francie replied. She picked up the calculator again, "$2,260.49 times $200. Amazing! $452,098."

"That's right," I said. "So, if we take those two numbers, $452,098 and $243,994 and average them because we don't know what your real rate of return would be over 30 years, you can see that you should have about $350,000 in savings after that time."

"I don't believe it," Francie responded, "and I was supposed to be good at math. You mean if I don't quit smoking, I'll burn up $350,000 by the time I retire?"

"That's right," I replied. "If you're serious about saving money, start by quitting smoking."

"Okay, so suddenly I have $200 each month to invest. Where do I invest it?"

"Ah, *that* I can talk to you about later on. But what's your first priority?"

I could see the glow in her eyes as the lightbulb went on inside her head.

"I guess, for the first year, I'd have to concentrate on getting rid of my credit card debts."

"Exactly," I responded triumphantly.

"Then, once the decks are cleared," Francie continued, "I could start to invest."

"As long as you don't fall back into any bad habits."

"My parents didn't raise any fools," said Francie in mock indignation. "I'll quit smoking even if it takes a few sessions with a hypnotherapist. In fact, poor Dr. Frost actually recommended someone to me a few sessions ago. I've got her name written down at home. If that doesn't work, I'll go see my doctor about setting up a nicotine-patch program that will help me withdraw. One of the women in my department at Quebec Power quit smoking two months ago using the patch system and she swears by it. On second thought, maybe I'll try the patch system first. Mind you, she also swears at the eight pounds she put on."

"Yes, that can be a problem," I said. "If you eat the money you were burning up before, you won't be any further ahead. And it won't do for you to improve your financial health by ruining your physical health. It's nice to be thriving on all fronts."

"Believe me," she said patting her stomach, "after the gourmet meal of information you've given me so far, I'll be careful about my food intake."

"I can see how Francie can benefit by quitting smoking," said Angie, "but what about people who don't smoke? How can Joey and I save money? $200 a month sounds so trivial and yet it seems a lot."

"Well," I said, "as I mentioned before, the same concept of quitting smoking applies equally to someone who stops drinking or bingeing on junk food. I think, for a lot of families, if just one or two 'habits' were changed, the extra money would be there. Smoking is the logical vice with which to start. In fact, if the government were smart, they'd introduce a two-tiered health care system under which one would pay much higher premiums if one were a smoker than a non-smoker."

"That makes sense," said Marlene. "After all, it's the smokers who put more pressure on the system. But how could you administer this?"

"You know," I said, "I thought of the concept of a two-tiered system quite a while ago. In fact, I brought it up on a radio talk show about six months ago when I was asked to comment on changes I would like to see in the tax system."

"What was the response?"

"Ironically, it was a daytime show and it seemed that every unemployed yahoo in the province called up to give me flak. Needless to say, they were all smokers. True, there were a couple of favourable calls, but by the end of the hour, I was sorry I had even started. The host of the show was happy though, because it improved his ratings! Anyway, how *do* you administer a two-tiered health care system? Like I said, the answer came to me just recently."

"How so?" asked Marlene.

"Well, I bought my daughter Jennifer a doge for her 16th birthday"

"A doge?" the other three asked in unison.

"Yes, doge. D-O-G-E. That's a dog with class." They all laughed.

"What did you get?" asked Francie.

"A border collie. He's really sweet. His name is George, and now that he's finally housebroken, he's a great companion. Except I can't get him out of the habit of chewing on my slippers. Anyway, when George was six months old, I had him neutered and I applied for a licence. It seems that the city has a two-tiered system where you pay a lot less if your dog has been 'fixed'."

"How do they check?" asked Francie.

"I'm coming to that," I answered. "On the back of the licence application form is a statement where the owner certifies the dog's status. If you state that your dog has been neutered, you must have your statement sworn and witnessed by a notary public or commissioner of oaths. I suppose most people think twice before lying."

"I get it," said Francie. "What you would do is have the health care form contain a similar affidavit..."

"Exactly," I continued, "you'd have to swear that you're a non-smoker and you'd be assigned a different code for your health insurance number than the smokers. Then when you went to visit a doctor or required hospital attention..."

"There would be some kind of penalty if you lied," said Angie.

"Such as perhaps losing some or all of your health care coverage," continued Marlene.

"That's right," I said. "The system would only work if there were severe penalties imposed for lying."

"I wonder if the government will ever introduce a two-tiered health care system?" mused Angie.

"I don't know," I answered. "I tend to doubt it because it makes too much sense." I looked at my watch. "Well, I think I'd better go back to work. But why don't we keep in touch?"

I reached into my purse and pulled out my business cards. Francie gave me hers while Marlene and Angie wrote down their addresses and phone numbers on scraps of paper which they then passed around. I looked down at Francie's card. It simply read Frances Chow, Systems Analyst with her employer's name, address and phone number.

"Francie," I said to her, "where did you get your education?"

"I have a Commerce degree from McGill University with Honours in Computer Sciences," she answered. "Why?"

"An Honours B.Comm?" I echoed. "So, why don't you indicate that on your card?"

She shrugged her shoulders.

"If you don't mind my saying so," I said, "I think you're making a terrible mistake, and you're not alone. All too often, I've noticed when I get a business card from another woman, there's no reference to her degrees. If you ever look at a *man's* business card, you can almost bet he'll have all the letters he can muster up after his name, almost down to his high school diploma. In so many cases, we women are our own worst enemies. With the traditional sex roles, we are perceived to have a lack of entitlement — not only to money, but also prestige. I've noticed that many financial advisors treat women with less respect than men. We have to learn to raise our self-esteem, and a good place to start is to *be proud of our accomplishments.*"

"You're right," Francie said. "I'm almost out of cards and when I have them reprinted, I'll include my degree. Well, this sure has been a profitable lunch. Mary, I don't know how to

THE FUTURE VALUE OF $1 INVESTED AT THE END OF EACH PERIOD

END OF YEAR	7% INTEREST COMPOUNDED AND DEPOSITS MADE				8% INTEREST COMPOUNDED AND DEPOSITS MADE			
	MONTHLY	QUARTERLY	SEMI-ANNUALLY	ANNUALLY	MONTHLY	QUARTERLY	SEMI-ANNUALLY	ANNUALLY
1	12.393	4.106	2.035	1.000	12.450	4.122	2.040	1.000
2	25.681	8.508	4.215	2.070	25.933	8.583	4.246	2.080
3	39.930	13.225	6.550	3.215	40.536	13.412	6.633	3.246
4	55.209	18.282	9.052	4.440	56.350	18.639	9.214	4.506
5	71.593	23.702	11.731	5.751	73.477	24.297	12.006	5.867
6	89.161	29.511	14.602	7.153	92.025	30.422	15.026	7.336
7	107.999	35.738	17.677	8.654	112.113	37.051	18.292	8.923
8	128.199	42.412	20.971	10.260	133.869	44.227	21.825	10.637
9	149.859	49.566	24.500	11.978	157.430	51.994	25.645	12.488
10	173.085	57.234	28.280	13.816	182.946	60.402	29.778	14.487
11	197.990	65.453	32.329	15.784	210.580	69.503	34.248	16.645
12	224.695	74.263	36.667	17.888	240.508	79.354	39.083	18.977
13	253.331	83.705	41.313	20.141	272.920	90.016	44.312	21.495
14	284.037	93.827	46.291	22.550	308.023	101.558	49.968	24.215
15	316.962	104.675	51.623	25.129	346.038	114.052	56.085	27.152
16	352.268	116.303	57.335	27.888	387.209	127.575	62.701	30.324
17	390.126	128.767	63.453	30.840	431.797	142.213	69.858	33.750
18	430.721	142.126	70.008	33.999	480.086	158.057	77.598	37.450
19	474.250	156.446	77.029	37.379	532.383	175.208	85.970	41.446
20	520.927	171.794	84.550	40.995	589.020	193.772	95.026	45.762
21	570.977	188.245	92.607	44.865	650.359	213.867	104.820	50.423
22	624.646	205.878	101.238	49.006	716.788	235.618	115.413	55.457
23	682.194	224.779	110.484	53.436	788.731	259.162	126.871	60.893
24	743.902	245.037	120.388	58.177	866.645	284.647	139.263	66.765
25	810.072	266.752	130.998	63.249	951.026	312.232	152.667	73.106
26	881.024	290.027	142.363	68.676	1042.411	342.092	167.165	79.954
27	957.106	314.974	154.538	74.484	1141.381	374.413	182.845	87.351
28	1038.688	341.714	167.580	80.698	1248.565	409.398	199.806	95.339
29	1126.168	370.375	181.551	87.347	1364.645	447.267	218.150	103.966
30	1219.971	401.096	196.517	94.461	1490.359	488.258	237.991	113.283
31	1320.555	434.025	212.549	102.073	1626.508	532.628	259.451	123.346
32	1428.411	469.320	229.723	110.218	1773.958	580.655	282.662	134.214
33	1544.064	507.151	248.120	118.933	1933.645	632.641	307.767	145.951
34	1668.077	547.700	267.827	128.259	2106.587	688.913	334.921	158.627
35	1801.055	591.164	288.938	138.237	2293.882	749.823	364.290	172.317
36	1943.646	637.750	311.552	148.913	2496.724	815.754	396.057	187.102
37	2096.544	687.685	335.778	160.337	2716.400	887.120	430.415	203.070
38	2260.496	741.207	361.729	172.561	2954.310	964.369	467.577	220.316
39	2436.300	798.576	389.528	185.640	3211.966	1047.986	507.771	238.941
40	2624.813	860.067	419.307	199.635	3491.008	1138.495	551.245	259.057
41	2826.954	925.977	451.207	214.610	3793.210	1236.466	598.267	280.781
42	3043.707	996.623	485.379	230.632	4120.494	1342.512	649.125	304.244
43	3276.130	1072.346	521.985	247.776	4474.943	1457.299	704.134	329.583
44	3525.354	1153.510	561.199	266.121	4858.811	1581.549	763.631	356.950
45	3792.595	1240.506	603.205	285.749	5274.540	1716.042	827.983	386.506
46	4079.154	1333.754	648.203	306.752	5724.774	1861.620	897.587	418.426
47	4386.429	1433.702	696.407	329.224	6212.377	2019.199	972.870	452.900
48	4715.917	1540.833	748.043	353.270	6740.452	2189.768	1054.296	490.132
49	5069.224	1655.662	803.358	378.999	7312.356	2374.397	1142.367	530.343
50	5448.071	1778.742	862.612	406.529	7931.727	2574.245	1237.624	573.770

THE FUTURE VALUE OF $1 INVESTED AT THE END OF EACH PERIOD

END OF YEAR	9% INTEREST COMPOUNDED AND DEPOSITS MADE				10% INTEREST COMPOUNDED AND DEPOSITS MADE			
	MONTHLY	QUARTERLY	SEMI-ANNUALLY	ANNUALLY	MONTHLY	QUARTERLY	SEMI-ANNUALLY	ANNUALLY
1	12.508	4.137	2.045	1.000	12.566	4.153	2.050	1.000
2	26.188	8.659	4.278	2.090	26.447	8.736	4.310	2.100
3	41.153	13.602	6.717	3.278	41.782	13.796	6.802	3.310
4	57.521	19.005	9.380	4.573	58.722	19.380	9.549	4.641
5	75.424	24.912	12.288	5.985	77.437	25.545	12.578	6.105
6	95.007	31.367	15.464	7.523	98.111	32.349	15.917	7.716
7	116.427	38.424	18.932	9.200	120.950	39.860	19.599	9.487
8	139.856	46.138	22.719	11.028	146.181	48.150	23.657	11.436
9	165.483	54.570	26.855	13.021	174.054	57.301	28.132	13.579
10	193.514	63.786	31.371	15.193	204.845	67.403	33.066	15.937
11	224.175	73.861	36.303	17.560	238.860	78.552	38.505	18.531
12	257.712	84.873	41.689	20.141	276.438	90.860	44.502	21.384
13	294.394	96.910	47.571	22.953	317.950	104.444	51.113	24.523
14	334.518	110.068	53.993	26.019	363.809	119.440	58.403	27.975
15	378.406	124.450	61.007	29.361	414.470	135.992	66.439	31.772
16	426.410	140.172	68.666	33.003	470.436	154.262	75.299	35.950
17	478.918	157.356	77.030	36.974	532.263	174.429	85.067	40.545
18	536.352	176.141	86.164	41.301	600.563	196.689	95.836	45.599
19	599.173	196.674	96.138	46.018	676.016	221.261	107.710	51.159
20	667.887	219.118	107.030	51.160	759.369	248.383	120.800	57.275
21	743.047	243.651	118.925	56.765	851.450	278.321	135.232	64.002
22	825.257	270.468	131.914	62.873	953.174	311.366	151.143	71.403
23	915.180	299.781	146.098	69.532	1065.549	347.843	168.685	79.543
24	1013.538	331.822	161.588	76.790	1189.692	388.106	188.025	88.497
25	1121.122	366.847	178.503	84.701	1326.833	432.549	209.348	98.347
26	1238.798	405.131	196.975	93.324	1478.336	481.605	232.856	109.182
27	1367.514	446.979	217.146	102.723	1645.702	535.755	258.774	121.100
28	1508.304	492.722	239.174	112.968	1830.595	595.525	287.348	134.210
29	1662.301	542.723	263.229	124.135	2034.847	661.501	318.851	148.631
30	1830.743	597.379	289.498	136.308	2260.488	734.326	353.584	164.494
31	2014.987	657.122	318.184	149.575	2509.756	814.711	391.876	181.943
32	2216.515	722.426	349.510	164.037	2785.126	903.441	434.093	201.138
33	2436.947	793.809	383.719	179.800	3089.331	1001.382	480.638	222.252
34	2678.057	871.836	421.075	196.982	3425.389	1109.491	531.953	245.477
35	2941.784	957.127	461.870	215.711	3796.638	1228.823	588.529	271.024
36	3230.252	1050.356	506.418	236.125	4206.761	1360.544	650.903	299.127
37	3545.779	1152.264	555.066	258.376	4659.830	1505.938	719.670	330.039
38	3890.905	1263.658	608.191	282.630	5160.340	1666.426	795.486	364.043
39	4268.407	1385.420	666.205	309.066	5713.261	1843.575	879.074	401.448
40	4681.320	1518.517	729.558	337.882	6324.080	2039.115	971.229	442.593
41	5132.968	1664.002	798.740	369.292	6998.859	2254.954	1072.830	487.852
42	5626.983	1823.030	874.289	403.528	7744.296	2493.199	1184.845	537.637
43	6167.341	1996.861	956.791	440.846	8567.791	2756.178	1308.341	592.401
44	6758.388	2186.872	1046.884	481.522	9477.516	3046.457	1444.496	652.641
45	7404.878	2394.571	1145.269	525.859	10482.502	3366.872	1594.607	718.905
46	8112.015	2621.602	1252.707	574.186	11592.722	3720.549	1760.105	791.795
47	8885.485	2869.767	1370.033	626.863	12819.197	4110.942	1942.565	871.975
48	9731.513	3141.031	1498.155	684.280	14174.100	4541.863	2143.728	960.172
49	10656.903	3437.546	1638.068	746.866	15670.879	5017.520	2365.510	1057.190
50	11669.102	3761.661	1790.856	815.084	17324.391	5542.556	2610.025	1163.909

thank you enough. I feel that my life is about to change. First off, I'm going to take your advice and quit smoking and pay off my credit cards. In fact, I'll make darned sure I don't get into any trouble." Francie swiftly reached into her purse and pulled out a pair of nail scissors along with her MasterCard which she placed on the table next to her Visa. "Watch this," she said as she swiftly cut up her cards. Spontaneously, we all began to clap as heads swivelled around the restaurant to better see this strange group of women staring down at two extremely dead credit cards.

"There," said Francie, "no more can I be tempted by the devil." We laughed again.

All of a sudden, her face lost its colour. "Oh my goodness," she gasped, bringing her hands up to her face.

"What's the matter?" asked Marlene.

"I just tore up my credit cards," responded Francie. "I...I haven't got enough money to pay for my share of lunch..."

"That's okay, Francie," said Marlene. "I'm sure the rest of us won't mind putting in another $4.00 each."

"No problem," said Angie, "I'm sure you'll be able to pay us back *with compound interest* in the years to come."

THE COMPOUND VALUE OF INVESTING THE MONEY SAVED BY QUITTING SMOKING (OR REDUCING OTHER INDULGENCES SUCH AS COCKTAIL CONSUMPTION OR JUNK FOOD, ETC.): ASSUMED $200/MONTH ($6.67 PER DAY)

TIME PERIOD	20 YEARS		30 YEARS	
At a Rate of Return of	7%	10%	7%	10%
With a Growth Factor from Table for $1/Month	520.93	759.37	1,219.97	2,260.49
Results in Future Value of $200/month	$104,186.00	$151,874.00	$243,994.00	$452,098.00

TABLE EXTRACTS FROM: HENRY B. CIMMER'S MONEY MANAGER

Chapter Four
Happiness is Burning the Mortgage

It may come as somewhat of a surprise that Marlene was the cohesive force who kept us all together. She was the one with whom the rest of us initially seemed to have the least in common. I suppose it's not unusual for ships to pass in the night, as it were, never to cross each other's paths again. After all, how many times have you exchanged business cards or phone numbers with someone, promising to keep in touch and nothing ever happened?

Two weeks after Dr. Frost's funeral, Marlene called my office and invited me to her house for afternoon tea the following Saturday. She mentioned that Angie had already agreed to come and she was hoping to get in touch with Francie, too. She told me her husband was going to be out of town at a golf tournament in Fort Lauderdale and that her two children, Cheryl and Billy, were away at university. I could tell, even on the phone, that, in spite of her comfortable lifestyle, she was lonely, and I accepted her invitation without hesitation.

Marlene and Tom lived in a beautiful home in Lower Westmount. The house had been built in the late 1800s and had undergone several renovations over the years. Each owner had, however, preserved the tasteful quality of the Victorian architecture with its high ceilings and odd shaped rooms. In fact, many of the windows still contained the original panes of glass, somewhat distorting the view, while conveying an aura of graceful aging. The curved oak staircase that led from the main floor to the upstairs bedrooms was a wonder to behold.

It was a cool and somewhat cloudy day so we took our

refreshments into the atrium—a glass-enclosed room that looked out on Marlene's spacious backyard. The conversation that afternoon was light and pleasant. I'm afraid Marlene, Angie and I talked a bit too much about our children, leaving poor Francie with little to contribute.

Fortunately, it seems one of us was usually able to tell when her attention would start to wander and the topic of conversation was gently steered in other directions. Francie proudly informed us that she had now officially been a non-smoker for three weeks, four days and eleven hours, and was coping very nicely, thank you very much. She was still wearing a nicotine patch on her arm and made a point of declining Marlene's offer of a second helping of raisin pie and custard.

I must confess I took some secret pride in having helped her break the smoking habit, and I fervently hoped she would be successful in the long run. We all had a good laugh when she reached into her purse and, with great solemnity, repaid each of us what we had laid out for her lunch, after she had ceremoniously destroyed her credit cards. Marlene went up an extra notch in my estimation when she accepted the proffered $5 bill without making a fuss about it. She could tell instinctively, as Angie and I could, that it meant a lot for Francie to pay us back. The afternoon sped by quickly and before we knew it, the lengthening shadows in the garden told us it was time to leave. On the way out, I felt Angie tugging at my sleeve.

"Mary," she said, "would it be okay if I came to see you next week on a professional matter? I mean, I'll be glad to pay for your time..."

"No problem," I replied. "Why not call me Monday morning and we'll set something up? I don't have my Daytimer with me, but I'm sure I'll have some time on Tuesday or Wednesday."

"That would be great," she said with a sigh.

I couldn't help but wonder what was troubling her, because the weight of the world seemed to fall off her shoulders when I agreed to see her so promptly.

$s

The following Monday, Angie called and we set up a meeting for Wednesday at noon. The advertising agency she worked for had its offices only about three blocks from mine and I offered to send out for sandwiches so she could get back to work on time.

Louise, my secretary, announced Angie's arrival promptly at noon that Wednesday and I came out into the reception area to greet her. I escorted her into my office and we sat down on the couch at the opposite end of the room from my desk. I felt she would be much more comfortable in that setting than if I were to seat her in one of my client chairs. Besides, the coffee table seemed a perfect place for us to enjoy our lunch.

"I hope tuna on whole wheat is okay with you," I said. "It's my favourite, and the little shop downstairs does a super job."

"Tuna's great," she said.

"Would you like coffee or tea?"

"Coffee will be fine, if it's no trouble."

I went into my combination storage/kitchenette area and returned moments later with two mugs. We both took our coffee black with a half teaspoon of sugar.

"So, how can I help you?" I asked, knowing Angie's time was limited.

"Well," she said, "I've got a financial question and I'd like your advice."

"What is it?" I asked.

"Joey and I can't seem to agree whether it's more important for us to put some savings into paying down our mortgage or whether we should have RRSPs. Last year Joey didn't even consult me. He came home one day in February and said he was going to take $3,000 out of our joint savings account to buy an RRSP. I was really hurt, especially since I don't know a whole lot about what an RRSP is. I mean, I know it's some kind of savings plan for retirement, but I'm afraid I've never paid enough attention..."

"Don't apologize, you're not alone," I interrupted. "In fact, I think if more women started asking questions, we'd all be a lot better off. After all, you can't know something unless you check it out first. Do you know whether Joey bought the RRSP in his name or yours?"

"I don't know. I never thought to ask," Angie said. "Does it matter?"

"Maybe, maybe not. How strong is your marriage?"

"Now there's a blunt question if I ever heard one."

"I know," I said, "but there's no point in beating around the bush. Believe it or not, there's more to financial consulting than just dealing with dollars and cents. After all, you know that 50 per cent of all marriages end in divorce. Can I read you something?"

"Sure." Angie shrugged.

I reached for my little notebook. "Remember, when we had lunch that day I told you that when I read something interesting, I clip it or jot it down for reference." I flipped through the pages. "Ah, here we are. There's an interesting book that came out a while back called *Women and Money* by an American attorney, Anita Jones-Lee. Listen to this. She has quite a way with words. In fact, there are *two* quotes I found sufficiently interesting to record. First, she explains how women are 'straddling, placing one foot inside the marriage on the sacred ground of hope and the other, disloyal foot in the divorce court'."

"Ha," said Angie.

"Here's the second quotation. 'Perhaps there is no greater recipe for disaster than the mixture of money and love relationships. Money, whose language is calculation, cannot understand love, whose language regards 'calculation' as calculating—therefore anathema to love.'

"I suppose she's got a point," said Angie emphatically. "Well, in answer to your question, I think our marriage is pretty good. I suppose Joey and I don't communicate as well as I'd like, but I think that's a pretty common problem."

"Yes," I agreed, "it's the standard complaint that I hear from so many people, men and women alike. Like John Gray put it in his book, *Men, Women and Relationships:* men are from Mars and women from Venus. We come from different planets."

"An interesting theory," said Angie. "Who knows? He may be right."

"Just for fun," I said, "let me ask you something."

"Okay."

"When Joey first told you about the RRSP, did he say to you *I bought an RRSP* or did he say *I'm going to buy* an RRSP?"

Angie thought for a moment. "I think he said 'I'm going to buy'. Why?"

"Did you question him?"

"No. I suppose I should have."

"Did you ask to discuss it or bring up alternatives?"

"No," said Angie, getting on the defensive, "he had made up his mind."

"Aha," I said, raising a finger in the air to emphasize my point. "You only *think* he had his mind made up."

"What do you mean?" asked Angie with a puzzled frown on her face.

"You see," I replied, "it's all part of the difference between how men and women communicate."

"How so?"

"My experience is that women have a tendency to discuss matters before coming to a conclusion. We tend to look at all the pros and cons; bat things around; think for a while; maybe even change our minds, and eventually we decide based on what we feel is best. And we're willing to involve other people such as our spouses or partners, throughout the process.

"On the other hand, according to Gray, men operate differently. They think things out independently. They may ask the odd question from a friend or colleague, or even a spouse, but they rarely say anything until they have *almost* made up their own minds. And here's the important point. *When they finally say something, it sounds to us women like they've made a firm decision, whereas in reality, their statement is simply a trial balloon.*"

"A trial balloon?" asked Angie still puzzled.

"When Joey said to you, I'm going to put $3,000 into an RRSP, he was actually *asking you for your input. You could probably have changed his mind if you had wanted to.*"

"Really?"

"Yes."

"Without a fight?"

"Sure. All you needed to say was, 'Well, do you really think that's a good idea? Perhaps we should consider using the $3,000 to pay down our mortgage.' This probably would have opened the topic for discussion and the two of you could have decided together or agreed to seek independent advice. Instead, you thought that his mind was irrevocably made up and so you didn't question his 'decision'."

"But how can you be so sure he wanted my input?"

"If he really didn't want your input, what would he have said?"

I could see the glow of instant comprehension as her face suddenly lit up. "I guess he would've told me that he'd *already done it.*"

"Exactly," I replied, nodding my head with emphasis. "The fact that he said he was *going* to do it, meant he was really open for your input."

"Then why didn't he ask?" wailed Angie in frustration.

"Because he had never been taught *how* to communicate with a woman. After all, men are from Mars..."

"I know, and women are from Venus. What's that book again?"

"*Men, Women and Relationships* by Dr. John Gray. I've got a copy here on my bookshelf," I said as I rose to get it. "I'll lend it to you if you want, but I strongly suggest you buy your own copy."

"Joey will never read it," sighed Angie.

"You never know," I said. "But if *you* do, you'll understand *him* better, and it'll be a start in the right direction. If your relationship is fundamentally sound..."

"Oh, it is."

"Then I'm sure you'll get something out of it. Besides, you may not get him to read the whole thing, but a few choice pages can make a lot of difference. The book is easy to read and uses some light-hearted humour to help men and women understand and appreciate each other's differences rather than wanting each to change to be more like the other."

"That's really interesting," said Angie, "but can we get back to my question? Our mortgage is coming up for renewal in 10 days and the good news is that rates are lower now than when we took it out. We've been paying 9 per cent. But I'm confused. Should we go for a six month term, one year, two years, five years? What do you think? In which direction is the interest rate going to move? I don't read financial papers but I hear these commentators on T.V. and everybody seems to have a different view."

"Well, Angie," I said, "the problem is, nobody has a crystal ball. I think the government would like to encourage a low interest environment which would help keep inflation down, but the problem is there are so many external forces out there, it becomes really difficult to predict. If the American government raises interest rates and the Canadian government doesn't, this means that international investment will move to the United States instead of Canada."

"Because the return is higher?"

"Exactly."

"Then if money moves out of Canada, the Canadian dollar falls, right?"

I could see she was a quick study. "That's true. And what happens if the Canadian dollar falls?"

"Imported goods become more expensive," she replied after a moment's hesitation. "I heard this interview on CBC's 'Business World' that explained all that."

"I can see you're well on your way towards becoming an economist yourself."

Angie blushed. "So, the Canadian government would have to raise interest rates in order to keep things in balance."

"You've got it. And that's just one example. Many international factors can also affect interest rates. Wars, natural disasters and so on."

"I guess that's what they mean when they talk about a global marketplace."

"That's right."

"So that still doesn't tell me what to do."

"Well, I can only give you *my* view, for what it's worth."

"That's why I'm here."

"Okay, let's assume the rate for a five-year mortgage today is 7 per cent. How much lower could the rate possibly go?"

Angie shrugged her shoulders. "I don't know. Probably 1 or 2 per cent."

"That's right," I replied. "I'd agree with that. On the other hand, how much higher can rates go?"

"I don't know," she replied after a moment's hesitation. "I suppose the sky's the limit."

"Exactly," I responded. "Remember when interest rates were 16, 20 or even 22 per cent a little over 10 years ago?"

She nodded. "So what you're saying to me is we're better off locking into a long-term rate."

"You've got it," I said again. "If you lock into, say, a five-year term, at least you know where you stand for an extended period of time. You've got security against exposure to a sudden increase in rates."

"But what if rates drop?"

"Then you lose a bit and you end up paying more than you have to. But what you're really paying for in this case is insurance."

"I never thought of it that way."

"Let's assume that you do lock in for five years at 7 per cent and the rate drops to 6 per cent. Your loss is 1 per cent over a four-year period. What that 1 per cent is...it's the equivalent of an insurance policy."

"I get it," she said, "and we get the peace of mind of knowing what our payments will be for a whole five years. I think your suggestion makes a great deal of sense."

"I should hope so because anything else would just be wild guessing."

"Okay, I think you've answered my question." She started to rise.

"Wait a second," I said, "that's the easy part."

"What do you mean? I'm going to suggest to Joey that we renew our mortgage at the five year rate."

"What about the amortization? Haven't you discussed that?"

"How do you mean amortization? Mortgages are paid off over a 25 year term, aren't they? And we've already been paying for seven years. That leaves us with about 18 years to go."

"Ah ha," I said, "that's my point. There's a big difference between the 'term' of a mortgage and its 'amortization' as you'll see in a minute. How old are you?"

"I'm 39."

"And Joey?"

"41. Why?"

"At your ages, *you should target to have your mortgage paid off over eight years—not 18.*"

"Really?"

"You bet. Remember when we had lunch and I talked to Francie and the rest of you about the power of compound interest?"

Angie nodded.

"Well, extending or amortizing your mortgage beyond the point that you absolutely have to is *compound interest in reverse.* Except the bank gets the benefit."

"You mean, we're paying more over a longer period."

"Right again," I said, "and in Canada, it's especially important for us to pay off our mortgages because mortgage interest on a personal residence is not deductible for income tax purposes."

"I knew that," said Angie proudly.

"You see," I continued, now in full lecture mode, "all too often, Canadians are bombarded by financial material that comes out of the United States. Americans don't make a big deal about mortgage acceleration payments—that means getting rid of the mortgage quickly—because, in the U.S., you can deduct your interest on your tax return. That means that the American government subsidizes between 30 and 40 per cent of the average citizen's mortgage interest in the form of reduced taxes. That's why, in the U.S., it's not uncommon to have mortgage amortization periods of 30 years, let alone 25."

"So the Americans get a tax break and we don't."

"True," I said, "but I really wonder whether the American government is doing such a big favour for its people."

"I would think that any tax break is a favour."

"Right, but what happens if you lose your job? The economy is just as uncertain in the U.S. as it is here."

"I get it," said Angie. "I suppose, if you lose your job and you have no income to deduct your mortgage interest against, you're no better off."

"True," I said, "but it goes deeper than that. You see, *if your mortgage is paid off and you lose your job, you and your family can afford to live on a lot less.*"

"I never thought of it that way."

"Unfortunately, too few people do. The average Canadian family spends about a third of its disposable income on housing, but if the mortgage is eliminated, a family's cost of living drops dramatically."

"I can see where you're coming from," said Angie. "The mortgage payments take up almost two-thirds of my paycheque. Then again, I've been cut back from 40 to 30 hours a week at the agency." She paused. "How did you learn all this? Did they teach it to you in accounting school?"

I laughed. "No, not really. Surprisingly, you can learn more from real life experiences than you do in school. Do you remember the late '70s when Canada was experiencing a boom?"

"Vaguely," said Angie.

"Well, I remember my father telling me about a friend of his who had moved from Montreal to Calgary. This fellow was an engineer whose parents had both died rather young and left him some money—not a great fortune—I really don't know how much. Now, in boom-time Calgary, back then, everybody was speculating and investing in the junior oil stocks, but my father's friend did something different. He took his inheritance and paid off his house. Two years later, everything came crashing down and he lost his job. I remember my Dad telling me how his buddy was unemployed for three years and yet he and his family were able to manage."

"You mean, because their mortgage was paid off, their cost of living..."

"Right. I didn't mention this, but he also used part of his inheritance to buy two cars, one for himself and one for his wife. During his unemployed period, they obviously didn't upgrade their vehicles...but without house and car payments, you're right on, the cost of living isn't all that high."

"So Joey and I should pay off our mortgage." Angie thought for a moment. "But what if there's high inflation again? I once heard somebody say that in times of high inflation your house goes up in value and you pay it off with cheaper dollars. So, if there's any chance of an inflationary cycle, wouldn't we be making a mistake?"

"I see you've been listening to your share of financial commentators and economists. But here's the key point. If the government decides to reinflate so they can pay off their debts with cheaper dollars by printing money, what's going to happen at the same time is that *interest rates will go skyrocketing upward.*"

"So we wouldn't be any further ahead—and neither would the government."

"Right again," I said. "Paying off a mortgage as quickly as possible is a win/win situation. In times of uncertain economy when there is high unemployment, you are able to better regulate your family's cost of living because a fully-paid home is the best insurance policy against loss of income. In times of high inflation, a fully paid home..."

"Protects us against rising interest rates," interrupted Angela triumphantly. "But what about the RRSP?" she continued. "You still didn't answer the question of what's better, paying down the mortgage *or* buying an RRSP."

"It's an interesting question," I said. I walked over to my bookcase and pulled down Henry Cimmer's *Money Manager* and brought it back to the table.

"I remember that book," said Angie. "That's the one you used to show Francie what she could save if she quit smoking and invested the money instead."

"I'm going to use this same book in a couple of minutes to show you in black and white what you could accomplish by paying off your mortgage over the next eight years instead of 18. But before I do, I'll tell you something. In the 1980s, this fellow Cimmer designed a computer program to assist people in making the decision whether they should pay their mortgages off first or buy an RRSP. To do the calculations manually took over 40 steps, but the computer could do all of this in a matter of seconds."

"So, what was the conclusion?"

"I'm coming to that. I found when I used his program, that the results were about the same as long as you assumed that the investment return on your RRSP would be approximately the same as your mortgage rate."

"In other words it doesn't make much difference. Is that what you're saying?"

I nodded in reply. "For example, if you assume that your mortgage bears interest at 7 per cent and your other alternative is to buy a 7 per cent term deposit in your RRSP, it probably doesn't make a whole lot of difference."

"But what if you can earn more in your RRSP?"

"Well, obviously, in that case, the balance might swing in favour of investing in the RRSP. So today, if you could renew your mortgage at 7 per cent and not pay it off quickly and invest your extra money in an RRSP instead at 15 per cent, the RRSP is probably going to be the better choice."

"But doesn't a 15 per cent return involve greater risk?"

"Angie, you amaze me. You know a lot more than you give yourself credit for. You've hit the nail right on the head. If you could get a *guaranteed* 15 per cent return, then I would say to you, buy an RRSP and don't worry about paying off your mortgage. *But paying off a mortgage involves no risk while trying to earn 15 per cent involves **substantial** risk.* Beyond that, paying off a mortgage provides security, and today security is virtually synonymous with financial independence. Also, there's one other factor."

"What's that?"

"In 1991, the government changed the RRSP rules so that, if you don't contribute up to your allowable maximum in any given year, you can carry forward for up to seven years and catch up. On the other hand, if you miss a year's opportunity to pay down your mortgage..."

"You're paying out more interest than you need to," added Angie. "But I'm still not sure I understand exactly how RRSPs work..."

"And I'm not so sure you really need to know everything right now," I said. "I'll be happy to explain the ins and outs of RRSPs to you at the proper time, but I would strongly recommend that you and Joey target to become mortgage-free as quickly as possible. And then you can catch up on these RRSP investments down the road."

"With—what did you say? A six-year...no...seven-year carry

forward. I get it. But can you give me something concrete that I can take home for Joey?"

"I'll be happy to," I replied. "That's why I've got this copy of *The Money Manager* here on the table." I walked over to my desk and returned a moment later with some paper, a pencil and my little hand-held calculator.

"Is that your portable computer?" asked Angie with a laugh.

"No, as you can see I do use a computer," I said, pointing in the direction of my credenza, "but for some things, it's just as easy to make calculations in the old-fashioned way. Then again, it wasn't so long ago that these little calculators didn't even exist, let alone computers."

"I know," said Angie, "the technological advances in advertising layout and design techniques are mind-boggling too."

"Okay," I said, "how much do you and Joey owe?"

"Just over $80,000," Angie replied.

"Okay, your previous mortgage was based on a 25-year amortization at 9 per cent, right?"

"Yup," said Angie.

"Now," I said, "let's see." I picked up Cimmer's *Money Manager,* turned to the table called **Monthly Payments Required to Repay a Mortgage Loan of $1,000 Over Various Periods of Time** and looked down the 9 per cent column to 25 years. I showed the book to Angie. "You see here, it costs $8.28 per month to pay off $1,000 at 9 per cent over 25 years." She nodded. "Therefore, an $80,000 loan costs 80 times $8.28 or," I turned to my calculator, punched in some numbers, "$662.40."

"That sounds about right."

"Now," I said, "let's look at the table for 7 per cent. In order to pay off $1,000 over 18 years at 7 per cent your payments would be $8.10." I started to write as I spoke. "Over an eight-year term, the payments are $13.58." Angie nodded again. "Therefore, the monthly payment for $80,000 is 80 times as large. That's $648 a month over 18 years, $1086.40 over eight years. Now the annual cost is 12 times the monthly cost." She nodded yet again. "Over 18 years, we're looking at $7,776 a year, while over eight years we're looking at $13,036.80. Now the total cost: $7,776 times 18 years amounts to $139,968, while $13,036.80 over eight years amounts to only $104,294.40."

"I get it," said Angie, "the annual payments are much higher over the first eight years, but we're paying for 10 years less."

"Well put," I said. "So, now let's look at the trade-off. The monthly payment over eight years is $438 more than the monthly payment over 18 years."

"I see that," said Angie.

"But look at the savings in interest. The total interest over 18 years is just under $60,000; $59,968 to be exact. Over eight years, the interest is only $24,294.40."

MONTHLY PAYMENTS REQUIRED TO AMORTIZE A MORTGAGE OF $80,000 @ 9 PER CENT OVER 25 YEARS

80 x $8.28 (factor for $1,000 mortgage loan at 9 per cent from Cimmer's Money Manager)	=	$662.40

COMPARISON OF ANGIE AND JOEY'S MORTGAGE PAYMENT WITH 18 AND 8 YEAR PAYOUTS

$80,000 @ 7 PER CENT	18-YR AMORTIZATION	8-YR AMORTIZATION
Monthly payment for $1,000 mortgage loan from Cimmer's *Money Manager*	$ 8.10	$ 13.58
Monthly payment for $80,000, 80 times	648.00	1,086.40
Annual cost	7,776.00	13,036.80
Total Cost	**$ 139,968.00**	**$ 104,294.40**
Monthly payment over eight years	$ 1,086.40	
Monthly payment over 18 years	$ 648.00	
Difference	$ 438.40	
Total interest over 18 years	$ 59,968.00	
Total interest over eight years	$ 24,294.40	
Difference	$ 35,673.60	

"So," said Angie, "for the sake of an extra $100 a week over eight years we can save...almost $36,000. I see your point," said Angie. "Then, in only eight years' time, before Joey's even 50 years old, we'd have our house paid!"

"That's right. And you'd be able to save an awful lot in RRSPs starting in the ninth year."

"I get it. The $13,000 a year that we would have been putting down against the mortgage could start to go into RRSPs."

"Wrong."

"Wrong?"

"In fact, you and Joey would be able to put aside around $20,000 a year into RRSPs."

"Of course," said Angie, as the reason suddenly dawned on her, "because these payments are...tax deductible."

"If the two of you were to put in $20,000, the government would give you back around $7,000...and your net cost would only be $13,000," I added for reinforcement.

"And then we would be able to build up our RRSPs until Joey and I are 65 or 70...but where do we invest and how do we do all this?"

"All in due course," I said. "I'll be happy to explain RRSPs to you at the appropriate time, but I really think the two of you should focus on paying off your mortgage first. And be sure to talk to several different banks and trust companies. Look into the various types of mortgages, especially the ones with accelerated weekly payment plans. If you pay your mortgage weekly, you can pay it off even faster with less interest."

"But what about early retirement?" Angie asked. "What's this that we always see on T.V. about Freedom 55?"

"Unfortunately, Freedom 55 is simply a marketing program designed by a life insurance company to sell products. For most people, it just doesn't work that easily."

"Why's that?"

"Because as you yourself can see, you and Joey will need that extra 10 years from his age 55 to 65 in order to build up enough investment capital to retire comfortably. Unless you start saving and investing at a very, very young age, or earn a heck of a lot of money from employment, or run a successful business of your own, the chances of being able to retire at age 55 without suffering a reduced standard of living are pretty slim. It really bothers me that some of the advertising we're exposed to isn't all that realistic."

"You don't have to tell *me*," said Angie wryly. "After all, I work in the industry. But there's one other question."

"Ask, and then perhaps we should eat," I looked at my watch.

"I'm concerned about keeping you from your work."

"You're right, I can't be late so I'll make this quick," said Angie. "I see the merits of paying off our mortgage more quickly, but can we really *afford* the extra $438 a month? I mean, it sounds like a heck of a lot. On the other hand…and maybe I should have mentioned this earlier…since the agency cut me back to 30 hours a week, I've been doing a bit of moonlighting at home. I can charge a lot less than agency rates because I don't have their overhead, and besides, the stuff I'm doing is so small that the company I work for wouldn't really want to do it anyway. I've been averaging an extra $250 to $350 a month, and I hope it continues."

"I'm really glad to see you've taken that initiative, Angie. All too often when people get laid off or cut back, they roll over, play dead and hope the system will support them. That's what's wrong with this country. In a sense, our unemployment insurance and welfare systems are too darned good! Can you believe it? You only have to work for 12 consecutive weeks in order to collect unemployment insurance later on. And it used to be only 10 weeks. The government sure doesn't encourage people to be self-reliant. All this useless talk about job creation…"

"I know, I know," said Angie. "I hear my Dad grumbling all the time about the prevailing lack of work ethic and how immigrants like himself had a lot more on the ball than young Canadians do today. He's always complaining that there's lots of work including yard maintenance but no one is willing to do it. Not even our kids want to get their hands dirty any more. But, anyway, how can we be sure that Joey and I will be able to afford the extra $400 a month on our mortgage?"

"I guess we're going to have to do a little budgeting. I wonder if you can phone your office and ask for an extra half hour or so. We're on a roll and we may as well keep the momentum going."

"I'll call my boss," said Angie walking over to my desk and picking up the phone. "I'll tell him that I'll make up the time by coming in early tomorrow, and Friday, if necessary. But let's eat first. All this heavy number talk is making me hungry. Besides, I could use a break. You may be used to number-crunching, but I'm an artiste!"

CHAPTER FIVE

ARE BUDGETERS REALLY BORING PEOPLE?

ANGIE AND I ATE OUR SANDWICHES IN SILENCE, taking the opportunity to recharge our batteries for the job ahead.

"Tell me something," Angie finally said as I looked up with raised eyebrows to acknowledge the forthcoming question. "You know this man David Chilton, who wrote *The Wealthy Barber?*"

"Oh, sure," I said. "It's really a great book for 30-year-old people who need some motivation to get into good saving habits."

Angie nodded. "I know. A friend of mine read it. Mr. Chilton's message seems to be that you should save 10 per cent of what you earn and you don't really have to worry about anything else. I think the concept is called 'Pay Yourself First'."

"Quite true," I replied. "It was actually explained even earlier in a book called *The Richest Man in Babylon.* It works nicely for younger people, but I'm afraid it's a bit simplistic."

"You know, Mr. Chilton now has a video and I saw it advertised on T.V. on Canada AM. They showed outtakes and, in one scene, he refers to people who budget as 'not being much fun to be around'. He implies that if you like to budget, you've got to be boring. And he also implies that most people don't have the strength of character to actually sit down, prepare a budget and then follow it through."

I laughed. "I know what you mean. I've seen those ads lots of times. In my opinion, though, as I said, Mr. Chilton is too simplistic in his approach—especially if we recognize that people are not all the same age and we all have different circumstances. I read *The Wealthy Barber* and I think it's a good book, but I don't necessarily agree with everything he says. Now, detailed budgeting—day to day or week to week—can be pretty tiresome, but I believe that preparing a general budget once a year makes a lot of sense."

"Why's that?" Angie asked.

"Well," I replied, "if you don't budget, you'll find that unexpected costs will crop up and you won't be ready for them."

"Such as?"

"In a simple case, a vacation. Another example—what if you have a family car that's paid for and you've been driving it for several years?"

"So...?"

"Well, eventually you have to replace that car. Have you set aside some money for a downpayment on a new car?"

"I see what you mean. I remember when I was growing up my Mom, being from the Old Country, used the 'envelope approach' to financial planning."

"What's that?" I asked, puzzled.

Angie chuckled. "She used to have different envelopes into which she would put money each time my Dad brought home his pay. She'd have one envelope for the kids' education fund, another for the family holiday in the Laurentians, and a third, just as you said, to cover the cost of replacing the car every five or six years. Of course, she didn't think to put the money into the bank to earn interest, let alone into any other kinds of investments."

"Maybe not," I said, "but she showed a lot of common sense. In her own way, she was budgeting for non-recurring expenditures."

"So, how does one go about preparing an effective budget?" asked Angie. "I'm embarrassed to ask," she confessed, "but it's not something I learned in school."

I sighed. "You're right. I've often wondered why the education system teaches us the fundamentals like reading, writing and math when we're a young, impressionable, captive audience, but leaves practical application to the higher learning years. By then, further education is optional, and we've got other distractions, our attitudes have changed and we're not as open to new ideas and ways of doing things. I know it's starting to change. And some schools are offering health and lifestyle or career and life management courses, but it's all happening too slowly."

"I agree," said Angie.

"You know, in a way, it's funny," I said. "The statistics indicate in more than half of married households, the women actually pay the bills. But I suspect that all they're doing is the mechanical task of writing cheques, addressing envelopes and so on."

"Why do you think that is?" Angie asked.

"I'm afraid it starts with the school system. I think that women are intrinsically able to better use their brains than men until they are discouraged from using them at all. I read that in a book called *Women's Work*, written by two psychologists at The University of Calgary."

Angie laughed.

"Even if women go into a competitive field, they're usually conditioned to take a more supportive role. Sure, some of us have the freedom to aspire to higher management, but there is the glass ceiling to contend with. Our society sure doesn't fully expect women to have careers. When we work, it's considered a fail-safe just in case our husbands lose their jobs. The fact that we bear children reduces our likelihood of promotion or higher salary levels. And, if we take a year or two off for child rearing, it's very difficult to start in a career where we left off. It can take years to make up for the lost momentum. There's the old double standard. If a man shows on his résumé that he's changed his job frequently, the reaction of a prospective employer is often, 'Gee, you must be good, everybody wants you.' On the other hand, if a *woman* changes jobs frequently, often because she's been forced to accommodate her husband's transfer from one city to another, that same employer would reject her and say 'You've made too many changes.'"

"Do you see any hope for us?" Angie asked.

"I'm sorry to sound so negative, but as long as we live in a male-oriented society, traditional socialization will continue.

61

The good news, though, is that more and more women are starting their own businesses because they don't want to play men's games to scramble up the corporate ladder. Men usually have four ways to relate to women: mother, wife, daughter and sexual partner. In business, none of these roles respects a woman's position as a worker, let alone as management material."

"I'm afraid you're right," said Angie wistfully.

"Of course, it'll change in time. When the traditional 'old boys' like Marlene's husband eventually retire, we'll see some pretty big advances. Younger men are far less traditional as are men with professional wives or partners. It's amazing how difficult it is, though, for a lot of men to understand that, *if their wives have good jobs and are happy in their careers, that gives **them** the flexibility to consider career changes or sabbaticals.*"

"You're right again," said Angie. "There are benefits to the dual income family. You mentioned health and lifestyle and career and life management education programs. My daughter is 12. I hope these programs are further evolved by the time she gets into high school."

"I'm sure they will be. My daughter, Jenny, just completed her course in Grade 11. Part of the purpose is to give young adults, especially young women, the full range of job options and to counter the socialized gender restrictions of the past. Of course, I think there is some potential backlash."

"How?"

"I've read studies which say that in many cases, daughters of high-powered career women miss their homemade cookies, and they, in turn, set their sights too low. It's sort of like the concept of 'shirt sleeves to shirt sleeves in three generations'."

"I'm sorry," Angie interrupted, "I don't understand your analogy."

"Oh, it's like action and reaction. The phrase 'shirt sleeves to shirt sleeves in three generations' refers to the situation where grandfather, the first generation Canadian, is an immigrant. He works hard and starts a business, generally spending most of his time in shirt sleeves working in his manufacturing plant. His son, the second generation, receives a good education and he builds the business to a level far beyond what his father had set out to do. Of course, his function is mainly administrative and he wears a jacket and tie. By the time you get to the third generation, the grandson rejects his father's values as being too monetary. He wonders how he can compete and, in fact, questions whether or not he really wants to. He often ends up settling for a blue-collar shirt-sleeve type job."

"Ah, now I get it." Angie nodded her head. "How do you think we can influence today's daughters of career women to continue bettering themselves and not revert to their grandmothers' roles?"

"There are lots of ways," I said. "One way is to emphasize vocational psychology and put it into a proper context. Under the existing social framework, vocational psychology is a poor relative in counselling psychology compared to family, marital and interpersonal." I paused to take a deep breath. "We must concentrate on role modelling. We should bring women with non-traditional careers into the elementary schools to talk to students. Field trips would also be useful. We have to dispel the myth that women do well simply because they work harder. Our brains are just as well developed as men's. We also need some changes within business environments. In many cases, businesses are guilty of failing to adopt procedures, equipment, schedules and uniforms to accommodate the fact that women have different shapes and sizes compared to men and different social needs."

"Can you give me an example?"

"Sure, here's a very simple one. Let's assume that the average woman can drive a garbage truck as well as her male counterpart. What if the manufacturer builds the trucks to accommodate drivers who range between 5'6" and 6'4"? A woman who might only be 5'2" or 5'4" couldn't comfortably drive that truck."

"Are you suggesting that we aspire to driving garbage trucks?" asked Angie in mock horror.

I gave her 'The Look' and we both laughed.

"No, really," she said, "I get your point."

"Anyway," I continued, "we're getting a bit off track, but I should mention that I don't think everything is all bad. We've come a long way and the changes in our society which emphasize health care and the environment will favour the advancement of women into the next generation—even those women who don't choose to start their own businesses."

"I agree," said Angie as she pushed aside the remainders from lunch. "Okay, I'm ready to tackle the budget. Where do we start?"

I went over to my bookcase and returned to the table with another book. "This same Henry Cimmer who wrote that math book we used to figure out your mortgage also put together another book a few years ago called *Your Canadian Guide to Planning for Financial Security.*" I held it up and showed Angie the cover. "This book contains a number of worksheets people can use, even if they don't have a state-of-the-art computer, to make various calculations. I've used it myself for some of the applications. Take a look." I flipped through the book. "Here's a schedule he set up that shows you how to do a personal budget. Cimmer started with the various categories of spending that the government uses to calculate the Consumer Price Index...Ah here it is on page 53."

THE CONSUMER PRICE INDEX
HOW THE AVERAGE CANADIAN FAMILY ALLOCATES ITS DISPOSABLE INCOME
(BASED ON 1990 SPENDING PATTERNS)

CATEGORY	PERCENTAGE
Housing	31.4
Food	22.0
Transportation	13.8
Clothing	6.3
Recreation, reading & education	11.0
Tobacco & alcohol	4.9
Health & personal care	6.2
Other	4.4
TOTAL	100.0

"For the budget itself, Cimmer expanded the categories to include their components. For example, he broke down housing to include mortgage payments, property taxes, heating and so on. He distinguished between food eaten at home and away under food costs. Here's a blank schedule on page 50 we can use for your budgeting. The extra category he calls 'other' covers gifts to friends and family, insurance premiums, and so on—whatever doesn't fit naturally in another category. Give me a moment and I'll photocopy it so that we can use it as a model." I went out to the photocopier and a moment later handed Angie the blank schedule.

Schedule of Personal Expenses

HOUSING

Rent/mortgage payments		$_____
Mortgage principal	$_____	
Mortgage interest	_____	
Property taxes		_____
Heating		_____
Electricity		_____
Insurance		_____
Maintenance and improvements		_____
Furnishings and appliances		_____
Telephone		_____
Water		_____
T.V. rental or cable		_____
Other		_____ $_____

FOOD

At home		_____
Away		_____ _____

TRANSPORTATION

Public transportation		_____
Automobile		
Car payments/rentals		_____
Gas and oil		_____
Insurance		_____
Licence		_____
Repairs and maintenance		_____
Tires		_____ _____

CLOTHING

Purchases		_____
Laundry and cleaning		_____ _____

RECREATION, READING AND EDUCATION

Travel and vacation   _____

Club memberships and dues   _____

Miscellaneous   _____

Babysitting (non-deductible)   _____

Education   _____

   Tuition fees (for children not eligible for tax credits)   _____

   Books   _____

   Miscellaneous   _____

Reading material   _____   _____

TOBACCO AND ALCOHOL

Tobacco   _____

Alcohol   _____   _____

HEALTH AND PERSONAL CARE

Medicine & medical services not covered by insurance   _____

Medical and dental insurance premiums   _____

Dental care not covered by insurance   _____

Grooming   _____   _____

OTHER

Gifts to friends and family   _____

Insurance premiums

   Life (annual increase in CSV $_____)   _____

   Disability   _____

   Liability   _____

Other _____   _____   _____

TOTAL PERSONAL EXPENDITURES $ _____

Angie gasped. "Do I have to detail all this stuff? Maybe Chilton is right."

I chuckled. "Don't worry, Angie, it's easier done than said."

"But it's intimidating, Mary."

"Piece of cake. Even if it isn't penny perfect, your budget will give you a pretty good idea of where you stand. Besides, with a little concentration, you can estimate fairly accurately what you and Joey spend on different things during the course of a year, without even going through your cheque book."

"But thinking ahead a year at a time feels strange," Angie said. "I mean, we live one day at a time and I know what has to be paid each month. As a matter of fact, we live month to month."

"As do most people," I interjected. "Your sights are too near term, so, of course, you find it difficult to plan effectively for the future. Besides, the relevant numbers are not what you spend monthly, but what it costs for you to live annually. Then, you'll know better what you have to set your sights on as a sensible annual income."

"How do you mean?"

"Well, you yourself said you have some flexibility. The agency has cut your hours and you've started to do some moonlighting. In theory, you can work seven days a week. Or, more realistically, you might find five or six extra hours a week is more than enough. Also, Joey might be able to help. Perhaps he can take on some handy-work or help with more of the household chores if you're putting in a lot of hours. You won't know until you and Joey set some goals and objectives."

"Okay," Angie sighed, "let's do it." She picked up a pencil and the schedule. "Let's see now. Housing. First the mortgage payments. What was that number again?" She rifled through the papers and books on my coffee table and found the right page. "$1,086.40 a month times 12. That's $13,036.80. Whew. Until I wrote it down myself, I didn't really believe it."

"Few things are believable until they register in your head as your own truth," I observed. "Just remember that 7 per cent interest on $80,000 is $5,600. Therefore, if your payments are $13,036 and only $5,600 is interest…

"Only!"

I ignored the interruption. "$…7,436 is going towards principal repayment in just the first year. *This is a direct increase in your net worth in the short term.*"

"An immediate reward sounds good," Angie smiled. "Let's move on. Property taxes last year were $2,600, so I'll put in $2,700 to be conservative. Heating averages about $50 a month, so $600 a year. Electricity, another $50 a month; another $600. You know, this isn't so terrible after all. Insurance is about $700. Hmm, what do I do for maintenance and improvements?"

"Well, here's the point I tried to get across to you before," I said. *"Your budget doesn't have to be accurate down to the penny.* For example, are you aware of any major improvements you need to put in right now or in the near future?"

"Ah, I see. The other expenses that we have to deal with, but not necessarily this month so they're not usually factored in until they become sudden expenses with no reserve to cover them."

"I know I've said it before, but you really are a quick study, Angie. You're right on."

"Thank you, ma'am," she said with a little bow. "As for any major improvements, none. The house is pretty much under control. Besides," she grinned, "Joey is a traditional husband—he knows how to fix things around the house."

"So, why don't you just put in, say, $400," I suggested. "Do you need any furniture?" Angie shook her head. "So let's leave that one blank. What's your telephone bill like?"

"Um, we don't have a whole lot of long distance charges, and we just have basic service, so it's only about $20 a month. So I'll put in $240."

"Best be a little more generous on that one, just in case," I suggested.

"Okay, $300."

"Try $360."

"Done." She made the entry. "We don't pay separately for water so I'll leave a blank there. T.V. cable is $15 a month, $180 a year and...what else? I can't think of any other costs."

"What about food?" I prompted.

"Joey and I like to eat well. We're both good cooks, so our grocery bill averages about $100 a week, and that's of course $5,200 a year. We probably spend about $50 a week dining out. It's a tradition that every Sunday we take Marcie out, usually for Chinese. Um, let's put in $2,600 there."

"See how easy it is to budget?"

"But what if we're over-spending?"

"Well, you can cut back if you have to," I shrugged. *"Look at a budget as a spending proposal.* Some of the items are adjustable expenses and some aren't." I could see Angie mulling over that point for a moment. She obviously liked the approach.

"Okay," she said. "We're almost half way done. Public

transportation. We don't use that. Joey's car payments are $286.25 a month times 12 which is $3,435 for the year. Every four years, I get Joey's old car and we finance a new one. Is that okay?" She looked anxious.

"For now it is. If the two of you were closer to retirement, I would suggest you set up a special savings plan that would allow you to buy a brand new car when you retired."

"So we wouldn't have to make car payments afterwards, right?"

"Exactly. If you take care of a vehicle, you could probably drive it for quite a few years. But for now, I guess you're like most families and you're stuck with car payments. There aren't too many employers who provide company cars any more."

"Aren't you impressed that I remembered the amount of Joey's car payment?"

I laughed. "As I said, Angie, we women are often more financially aware than we give ourselves credit for. What about operating costs?"

"For the two cars, gas and oil runs around $200 a month, so $2,400. Our insurance is about $600 for each, $1,200 in total. Thank goodness Marcie doesn't drive yet."

"Well, you're lucky you have a daughter."

"You're so right. Only the young fellows have to pay higher premiums. It's another one of those times when it's good to be a female." We both chuckled. "Car licences run at about $120 and repairs and tires, I'd say about $750 for the two cars combined. This might be a bit low, but, then again, Joey does most of the fixing."

"Now, for clothing," I said.

"What do you think is reasonable?"

"Well, it's really your budget," I said, "but I suppose a little bit of input won't hurt. In their book, *Megatrends for Women*, Aburdene and Naisbitt refer to a 1991 *Glamour* survey which says that most women spend less than 7 per cent of their gross income on clothing. On the other hand, there are financial experts who believe that 10 per cent of a woman's salary is a reasonable amount to spend on clothing and image. One financial expert, Emily Card, said in a book she wrote that one should 'buy basics, borrow frills'."

Angie laughed. "Actually, I earn about $30,000 before tax and spend about $2,000 a year on clothes. Joey spends another $1,000 or so, and then there's Marcie's stuff. I think in total $4,000 should cover it. As far as laundry—the next item on the agenda—I do most of it at home, but we do send some stuff out. On average, I guess about $15 a month times twelve months, that's $180. Now, the next category is recreation, reading and education. What do we spend on travel and vacations?" She turned to me. "You know, in this case I'd like to put down what I would *like* to spend. Is that okay?"

"Of course," I replied, "as long as it's reasonable."

"If our vacation allowance averaged $200 a month, or $2,400 a year, we'd be in the ballpark. How do you like that for a good old male-oriented term? We both like to take a couple of nice driving trips during the summer, but during the winter break we tend to hang around here and spend time with the family, so $2,400 should cover it." She made the notation, then stopped cold at the next one. "Club memberships, that's for rich people. We don't have any. Onward. Miscellaneous entertainment, $100 a month; $1,200 a year. Fortunately, we're beyond the babysitting stage and don't have to pay tuition fees or for books, but I think, on balance, Marcie costs us about $100 a month for her allowance, various school charges and so on."

"Pop that into miscellaneous," I suggested.

"Okay, $1,200 for miscellaneous it is. Reading material. We buy the odd paperback book, but we get most of our stuff from the library. I'll leave that blank unless you think I should start a collection of financial planning books."

"No, I don't think that's necessary...yet."

"Tobacco and alcohol. Fortunately, we're both non-smokers so I can put a great big zero there. Under alcohol, Joey and I aren't big drinkers—the odd bottle of wine and he'll have a beer or two on a hot day—but, at most, it's about $20 a week, so I'll put down $1,040."

Angie paused for a moment to look at what she had already filled in, and I could see she was beginning to appreciate the picture I was talking about: the portrait of her family's financial future shaping up. I suspected she had never seen what her annual spending looked like. She was clearly originally intimidated by the blank schedule. I waited patiently for her to take a mental breather before diving right back in.

"Now, health care. What have we got here? Medicine and medical services not covered by insurance. Some prescription medicines here and there; Tylenol, cold remedies, whatever... maybe $600 a year. Joey has a medical and dental plan at work, and I think he said his payments are $300 a year. I guess our dentist soaks us for about $2,000 beyond the insurance coverage, and then for haircuts and stuff like that, we're probably looking at another $300."

I kept smiling and nodding patiently as I watched Angie work. My relief grew as she got closer to the end of the list.

"Let's see. Gifts to friends and family. I wish we could give more, but I think our Christmas gifts and such amount to about $800. That would include weddings, birthdays and stuff like that, even charitable donations. Now, life insurance," she stopped and looked sheepishly at me. "I have to confess, Mary. Other than a $50,000 policy that Joey has at work, we don't carry any."

I couldn't refrain from a loud, mental ouch which actually came out as a gasp.

"But we both *do* have disability programs through work," Angie continued hastily. "That would cover us for our take-home pay if we became disabled. I pay only $100 a year and Joey's costs $200, so that pretty well covers it. Except what should I do for life insurance?"

"Let's put in a question mark for now," I said. "We can deal with it after we total everything else that's entered. But there's one thing you've forgotten."

Angie re-examined the schedule with a perplexed look on her face. "What can that be?" she asked.

"Do you have your own bank account?" I asked gently.

"No," Angie replied, "I mean, we have a joint account from which I pay the bills and Joey has..."

I nodded. "Angie," I said, "I know you told me you and Joey

have a good marriage and I think you might have a little trouble with what I now want to say to you, but here it is anyway."

"Go ahead," said Angie, "I'm listening.

"Well, you know how so many marriages break down today. It's important for a woman to maintain an independent credit history, and to build a relationship with her bank manager, so a personal bank account becomes vital. Also, most financial advisors will suggest that you keep at least six months' living expenses in your separate account. I think more women have to learn to put themselves first. Money has to move up the ladder of women's values. Self-preservation is important. It includes not only making yourself more of a priority, but also ensuring you have enough money to sustain life, even in a worst case scenario. You've got to protect yourself against the unknown. Someday, it may be up to you alone to support yourself and maybe a child in the style you'd like to be accustomed to. You've no doubt heard that almost any financial advisor will tell you to pay yourself first. You've got to have your own independent savings so that..."

"Savings?" interrupted Angie. "I thought we were budgeting for expenses."

"Ah, we are," I replied, "but here's the key point. *Your savings are an expense, the exact same way as rent.* Even if your marriage stays sound, you should always have some money set aside for an emergency. Or should you decide that you want to treat yourself to something nice, you should have the right to buy it without having to ask permission."

"I see what you're getting at. So, you think I should incorporate a savings factor for myself under the 'other' category."

I nodded in agreement.

"How much should that be?"

I shrugged my shoulders. "That's up to you. One has to draw a balance between enjoyment of life today..." I paused and pointed to the section of the schedule dealing with recreation and entertainment, "...versus looking towards the future. It's a tough one," I continued. "Remember, women live between six and 12 years longer than their male counterparts. Statistically, you'll spend 22 years in retirement. In North America I believe

75 per cent of women are on their own by age 50, due to death of, or divorce from, a spouse. Eight out of 10 married women will be widows, so I think you *need* to look after yourself. It's *not* an *option*. If I may be blunt, the fact that, up till now, Joey hasn't seen fit to carry life insurance beyond what he gets at work is not a sign that he is a 'bad guy', but it does show that he isn't as financially aware as he should be. Women's financial needs are different in large scale from men's, because of the difference in life expectancies. And unfortunately, in general, women don't earn as much. Do you know that in this book I referred to before, *Women and Money* by Anita Jones-Lee, she says that there are only 110,000 women in the United States who earn more than $100,000 a year compared to 1.3 million men?"

Angie whistled in surprise.

"So, that's why I suggest if you can save, say $2,000 a year on your own, you'd be doing yourself a great favour in the long run. Anyway, let's see if $2,000 fits. We can always make adjustments, if we have to."

"Okay," Angie said as she pencilled in the number.

"Excellent," I replied. "You've done a great job and notice it only took 10 or 15 minutes. Remember, a family budget doesn't have to be completely accurate as long as the people preparing it put *some* thought into it. It's a good starting point. If nothing else, what you've done so far shows that, within a few years, you and Joey could be in a good financial position."

"What do you mean?"

"Well, even in the first year, your budget calls for mortgage principal payments of almost $7,500 along with other savings of $2,000."

"You mean my special fund?"

I nodded. "Remember, once your mortgage is paid off, even if nothing else changes, between the two of you, you'll be able to put $20,000 a year into an RRSP. And then your best friend will be compound income."

"Wow. I can hardly wait to get to that next step." Angie was becoming quite excited about the future prospects of the Larocca family.

"Okay," I said, "let's add it all up. Here, I'll do it." I took her schedule and my calculator and quickly punched in the numbers. "Would you care to guess at the total?" I asked after a couple of minutes.

"I sure hope it isn't much more than $50,000."

"Why that figure?"

"Well, on Joey's salary of $45,000 a year, he brings home a little more than $2,600 a month," she explained. "About $31,000 a year after taxes, unemployment insurance and Canada pension. Taking the cutback at my work into account, I can expect to earn about $26,000 a year and my take home pay will be just under $20,000. I haven't factored into this my income from moonlighting because that's uncertain at this point. So his 31 and my 20 comes to $51,000."

"Good," I smiled broadly. "As you would put it, we're right in the ballpark. Your total expenditures, as calculated, are about $50,600."

"That's great," she said sarcastically. "That gives us a cushion of a few hundred dollars! I feel so secure!"

"Hey, it's not so bad," I said. "Remember…"

"I know, I know. The principal payments against the mortgage and my special savings fund."

JOEY AND ANGIE LAROCCA
SCHEDULE OF PERSONAL EXPENSES

HOUSING

Rent/mortgage payments		$ 13,036
Mortgage principal	$ 7,436	
Mortgage interest	5,600	
Property taxes		2,700
Heating		600
Electricity		600
Insurance		700
Maintenance and improvements		400
Furnishings and appliances		
Telephone		360
Water		
T.V. rental or cable		180
Other		$ 18,576

FOOD

At home	5,200	
Away	2,600	7,800

TRANSPORTATION

Public transportation		
Automobile		
Car payments/rentals	3,435	
Gas and oil	2,400	
Insurance	1,200	
Licence	120	
Repairs and maintenance	750	
Tires		7,905

CLOTHING

Purchases	4,000	
Laundry and cleaning	180	4,180

RECREATION, READING AND EDUCATION

Travel and vacation	2,400	
Club memberships and dues		
Miscellaneous	1,200	
Babysitting (non-deductible)		
Education		
Tuition fees (for children not eligible for tax credits)		
Books		
Miscellaneous	1,200	
Reading material		4,800

TOBACCO AND ALCOHOL

Tobacco	0	
Alcohol	1,040	1,040

HEALTH AND PERSONAL CARE

Medicine & medical services not covered by insurance	600	
Medical and dental insurance premiums	300	
Dental care not covered by insurance	2,000	
Grooming	300	3,200

OTHER

Gifts to friends and family	800	
Insurance premiums		
Life (annual increase in CSV $_____)	?	
Disability	300	
Liability		
Other: *Special Savings Fund*	2,000	3,100

TOTAL PERSONAL EXPENDITURES	$	50,601

"You're not in bad shape," I continued, "but remember, your budget is not exact. While it's pretty easy to pinpoint your mortgage and car payments, people always tend to spend more on entertainment, clothing, travel and so on than they think. Then there are always hidden costs." I stared at the budget and slowly shook my head. Angie's face showed her concern.

"Are we in trouble, Mary?"

"No, you'll just have to be pretty careful. As long as your mortgage payments are made promptly and you save the first $165 that you take home each month to cover your $2,000 annual contribution to the 'Angie Larocca Special Fund', you can spend the rest of the money you and Joey bring home, as long as you don't go into debt. Juggle some of the adjustable costs if you have to, but don't take on any debt. You've got two good *forced savings plans* between your mortgage and your personal fund. The rest of your after-tax income is available for you to do with as you want, except we have one other matter to deal with—life insurance."

"Is that a major issue?" Angie asked with some trepidation.

"Not really," I replied. "You don't need a lot of coverage because you only have one dependent child and you're both capable of looking after yourselves. But consider this. If Joey were to drop dead today, what do you think you'd need?"

"Well," Angie thought for a moment, "it would be nice if I had the house paid for and maybe another $200,000 or so that would provide some income to cover the rest of my expenses."

"So your mortgage is $80,000. Add another $200,000. All told, $280,000 of coverage should be enough. Subtract the $50,000 that Joey has from his employer-sponsored program. That leaves $230,000. Let's round that up to $250,000, and that's after-tax money."

"What do you mean by after-tax money when you're talking about life insurance?"

"Under Canadian income tax law, life insurance premiums are usually not allowed as a tax deduction," I explained. "There is an exception in certain business situations, but that doesn't apply in your case. On the other hand, when an insured person dies, the proceeds are paid to the beneficiary tax-free. So, whatever you receive into your own hands from the insurance company is free and clear."

"Great, we have to wait until we're dead to get a tax break," Angie muttered. "Isn't that typical?"

I found myself convulsing with laughter. "For someone who hasn't given life insurance a whole lot of thought, your analysis isn't bad," I said as I got control of myself. "It makes sense that you would want to have a fully-paid home so you need $80,000 of mortgage insurance. As you said, you'd also like to have some capital. So $250,000 plus Joey's workplace coverage certainly seems adequate."

"Makes sense to me," she nodded.

"Now what if *you* died?" I asked. "What would you want Joey to have?"

"Well, if he only had one income coming in, it would be nice if the house were paid for, but he wouldn't need much more than that as long as he was able to work."

"Maybe not," I said, "but remember, you do a lot around the house, and he might want to have enough capital so he could hire a housekeeper. Besides, what's good for the goose is good for the gander. So, perhaps it would be nice if your life were insured for $250,000 as well. You know, the two of you aren't in bad shape. You only have one dependent child. A lot of people worry unduly about inflation, but in a few years your mortgage will be paid. Once Marcie is no longer a dependent, your clothing costs will drop as will your miscellaneous expenses. When you retire, you may find that you and Joey can get by nicely with one car instead of two, and a good deal of health and personal care costs are currently covered by the government once you reach age 65. Although it's probably not safe to count on it these days!"

"That's still a long way off," said Angie, "but I can see your point. By that time I won't need to have a special savings fund either, will I?"

"No, probably not. You might begin to enjoy spending it!" I agreed. "Well, if we eliminate the mortgage payments, the special savings and another $3,000 or $4,000 to account for Marcie no longer being a dependent, I can see that, in today's dollars, Joey and you would only need about half as much after you retire as you do today."

Again the light-bulb went on and her face absolutely glowed. "I get it," she said. "So many people get so caught up in worries about the future they become immobilized. They think it's impossible to build up enough capital to retire comfortably...so they don't even start."

"That's true. The biggest mistake you could make is to assume that, if your cost of living today is $50,000, it's automatically going to be $150,000 in 25 or 30 years' time. That's not the case at all. In fact, if inflation stays low, your cost of living in tomorrow's dollars could even be *less* than it is today. Once your house is paid, that is."

"Interesting—and comforting," said Angie, breathing a sigh of relief.

"It sure is. You probably won't need more than half a million dollars or so plus your fully-paid house in order to retire comfortably. And where do you think that's going to come from?"

Angie thought for a moment. "From the RRSP I guess. Once our house is paid...and we start putting in $20,000 a year...it won't take long..."

"No, it won't," I finished, "but we'll cross that bridge when we get to it. In the meantime, now you've got a game plan." I made a move to start cleaning up the various books and papers on the table.

"Wait a minute," Angie said, putting her hand on my shoulder. "We just agreed that Joey and I should each have $250,000 of life insurance coverage. You wouldn't happen to know how expensive it would be for each of us to get this, would you?"

"They don't publish insurance rates, Angie, so I can't just pull out a book and give you a figure," I replied, "but I don't think it's as expensive as you might think. With your needs and financial situation, the two of you don't need anything more than pure term insurance. You could probably get $250,000 of term insurance coverage each for about $800 a year. You're both in good shape, I assume, and you're both non-smokers. Term insurance is relatively cheap."

"Term insurance?" She shook her head. "I'm sorry to be so ignorant, Mary, but what is term insurance?"

"Don't apologize, Angie. In simple language, term insurance is a straight bet between the insurance company and the insured. The insured bets he or she will die. The insurance company bets he or she will live. So, for a ten-year term insurance policy at your ages, you'd probably pay $800 a year to entice a particular company to bet with you. They're willing to bet your few hundred against their $500,000—$250,000 for you and $250,000 for Joey. The reason is that maybe only one in a hundred forty-year-olds dies, and most of those who do aren't insurable anyway. So, it's a good bet from the insurance company's perspective."

"But if we're not going to die, why do we need the insurance?"

"Well, you never know. *Some* people die. Either of you could get hit by a truck for example, or suffer a sudden illness. It isn't likely either of you would be the one in a hundred to keel over, but it could happen and neither of you would want to take the gamble of leaving the other or your daughter without a decent financial buffer. Since we've put together a good short-term plan for you to pay off your mortgage, I suggest you and Joey each take out ten-year term insurance for $250,000 with each other as beneficiaries."

"I imagine we could get it from any insurance company or agent."

"Sounds simple enough, except you want to shop around."

"Huh?" She grunted. "Shop around for what?"

"The best rates you can get," I continued. "The insurance business is pretty competitive and every insurer offers a wide range of products. Actually, it can get pretty confusing and complicated."

She groaned. "More of this bean-counting. I didn't think you'd make me into an accountant in one afternoon."

"Now, Angie, get real. Technology is your friend here—specifically computers. There's a company in Ontario called CompuLife that provides a computerized price quotation service for insurance brokers and agents with monthly information updates. All the agent or broker has to do is type in your particulars: Female, 39, non-smoker, and the desired coverage, in your case $250,000 of ten-year term insurance. Then the computer spits out as many as 60 different quotations from various insurance companies."

"Finally, there's something that's going to take less than the rest of our lives to deal with," Angie smiled.

"Yes, computers certainly are wondrous things," I beamed. "Now, you'll want the opportunity to renew your ten-year policies at the end of the ten years without proving your health is good. It'll cost a bit extra to get this option, but it's worthwhile. The product I suggest for you and Joey is *ten-year renewable term*."

"Ten-year renewable term," Angie said under her breath as she wrote it down.

"I think we've pinpointed enough details that CompuLife should work for you. A friend of mine who has an office down the block and sells insurance showed me how it works and it's a dream. Though you might not necessarily pick the company that quotes the cheapest premiums. Most companies offer special rates for persons who don't smoke…"

"Actually," Angie interrupted, "we both used to smoke, but we quit together shortly after we got married."

I nodded my head and continued.

"Well, then, you both should qualify since most companies define a non-smoker as not using tobacco, generally in any form, within one year prior to the date you apply for insurance. Other insurers are small operations, and you might not want to take the risk of dealing with a company you've never heard of. But you'll hit names you recognize and you'll find, depending on circumstances, Sun Life might be a better bet for you than London Life. On the other hand, London Life or Imperial Life might come out ahead of Sun Life for Joey."

"Well, we're both in pretty good health, although I do exercise more than he does. Did you know I was hoping to run a marathon this summer? I'll have to shed a few pounds but the exercise should take care of that."

"No kidding," I said in surprise. "That sounds like a big challenge."

"Training is just one more thing to keep me busy, but it seems to magically brighten my spirits and I feel better inside and out," said Angie, gleaming.

"In any event," I continued, "you never know what you'll find. As I understand it, the various insurance companies try to balance their risks and they actually have sales—just like department stores. For example, a particular company at a given point in time might be trying to entice smokers between ages 50 and 55." I held up my hand to keep Angie from interrupting with the all-too-obvious question. "Odd, I know, selling to higher-risk individuals, except they figure they can balance their portfolio and earn a good premium for the risk. That same company, eager to attract this particular market, might not want to offer great deals for males between ages 20 and 25, so there's no way to know at any time which company is the best one unless you check."

"So, where do I get my hands on this program?" Angie asked.

"You don't," I replied. "Just find an insurance broker or agent who uses CompuLife and is willing to back up his or her recommendations with hard data on what the different companies are charging. If you want, I can suggest a couple of names to you."

"No, thanks, Mary. Come to think of it, I've got a cousin who owns her own insurance brokerage business. I'll call her Monday for some quotes."

"Good," I said. "I think we've accomplished enough for one day."

"Amen to that," Angie sang out.

"I just want to remind you, though, that I'm interested in more than just collecting a fee for the hour I spent with you. I want to see you stick to the program we talked about today. If your income were to change significantly one way or the other, or your family circumstances change—perhaps you get pregnant..."

"No chance," Angie interrupted. "Joey's had a vasectomy."

"Anyway, you've got a plan for now, and I would really like to see you move ahead."

"I appreciate your help, Mary," Angie said. "I'm really glad I met you, although I would've liked the initial circumstances to have been more favourable. I just hope I can get all this across to Joey."

"You will. Just be patient. Remember, a husband requires a great deal of care and feeding—just like a tropical flower. Take it slowly and I'm sure Joey'll see the logic of what we've talked about today."

"I think you're right," said Angie, glancing at her watch. "Well, only two more hours at the office and then I guess I'd better head on home to water my plant."

CHAPTER SIX

YOU BET YOUR LIFE

ABOUT A WEEK LATER, Angie called me bubbling over with enthusiasm. It seems on the way home from work that same afternoon we had our meeting, she stopped at a book store and picked up *Men, Women and Relationships* by Dr. John Gray. She read it, cover to cover, before even attempting to discuss with Joey the game plan she and I had developed together. Instead of pushing him for an immediate acquiescence, she gave him copies of the schedules we had prepared, and a couple of days to review them. Given the time to mull things over on his own, Joey became quite agreeable. He saw the logic of getting rid of the mortgage first to ensure an affordable cost of living in an uncertain economy and then catching up with RRSPs later on.

Angie confessed to me that she *did* tell Joey about her plan to put aside $2,000 a year on her own into a special savings fund. (It's great when this works out, but some women have found it's prudent to treat the account as their own business and choose *not* to tell their partners.) Interestingly, though, she decided to make a modification to the plan. We had discussed a monthly savings program of $165, which would total $2,000 at the end of the year. Angie's new idea was to set aside $200 a month for five consecutive months, take a month off, spend an extra $200 in month number six, and then repeat the process. In other words, her plan was to save $200 ten months a year and spend $200 two months a year.

"It's important for me to be able to reward myself along the way," she said. "I've got to have the chance to go out and buy myself something special once in a while. Or maybe something for Marcie. Or, you never know," she continued, "a little something for Joey."

It's too bad she couldn't see me smile. I was going to wait a few months and then, once she was accustomed to a savings program, I was going to make a similar suggestion. But she had hit on this important concept all on her own. *Saving money without rewarding yourself along the way isn't a whole lot of fun.* In fact, if there are no rewards to look forward to in the short or medium term, one tends to lose the incentive to save. It's too bad more financial planners don't think that way. Any time I suggest a mutual funds savings program (I'll deal with that later) to my clients, I suggest they take periodic sabbaticals from the saving process. Sure, all the statistics indicate that three out of four Canadians will live past retirement age, and it's important to plan for the future. But, on the other hand, it's also important to enjoy life *now.* You never know whether *you'll* be the unlucky person who gets hit by a bus.

Speaking about getting hit by a bus, I asked Angie if she had done anything about the life insurance issue.

"Oh yes," she said. "Even on that, Joey was in agreement...at least up to the point where he 'authorized' me to get some quotes on a quarter of a million dollars of coverage for each of us.

"I made an appointment with Amanda Mastronardi, my cousin who owns her own insurance brokerage firm," Angie confirmed, "and I was able to drag Joey over to see her Thursday night. She agreed with you that a 10-year renewable term was the best way for us to go, and she reinforced your plan of having us pay off our mortgage within that time frame. She confirmed we could review our situation at that time, or earlier if circumstances warranted. She said her agency was one of hundreds of independent agencies across the country that subscribes to CompuLife, and she was impressed we knew about the service.

"I chose Westbury Canadian, at an annual cost of $327.50. In Joey's case, the lowest premium was with Western Life, but Marie recommended Laurier Life because of their lower renewal costs. Between the two of us, you were right. Our annual insurance cost will be almost exactly $800.

"I was surprised," she continued, "at the number of companies charging well over $1,000 a year for the same coverage. When we saw that, Joey and I realized how important it is to shop the market for insurance...or anything else for that matter. We arranged to pay our premiums monthly as an automatic debit to our joint bank account. It cost a bit more to do it this way but it helps us manage our cash flow."

I was amazed at how quickly Angie had started to pick up the jargon of the financial planning world, and I laughed to myself.

"I must admit, though," Angie went on, "I resent paying for something I never want either of us to collect, but when I take a step back and examine our situation, I can see how important adequate protection is. I also asked Joey about his disability insurance coverage and was shocked when he admitted that his company had eliminated the plan three months ago as a cost-cutting measure. He didn't want to 'worry me' he said.

"Instead of getting mad, I explained, quite patiently (thank you Dr. Gray), that we're in this life together and disability insurance is important so we can protect each other as well as Marcie. Amanda promised to get back to us next week with a proposal that would give us $3,000 a month if Joey became disabled for more than six months and $2,000 a month if it happened to me. This pretty well corresponds to our take-home pays and Amanda told us disability insurance receipts are not taxable."

"That's right," I said, finally able to get a word in edge-wise. "We should have talked more about disability, but you said you were covered, so I let it go. Single women also need disability coverage, although, if they have no dependents, they don't often need to carry much life insurance. Do you have a fax machine handy?" I asked.

"Sure, why?" replied Angie.

"Would you mind sending me copies of your CompuLife quotations? You and I are almost exactly the same age and I'd like to review my *own* coverage in the next little while."

"Of course," said Angie. "I keep forgetting you've got Jennifer to worry about. I'll fax the papers over to you tomorrow."

"Thanks," I said. "I'm glad everything worked out for you."

We exchanged pleasantries, and eventually got off the phone. True to her word, Angie faxed over the CompuLife life insurance quotes the following day. I include them here for your reference. Shopping the life insurance market is really quite easy to do. Ironically, you may not get the best deals from the largest companies. It's because their advertising costs tend to be relatively high. It's also expensive for them to support a network of captive agents across the country who essentially promote their products only.

You may find you get a much better deal from a smaller company that operates through independent brokers. Their advertising costs are less and they don't have to foot the bill for a large sales force. However, it's important to balance this against the stability and history of the company when making a final choice. Just make sure your own agent or broker is someone you trust, and the insurance company you decide to deal with is reputable and solvent. I might add that life insurance companies don't usually go broke the way other financial institutions do from time to time. The industry itself provides some pretty good guarantees just in case. Skim the next couple of pages and you'll see how easy it is for you to handicap your own insurance bets.

COMPULIFE SOFTWARE INC.

Term Survey—10 Year Renewable
Face Amount: $250,000
Proposal for Angie Larocca   Prepared by Amanda Mastronardi
Age Last Birthday: 39   Age Nearest Birthday: 39   Female Non-smoker

---

EMPIRE LIFE INSURANCE COMPANY
TERM 10/10

	GUARANTEED
Age 39	310.00
Age 49	922.50

RENEWABLE TO 59   CONVERTIBLE TO 49

WESTBURY CANADIAN LIFE INSURANCE COMPANY
TERM 10 –10 YEAR R & C TERM

	GUARANTEED
Age 39	327.50
Age 49	812.50
Age 59	1,902.50
Age 69	5,430.00
Age 79	18,252.50

GIC OPTION INCLUDED FOR AGES UP TO 55
RENEWABLE TO 80   CONVERTIBLE TO 70

THE MARITIME LIFE ASSURANCE COMPANY
TERM 10 – CONVERTIBLE (NON-RENEWABLE)

	GUARANTEED
Age 39	332.50

RENEWABLE TO 49   CONVERTIBLE TO 46

RELIABLE LIFE INSURANCE COMPANY
YRT-95 – LEVEL PREMIUM FOR YEARS 1–10

	CURRENT	GUARANTEED
Age 39		337.50
Age 49	767.50*	1,387.50
Age 50	870.00*	1,475.00
Age 51	1,012.50*	1,557.50
Age 52	1,202.50*	1,642.50
Age 53	1,460.00	1,750.00

RENEWABLE TO 95   CONVERTIBLE TO 65

LAURIER LIFE INSURANCE COMPANY
ULTRA TERM 10 – 10 YEAR R & C TERM

	GUARANTEED
Age 39	339.50
Age 49	777.00
Age 59	1,984.50
Age 69	5,199.50

RENEWABLE TO 75   CONVERTIBLE TO 65

FINANCIAL LIFE ASSURANCE COMPANY
CHOICE TERM 10

	GUARANTEED
Age 39	340.00
Age 49	1,032.50
Age 54	1,380.00
Age 59	2,082.50
Age 64	2,870.00
Age 69	4,302.50

RENEWABLE TO 80   CONVERTIBLE TO 65

LEGEND: * VALUE PROJECTED, NOT GUARANTEED
NOTE: EVERY EFFORT HAS BEEN MADE TO ASSURE THE ACCURACY OF THIS INFORMATION BUT WE CANNOT
GUARANTEE ACCURACY AND ARE NOT LIABLE FOR ERRORS OR OMISSIONS

COMPULIFE SOFTWARE INC.

Term Survey—10 Year Renewable
Face Amount: $250,000
Proposal for Joey Larocca   Prepared by Amanda Mastronardi
Age Last Birthday: 41   Age Nearest Birthday: 41   Male Non-smoker

---

WESTERN LIFE ASSURANCE COMPANY
WESTERN 10

	GUARANTEED
Age 41	456.00
Age 51	1,685.00
Age 61	4,157.50
Age 71	8,600.00

RENEWABLE TO 75   CONVERTIBLE TO 65

EMPIRE LIFE INSURANCE COMPANY
TERM 10/10

	GUARANTEED
Age 41	467.50
Age 51	1,540.00

RENEWABLE TO 61   CONVERTIBLE TO 51

LAURIER LIFE INSURANCE COMPANY
ULTRA TERM 10 – 10 YEAR R & C TERM

	GUARANTEED
Age 41	472.00
Age 51	1,432.00
Age 61	4,142.00
Age 71	8,032.00

RENEWABLE TO 75   CONVERTIBLE TO 65

THE MARITIME LIFE ASSURANCE COMPANY
TERM 10 – CONVERTIBLE (NON-RENEWABLE)

	GUARANTEED
Age 41	475.00

RENEWABLE TO 51   CONVERTIBLE TO 48

TORONTO MUTUAL LIFE INSURANCE COMPANY
10 YEAR RENEWABLE & CONVERTIBLE TERM

	GUARANTEED
Age 41	485.00
Age 51	1,685.00
Age 61	4,157.50
Age 71	8,600.00

RENEWABLE TO 75   CONVERTIBLE TO 65

AMERICAN LIFE INSURANCE COMPANY
TERM PLUS II – 10 YEAR TERM

	GUARANTEED
Age 41	487.50
Age 51	1,615.00

ORIGINAL AGE ENHANCEMENT OPTION <= 1.5M
RENEWABLE TO 61   CONVERTIBLE TO 61

LEGEND: * VALUE PROJECTED, NOT GUARANTEED
NOTE: EVERY EFFORT HAS BEEN MADE TO ASSURE THE ACCURACY OF THIS INFORMATION BUT WE CANNOT
GUARANTEE ACCURACY AND ARE NOT LIABLE FOR ERRORS OR OMISSIONS

88

CHAPTER SEVEN
DIVORCE: WHO GETS THE DOG?

I DIDN'T SEE MUCH OF MY NEW-FOUND FRIENDS in the months that followed my discussions with Angie. Before I knew it, tax time was upon me and I was waist deep in tax returns. Do you think tax simplification will ever happen? Half of me fervently hopes so, while part of me rejoices in the lucrative make-work project that the government has created for this nation's accountants.

Accounting and tax are great recession-proof businesses. After all, people need the services of accountants whether times are good or bad. It doesn't really matter whether the ink runs black or red. It isn't glamorous (as I said at the beginning of this book, did you ever watch L.A. Accountant or Street Audit? Me neither!) but it's a living, and a good one at that.

I suppose if they ever decided to simplify taxes, I can help them reduce the form to only two lines:

Line 1 –What did you earn? $ _____
Line 2 –Send it in.

By the second or third year though, they won't be able to resist making things more complicated. The form will then read:

Line 1 –What did you earn? $ _____
Line 2 –Add 10 per cent $ _____
Line 3 –Send it in

But I digress. May and June were busy months because that was the year Jennifer was graduating from high school. First, there was the feverish preparation for her graduation party followed by the tense weeks during which I tiptoed around the house as soundlessly as possible so she could concentrate on studying for her finals. We finally did manage three weeks together in July up in the Laurentians. I rented a friend's country house and we spent our time swimming, canoeing and reading.

I thought I was well-rested, until I got back to the office and saw the volume of paper that had accumulated in my absence. It was almost enough to make me want to run away to some South Sea island and spend the rest of my life living on coconuts and bananas (as long as there weren't any terrible bugs).

It took a couple of days, but I eventually regained my composure and started methodically wading through the pile. During the latter part of July and August that year it rained a lot and while summers in this country are too darn short as it is, I took some consolation in the fact that there wasn't much temptation to take me away from my work.

One morning in mid-August, Marlene called, sounding so distraught I didn't immediately recognize her voice.

"Tom's left me, and I don't know what to do," she cried over the telephone.

I managed to calm her down and offered to see her that very afternoon. I made sure she knew how to find my office and did my utmost to clear my desk in anticipation of this unexpected turn of events. When I went out for a brief break at lunch, I stopped at the neighbourhood convenience store and bought a fresh box of Kleenex, which I placed discreetly on the coffee table next to the couch in my office. I had a feeling Marlene was going to need it.

I was somewhat surprised that afternoon when I came out to greet Marlene, that she looked every bit as elegant and composed as ever. I breathed an inward sigh of relief as I recognized that Marlene had an inner strength that would stand her in good stead over the troubled months (and years?) ahead.

In times of deep trouble, the best thing any one of us can do is to take a deep breath and tell ourselves "this, too, shall pass". Sometimes it's hard at the time to convince ourselves of that, but in the long run we often look back on the disappointments, and even the tragedies in our lives, with the recognition that we've emerged stronger and better. I asked Marlene to take a seat on my comfortable sofa and offered her a cup of coffee or tea.

"Maybe a bit later," she said. "There's so much I want to ask you...and I don't want to waste your time..." Her voice trailed off and I rushed to assure her I wasn't doing anything pressing anyway, and had plenty of time to talk to her.

"He wants us to sell the house," she began, "and he's offered me half. And he said he'll pay me $15,000 a year for the next three years. I can keep my jewellery and..."

"Wait a minute, Marlene," I interrupted, holding up both hands in a fervent plea to stop the runaway freight train before it got really out of control. "Let's start at the beginning. What happened?"

Her composure began to slip.

"I...We...We haven't had the best relationship now for quite a number of years," Marlene began. "Tom was busy climbing the corporate ladder while I stayed home, looked after the kids and functioned as his hostess and social secretary—entertaining clients and associates. Gradually, I also became quite involved in volunteer charity work, primarily in the arts. I'm afraid I wasn't all that interested in what Tom was doing and I guess he must have found me somewhat boring as well. We..."

"What does Tom do?" I asked.

"He's regional vice-president for one of the chartered banks. He's fluently bilingual. Believe it or not, even though our name is Henderson, he grew up speaking French before he even learned English. His mother's maiden name was Laperrière.

"The banks seem to make money even when the economy is down," she continued, "and I don't know what he earns, but it wouldn't surprise me if it's upwards of $200,000 a year. I don't know. It could even be more. I know Tom wasn't always faithful to me, and if truth be told...but anyway, we've got two lovely children, a beautiful home and..."

Her voice trailed off and the only sound in the office was the gentle 'whoosh' as the first Kleenex rapidly departed from its container. I waited quietly for Marlene to regain her composure.

I felt it was better not to say anything at all. Usually, given a bit of breathing space and a sympathetic ear, a woman can solve her own problems.

By the way, this is something most *men* don't realize. They think when a woman starts to complain about things, she wants the man in her life to fix everything. But that's not the case. What women are usually looking for is a sounding board off which to bounce their ideas. It helps us focus because sometimes the problems we *start* off talking about aren't the *real* problems that are bothering us. It just takes us a while to get around to the core issues. Men, on the other hand, internalize their problems and rarely talk about them until they think they've got solutions. And then women tend to get upset because they weren't consulted. After all, *we* don't like to be handed a 'fait accompli'. So, with men feeling that they are constantly being 'dumped on' by women who presumably want their problems solved, and women being made to feel like unintelligent second-class citizens who don't have a voice in anything important, there's naturally lots of friction. War often erupts between the Martians and the Venusians. And all this is really so easy to resolve! Women simply have to learn to reinforce the fact that they're *not* looking for their men to solve all of their problems. Nor are they dumping on them or holding them responsible for the many things that tend to go wrong in our day-to-day lives. I mean, it's not the husband's fault that little Sam forgot his ski pants at the daycare and it's -25° outside. If men could just learn a bit of patience and let their women blow off steam and not take it personally, life would become much more pleasant. On the other side of the coin, *women* don't want to hear, *I've* decided we're going to go on a week's cruise to Bermuda this winter. (You bet she'd *love* to go to Bermuda, but she wants to be part of the decision.) Communication, communication, communication...But again, I digress. This is Marlene's story I'm supposed to be telling here and it seemed that, in her case, things might have gone more than a bit too far for her relationship with Tom to be salvaged.

"So, Marlene, what happened?" I asked gently.

"Well, last Friday, Tom came home and told me he was

leaving. It appears he's been having an affair for the last two years with one of the department heads in his office."

"And you're sure this isn't just another fling?"

"Not this time," she said, tearfully, reaching for another Kleenex. "He was so damn smug and self-righteous. It's not the sex, he told me. It's that *she's interested in what I do. We've grown apart, and this is my last chance,* he said... Anyhow," she shrugged, "two years is a long time to carry on an affair."

"You don't think counselling would help?" I asked.

"I suggested it, but he told me he had made up his mind. Oh, he's got it all planned. As I told you, he wants to sell the house and split the proceeds and he's offered me $15,000 a year for the next three years so I can 'get back on my feet'. When I asked him what he expected me to do, he shrugged his shoulders in that infuriating Gallic way of his. He did offer to pay the children's tuition and living expenses while they are away at university. All heart, that man."

"Have you talked to a lawyer?"

"Oh, that won't be necessary, he told me. He doesn't want me to go through any 'unnecessary expenses'. His lawyer will take care of *everything*. And he'll pay the bill."

I shook my head slowly as I collected my thoughts.

"Well, the first thing I can tell you, Marlene, is that you need your own independent counsel. Typically, when one spouse wants out of a marriage, he or she—and it's usually he—thinks it can be accomplished one-two-three, no fuss, no bother, all the dirt quickly swept under the rug. But it doesn't usually work that way, especially if there is a fair amount of money involved, or other issues, such as who's going to have custody of the children, and so on.

"The good news from all this is, at least *you* don't have a problem in connection with the children. I think the most important point is to keep *their* trauma down to an absolute minimum. They're old enough to form their own judgements. If Tom's relationship with this other woman becomes permanent, now that it's out in the open, the children must have the opportunity to make their own decisions as to whether or not they like her. One of the worst mistakes *you* could make is to poison their minds against her or their father. I think you should do your best to contain your bitterness and not involve them."

"I suppose you're right," said Marlene. "It won't be easy; you see, everything is happening at once. The kids are both leaving home to go to school and Tom is gone. I've never been so alone. I really don't know what I'm going to do."

"Oh, Marlene, I know it hurts, but I also truly believe you've got the inner strength to see your way through this. It's important for you to remember that *in the long run, things do work out*. But for now," I went on, "it's imperative to realize that you need your own independent representation. On the one hand, you can't let Tom rush you into a settlement that isn't fair, and on the other, if he starts to adopt delaying tactics to wear you down, you can't make any rash concessions. Having your own lawyer on your side will help you get a fair deal."

"Off the top of your head," Marlene asked, "what do you think of what Tom's offered?"

"It's a bit hard for me to answer that question without knowing all the details about your combined net worth and what Tom's income is. But, off the top of my head, as you so aptly put it, I think what he's offering is much too low. You see, in most jurisdictions, the rule of thumb on marriage breakdown is that both spouses are supposed to split equally the assets that have been accumulated during the marriage. Now, I don't know what investments you and Tom have, but if he's an executive with a large bank, he has an employee pension, and you'd be entitled to some of that as well."

"Really?" Marlene asked. "Even if he won't get it for a number of years yet?"

"That's right. The rules include pensions and registered retirement savings plans as part of family assets subject to distribution. By the way, if Tom plays coy in disclosing his financial picture, one of the things that your lawyer would be trained to do is to get the facts. The law requires full disclosure. Now, again, the 50/50 rule is a rule of thumb, and if the parties can't work out an equitable arrangement between themselves, the courts have the power to award more or less.

94

"Personally, I have great difficulty in rationalizing the kinds of awards that some women receive when they get divorced from extremely wealthy husbands. I mean, just because one's husband may have been a movie star or a business tycoon, shouldn't necessarily entitle a former wife, especially one who has only been with him a short time, to a settlement of millions of dollars. On the other hand, in cases like yours, where you 'held down the fort', so to speak, for all the years during which your children were growing up, so Tom could be free to pursue his goals of achieving promotions and growth within his firm, there should be an equitable reward. And it's pretty clear to me $15,000 a year for three years just so you can 'get back on your feet', the way he put it, isn't very much for your years of investment in the family partnership compared to his income and, presumably, his net worth. Have you any assets of your own?"

Marlene thought for a moment. "Actually, not that much. I have $25,000 I inherited from my maiden aunt two years ago, which Tom invested in my name in a five-year term deposit with his bank. I'm still getting about 8 per cent interest." Suddenly her face lost all its colour. "Does Tom get half of that?" she asked, horrified.

"I don't really know," I said, "but you can find out from your lawyer. If my memory serves me right, after a marriage breaks up, an inheritance usually stays with the party who received it unless the other party can show that the inheritance was incorporated into the lifestyle of both parties while they were still married."

"What you're basically saying is that if the income from the inheritance was needed by Tom and myself to cover our living expenses, I might have to give some of that up."

"Right," I said. "Now, in your case, the inheritance was small. But, hypothetically, what if someone inherits $500,000 after three years of marriage and then the marriage breaks up 15 years later? Then it's certainly possible, in fact probable, that the inheritance has been factored into the joint lifestyle, and the person who actually received it may have to give up part. But it's a negotiating point, although in your situation, I think there's almost zero chance of Tom taking any part of it away from you.

Have you saved any additional money of your own?"

"Not really," she said, going on the defensive. "I mean, Tom always gave me enough to pay the household bills..."

I sighed. "It's too bad most women aren't better prepared."

"How so?"

"This may sound somewhat callous, but I think every woman who is dependent on her husband by virtue of the fact that she doesn't have an outside business, job or career, should try to sock away enough money to cover six months' living expenses on her own. This would be a welcome life-line in the event the requirement to become self-sufficient suddenly arises."

"You're right—that is a rather callous suggestion."

"Maybe so," I said, "but so many marriages do end up in divorce and there is also the chance of an unexpected health, legal or financial problem that can make a woman wish she had her own resources to fall back on. All too often, it's the woman who is saddled with the responsibility of raising young children on an insufficient income. Even when she's fortunate enough to obtain a judgement for child support, in more than half the cases, she never receives a penny."

"That's really unfair," exclaimed Marlene.

"Of course it's unfair, but it's a fact of life. At the provincial level, it seems that governments are finally starting to take steps to enforce maintenance orders. A number of the provinces are looking at reciprocal legislation so that if a deadbeat parent moves from one province to another, a court order in the first province would become enforceable in the second."

"You mean, if a man moves from, say, B.C. to Ontario, leaving behind an obligation to a former wife, the Ontario courts would help enforce the B.C. judgement?"

"You've got it. The downside is that the former wife usually has to incur time delays and possibly prohibitive legal expenses," I said. "You know the old saying, 'the Lord helps those who help themselves', and as calculating as it may sound, I recommend to all married women—even those who consider themselves happily married—that they maintain some financial resources of their own."

"And learn some financial awareness," Marlene added

ruefully. "Even if I had some money, I wouldn't have a clue what to do with it. Mary!" she exclaimed as she started to cry again, "what *am* I going to do? I have no job, no skills, and don't know the first thing about business or anything. Maybe I'll just take whatever Tom gives me and when it runs out, I'll kill myself!"

"Now don't you dare talk like that, Marlene. You're an intelligent woman and I know you'll land on your feet. You're not alone and there are at least 15 to 20 productive years ahead of you. But try not to be so self-defeating. Lots of women have had to learn to handle divorce and widowhood, and so will you. And believe me, when this is all over, you'll be better off than a great number of them. Now let's approach this constructively. Do you want to take a break and have coffee?"

"Yes, that would be nice," Marlene said. I could see she was making a conscious effort to get a grip on her emotions. "Do you have any tea?"

I nodded.

"Milk and one level spoon of sugar, please."

I walked over to my desk, picked up the phone and asked Louise, my secretary, to bring us coffee and tea. Most of the time, I get my own drinks for myself and my clients. I don't view the fact that I could 'order' my secretary to bring me beverages as a power trip. But, once in a while, it's good to realize when one should make an exception to a rule, and this was one time when I didn't want the flow of conversation to be unduly interrupted. A few moments later, when Louise knocked on the door and entered carrying a tray, I could see she appreciated my position, as she surreptitiously glanced at the mountain of soggy Kleenex building on the corner of my coffee table.

Marlene and I were soon sipping from our cups, each of us lost in our own thoughts.

"So, you really think I should get myself a lawyer?" she finally asked.

"You bet I do," I answered.

"Will a lawyer help me with the tax implications? I mean, I don't even know what happens when Tom...if Tom...gives me any money."

I couldn't help chuckling.

"What's so funny?" asked Marlene.

"Well, to be honest with you," I said, "and this is kind of a subjective thing, I find, in general, divorce lawyers who also call themselves 'family law practitioners', tend to know very little about income tax. They'll probably refer you to an accountant or to a tax lawyer in their firm. They see *their* job as simply getting you the best deal possible under the circumstances, and they pride themselves on their negotiation skills."

"So, a divorce lawyer is not the right person to give advice on tax. I wonder why that is," Marlene mused.

"It's because most lawyers who aren't involved in tax practice are afraid of—and even hate—income tax. And it's not only the divorce lawyers. I've dealt with many corporate lawyers who set up companies and do contracts who haven't the foggiest idea of what the tax implications are in the deals they put together. The same holds true for many lawyers who specialize in real estate."

"So, how do they keep from getting into trouble?" Marlene asked incredulously.

I laughed. "Generally it's because their *clients* know even less than they do." For the first time that afternoon Marlene smiled—tentatively. "In the larger firms, though," I continued, "the lawyers who practise within their respective specialties consult with their confréres who are tax specialists. But the large firms often tend to be expensive. After all, they have high rent and large overhead."

"What would you recommend, considering I obviously have limited resources?"

"*I* can certainly tell you what the tax implications are, if you'd like me to. And I can work together with your 'family' lawyer so you'll understand the full implications of the final settlement agreement before you sign it. I think whichever lawyer you choose will be relieved to know that he or she..."

"She."

"*She* won't have to worry about taxes."

"Can *you* give me a bit of an overview now?"

"Sure," I said, "but I'll keep it brief. If you really want to know a bit more about how the income tax system works regarding separation and divorce, I can recommend something to you." I went over to my bookcase and retrieved a book with a blue cover that I handed to Marlene.

"*The Canadian Tax and Investment Guide* by Henry B. Zimmer," she read. "My goodness, I don't want to read that. I can assure you, I have no desire to become a tax expert."

"This book isn't designed to make you a tax expert," I replied. "In fact, it's written for lay people, and consists of a series of different topics. Right at the beginning, Mr. Zimmer says you don't have to read the book cover to cover. For example, if you don't own your own business, the chapters on business income have no bearing on your circumstances. There is, however, a chapter here which is only 10 or 15 pages long on the subject of separation and divorce. He summarizes the tax rules in simple layman's language."

"Oh, I'm sure I can handle 10 or 15 pages, as long as there's not too much jargon."

"That's the beauty of the book," I said. "It truly *is* written in simple language, and there's even a glossary of terms at the end if the reader should happen to get stuck, or wants to refer back to something that he or she isn't clear on."

"Can you lend it to me for a day or two?"

"No problem," I said, "but if you'd like, I can also give you a summary of the relevant points in just a couple of minutes."

"Please do," said Marlene. "The more I understand, the easier it'll be for me to get my act together."

"All right then. Let's assume that a marriage breaks down and a husband transfers property or agrees to make payments to a wife."

"Okay," she nodded.

"Now, there are two kinds of payments. The first is alimony or a separation allowance that is paid on a periodic basis— generally monthly."

"You mean like the $15,000 a year Tom wants to give me for the next three years?"

"Right," I said. "When alimony or maintenance payments are made, they are tax-deductible to the payer and they are taxable income to the recipient. If Tom is earning over $70,000 a year, which you've told me he is, he's probably in a 45 to 50 per cent income tax bracket. It would therefore cost him only 50 or 55 cents on the dollar to make these payments to you."

"So that's what tax-deductible means. What you're telling me is that, for income tax purposes, it's as if he earns $15,000 a year less."

I nodded.

"And, therefore, his income taxes are between 45 and 50 per cent less on that $15,000."

I nodded again.

"So, he's really only offering me $7,500 or $8,000 a year out of his own pocket?"

I nodded a third time.

"That's not very much at all in his circumstances."

"Well," I said, "that's why it's so important for you to understand the income tax implications and why you need your own lawyer."

"Now, what happens on my end?" Marlene asked.

"When a wife receives alimony or maintenance for her children, whatever she gets is taxable as income. On the first $30,000 a year, she can count on giving the government about 25 per cent. But if she were supporting children, she would have additional tax benefits."

"Now that doesn't apply to me. Are you really saying the government would take away a *quarter* of what Tom gives me?"

"That's right. *And that's assuming you have no other income.* What if you went out and got a job or started a little business that generated $30,000 a year for yourself?"

"I wish," said Marlene.

"It's not out of the question," I continued, "and I'll get back to that a little later on. The point I want to make, though, is this. If you were earning $30,000 a year from a job, a business or even from investments, and *then* you got $15,000 in alimony *on top,* the *government would take away 40 per cent of the additional amount.*"

"You mean I'd only be left with $9,000 a year?"

"Exactly."

"So, what's more reasonable?"

"Well, I don't know for sure, until I find out what Tom's income and net worth is."

"Net worth?"

"Yes, what he owns minus what he owes."

"Oh, like assets minus liabilities."

"Are you sure you don't want to become an accountant?"

"No offence, but that's pretty far removed from my interests."

It was good to see Marlene beginning to relax and regaining composure.

"Okay," she continued. "You've explained what happens when a husband pays alimony and maintenance, but what about the alternative?"

"You mean the second type of payment...a lump sum?"

"Yes, if that's what you call it."

"Ah, here the story is the opposite. If a husband gives a wife a lump sum settlement, he doesn't get a deduction for it and she doesn't have to pay tax."

"So the money is free and clear?"

"That's right. If it's a monetary lump sum."

"Are there other kinds?"

"Yes, and I'll get to that in a moment. But just to be sure you understand, let's assume Tom gave you $200,000 in cash as a lump sum. He wouldn't get a deduction and you wouldn't have to pay tax."

"That's great."

"In a way it is, but there's one other thing you should keep in mind."

"What's that?" Marlene asked.

"When you invest the $200,000, the *investment income will be taxed* on an ongoing basis. So if you earned $15,000 a year from the $200,000, you'd have to pay the same taxes we talked about earlier."

"That's not so good, is it?"

"It is and it isn't. Taxes are a way of life and we have to live with them. The one advantage to a lump sum is that, if we can assume for a minute that $200,000 would generate $15,000 a year, you would then have your income *indefinitely* and not just for three years the way Tom suggested."

"You're right," Marlene said snapping her fingers as my message sunk in. "This way my income would become *permanent* instead of *temporary.*"

"Exactly," I said. "In general, a lump sum is better than periodic payments. That's as long as your former spouse has the lump sum to pay over. There's another benefit, too."

"What's that?"

"If you have a lump sum, then the assets become yours to control and you don't have to worry about what happens to your former husband."

"You mean, if he loses his job..."

"Or decides to run off to Mexico, or dies prematurely, and so on."

"I see where you're coming from. What happens if the house is sold, or he transfers his share to me?"

"Fortunately, there are no taxes on the sale of what's called a principal residence. So, if the two of you sell the house jointly and split the proceeds, that money is tax free. Of course, if there were a mortgage on the house..."

"There isn't."

"I didn't think so, but if there were, the debts would have to be paid first before you two could split the residue."

"Residue?"

"What's left over. Sorry, sometimes I can't help being an accountant! Even if Tom were to transfer *his* share of the money from the sale of the house to you, that would also be a tax-free transaction."

"Do you think that's possible?"

"Well, again, I don't know all the facts yet. But my intuition is there's a good chance that, in the final settlement, you'll wind up with the house."

"But what do I do with it? It's so big. The memories..."

"Your best bet is probably going to be to sell it, although you must never give the impression that you're being *forced* to sell or the real estate community will come down on you like vultures on a dead rabbit."

"How so?"

"The word gets out when there's a distress sale, and buyers and their agents are eager to take advantage. Play it cool and when you do eventually sell the house, my advice is to buy something else, smaller and maintenance free."

"You mean like a luxury condo?"

"Right. Where you won't have to worry about lawn maintenance, snow removal and so on."

"Why shouldn't I invest the money instead in the bank or buy some stocks or bonds, not that I know anything...?"

"Well, you should invest *part* of it so you'll have some income to live on, but I don't think it makes sense for you to invest the whole thing and then rent."

"Why not?"

"In this respect, the tax system is your big enemy. If you invest your money, whatever you earn is *taxable,* but your rent, on the other hand, is *non-deductible."*

"Oh, I see," said Marlene. "That's a double-whammy, isn't it?"

"You'd better believe it. Let's assume you have $100,000 and earn $10,000 on it."

"You mean 10 per cent? Can I really get that much with no risk?"

"Maybe, maybe not. For now, let me just use 10 per cent as an example."

"Okay, I'm earning $10,000. Now what?"

"Well, let's assume you also find a job that puts you into a 40 per cent tax bracket."

"I see. What does that mean?"

"It means that, on the $10,000 you earn from your investments, you'd only keep $6,000."

"Oh."

"Now, what if your rent is $500 a month?"

"I'm not so sure you can rent a great apartment for that kind of money. I'm used to living in Westmount."

"True," I said, "but this is just a 'for instance'. So, what if your rent *was* $500? *It would take your entire after-tax investment income to cover your rent.*"

"While, on the other hand," Marlene continued, "if I invested that $100,000 in a condo instead, *I could probably have a much nicer place to live.*"

"And you'd be living virtually rent-free; leaving aside condo fees, it would be your own home."

"I can see what you're saying," said Marlene sadly. "I'll have to think about all this, but I understand your basic message. Income is taxable while personal rent is not deductible and that's not a good thing! What happens then, if I were to receive other property from my husband?"

"Such as?"

"Well, I think he owns shares in the bank through some employee program."

"What will *usually* happen, in that case, is that he will have to pay the tax on any capital gain when he makes a transfer to you."

"Capital gain?"

"Yes, the difference between his cost and the fair market value at the time he transfers those shares to you."

"Oh."

"On the other hand, in one way, you'd have to share in that tax."

"How so?"

"Well, if his lawyer is any good, and I'm sure he will be, he'll argue that, in the same way as you have to divide *assets* when a marriage breaks down, you also have to divide *liabilities*. And if, for example, Tom's capital gains tax is $10,000 when he transfers shares to you, his lawyer will argue that he should transfer $5,000 less in total value, so *you* pay your share of the tax indirectly."

"Is that fair?"

"It is, as long as the total property settlement is fair. In the same way as assets grow in a marriage, so do potential tax liabilities, and if you're going to share in one, you must share in the other."

"I suppose that makes sense, but that's something else I've got to think about."

"Well, you'll have plenty of time, but I certainly think covering some of these points early on will be helpful to you."

"As long as I can keep everything straight."

"That's why I want you to read that chapter in Zimmer's *Tax and Investment Guide*. If you go through it once or twice, all of the tax stuff will become crystal clear."

"I do hope you're right."

"At least give it a try."

"Okay," said Marlene. "I'll take the book with me, but I have one other question. This one's on stocks…I probably have a lot more to ask you, but I hardly know where to begin."

"That's okay, take your time. We're really doing quite well."

"All right then," said Marlene with a deep sigh, "what if I receive these bank stocks and then their value changes?"

"Nothing happens until you sell," I said. "If the stocks go up in value, *you'll* have to pay the tax on *your* capital gain. Under the present tax rules, three-quarters of any profit is added to your income."

"That's a bit of a tax break, isn't it?"

"It's because the government wants to subsidize situations where people invest in growth-producing property."

"Oh, but what if the stock drops?"

"If the stock drops, then three-quarters of your capital loss can be claimed as a tax deduction, but only if you have offsetting capital gains."

"And if I don't have any capital gains?"

"Then you have to wait until you make such gains later on."

"What if I never do?"

"There's a special rule that allows you to offset an unused capital loss against other income in the year of death."

"But that's not much good, is it?"

"It's better than nothing," I said, "although, indirectly, you've led up to a key point. In any case where a wife receives stock in a company under a settlement, she might be better off selling a good chunk of it at the very outset and then…"

"I know," said Marlene brightly, "diversifying."

"Yes. How did you know what I was going to say?"

"I've heard the odd financial commentator on T.V. and read an article here and there. I'm not *totally* uninformed, although, as you know, this subject didn't really interest me before."

"Welcome to the real world," I said with a smile.

"I have a friend who's in the same position as I am—getting divorced—and her husband has offered her an interest in his business. What do you think of that idea?"

"Was she active in the business?"

"No, not to my knowledge."

"Well, there's one important personal rule I'd like to share with you and I think all women should adhere to it."

"What's that?"

"Never put your money where your brain isn't welcome."

"That's well put," Marlene said. "Did you make it up?"

"I wish I could take the credit," I replied, "but it's one of the many good quotes I've written down in my notebook and then memorized from a book called *Women and Money* by Anita Jones-Lee."

"I seem to recall you mentioned that book on that day...it seems ages ago...when we first met and had lunch. Poor Dr. Frost."

"Yes, poor Dr. Frost is right...But at least some good came out of that."

"Yes," Marlene agreed, "the four of us are really becoming close friends, even though we're all so different."

"We can learn a lot from our respective differences," I said.

"So, what should my friend do? The one whose husband offered her a share in his business."

"Well, it's tough for me to answer that question when I don't know the circumstances. But I, for one, wouldn't be comfortable if I wound up with a minority share in an ex-husband's business. Maybe he can keep the whole business and borrow against its value in order to give her an equitable lump sum instead. I know there's the odd time when a husband and wife are partners in a business, then they get divorced and they're still able to keep the business running profitably together, but I think that's pretty rare. For the most part, I think it's better to adopt the philosophy 'when it's over...' "

"It's over," concluded Marlene.

"Right."

All of a sudden, she started to cry again. I waited.

"But even if I get the house and maybe $100,000 or so, what am I going to do?" she wailed. "I certainly can't live on the income and if I eat into capital, it'll all be gone in three or four years."

"The first thing is not to make any fast moves. There will be real estate agents after you to buy property and probably other people wanting you to invest in any number of business and investment ideas. Be careful. Make sure you're ready to make clear, well-informed decisions. Don't jump into things without fully researching them, and be 100 per cent comfortable with your decisions."

Marlene nodded. "I can see what you mean. A real estate agent already dropped by—I don't know how he found out so soon!"

"It doesn't surprise me. Anyway, Marlene, your problem is not uncommon," I said. "It's not an infrequent occurrence for a wife to end up following a divorce with a house and very little in savings. The key point, I think, is *you've got to invest in yourself.* After all, as I said earlier, your life is far from over."

"What do you mean invest in myself?"

"Well, what I'm about to suggest is something I can virtually guarantee you're not going to accept immediately. It'll take some time to digest this, but I think it's important."

"Okay, I promise to listen. What are you getting at?"

"I'm going to tell you about one of the relatively rare circumstances when *it pays to get yourself into debt."*

"Go into debt?" Marlene gasped incredulously.

"Yes. There are times in a person's life when it pays to borrow money in order to invest in oneself. Let me give you an example. A number of years ago, I was involved in a church group and one of the members was a young fellow who worked for the city in what he himself described as a rather boring capacity."

"What did he do?"

"Would you believe his department was involved in selecting names for streets in new subdivisions?"

"No kidding? A separate department? No wonder the government is in so much trouble!"

"Be that as it may, that's what his job entailed."

"So, what happened?"

"Well, this fellow had a Bachelor of Commerce degree with a major in urban planning, but he told me he had good math skills and wanted to become a Chartered Accountant."

"So, why didn't he?"

"Wait. I'm getting to that. To become a CA requires at least two years of working in an accounting firm while taking courses at night, followed by an intensive examination process."

"He didn't think he could do it?"

"It wasn't the exams that worried him. It was the fact that he'd have to leave his $40,000 a year job and take a cut in pay of around 50 per cent to article in an accounting firm."

"And..."

"He felt he just couldn't afford to do it. He was married and had two young children. His wife was only able to work part-time, and he felt he needed all his income."

"So, he was stuck?"

"Not really. I reminded him that giving up $20,000 of income each year for two years would only cost him $12,000 a year after tax."

"Yes, you're right," said Marlene. "If he were earning $20,000 instead of $40,000, his tax would be substantially less. What else did you say?"

"I suggested that he could arrange a personal line of credit of $24,000 to cover his shortfall over the following two years and then he could afford to go into the CA program. He could draw against this line of credit during his apprenticeship period to pay his ongoing bills."

"But at the end of two years, he would have been $24,000 in debt," said Marlene with a puzzled look on her face.

"But if he was successful in passing the exams, he would be a Chartered Accountant..."

"With a much higher income-earning potential," finished Marlene as she suddenly understood what I was getting at.

"This is the concept I want to share with you. *Sometimes it pays to go into debt if you're going to be investing in yourself.* With the kind of income that a CA can earn, he could've had that debt paid off in no time at all."

"Did he take your advice?"

"Unfortunately, he didn't. And to this day when I see him, he complains bitterly about how unfairly the world treats him. You know the old saying, 'you can lead a horse to water'..."

"I know, 'but you can't make him drink'. So how does all this apply to *me?*"

"Well, I guess this is something you don't have to deal with immediately, but do you have any idea of what you'd like to do? Even if it took you a couple of years to get there."

"Actually, I do have *one* idea that I've thought about occasionally over the years. I've volunteered with the Quebec Young Artists League and also the Montreal Museum of Fine Art and I've gradually learned a fair amount about art. I now sit on the Art Selection Committee for the Museum and I help judge art at various shows."

"So what's your idea? Do you want to share it with me?"

"Why not?" Marlene said with a weak smile. "It's like this. My husband's bank has quite an extensive art collection."

"Yes, many of the chartered banks do."

"And every few months they rotate the pictures in the executive suites. Sometimes Tom used to tell me how he hated a particular picture, but other times he was really happy."

"Go on," I said hesitantly, not sure what she was driving at.

"Here's my idea," Marlene said. "Most businesses can't afford to have extensive art collections which they can rotate, and most executives don't know a whole lot about this subject anyway. So, I thought there would probably be a good market for someone to go around to different businesses and rent artwork to them."

"An art rental business," I said. "How clever."

"Yes, for the most part, I suspect the market would be in prints, but in some instances a business may want to rent some originals."

"Makes sense to me," I said.

"And I also think there might be an opportunity for me to find some good young artists and get them some exposure."

"How so?"

"Well, let's assume an artist is just starting out and is producing good work, but hasn't yet reached the point where he or she is being carried by a gallery. I'm sure I could take some of his or her works in exchange for a small monthly rental. In turn, I would rent these pictures or sculptures to appropriate clients and if someone wanted to *buy* a particular work, I could arrange for the sale. The artist would be paid and I'd receive a commission, as well."

"That sounds like a good business plan to me, as long as you don't have to invest too much money up front in inventory."

"No, I don't think I'd have to. But, before I do anything like that, I'd like to take some courses at the École des Beaux-Arts. They're offering a special two-year program in art appreciation and design. I can use the knowledge and also get some credibility."

"Ah ha!" I said. "Your idea of an art rental business parallels beautifully the concept I tried unsuccessfully to get across to this would-be accountant acquaintance of mine a few years ago.

"Let's assume you had an equity of $100,000 in your home, just to take a simple example, and you needed $20,000 a year to cover your living expenses. You could arrange a $40,000 mortgage on your home which would give you the cash flow you'd need to go back to school for two years in order to *invest in yourself.* At the end, you'd be able to start your business. On the surface you'd be $40,000 in debt, although your *income-earning potential would be that much higher.* Do you follow me?"

"I sure do," Marlene said.

"You could then start to pay off that $40,000 over the next eight to 10 years from your earnings."

"Just for fun, could you give me an idea of what that would cost?"

"Just a second," I said as I went over to get Henry Cimmer's *Money Manager.* "Okay," I mused as I rifled through the pages, "to pay off $1,000 at say 7 per cent over eight years costs $13.58. Therefore $40,000 would cost 40 times $13.58..." I reached for my little calculator, "...$543 a month."

"Not an insurmountable fortune, I suppose," said Marlene, "if I had a good business going."

"Of course, you might have to borrow another $20,000 or so for inventory, but you could cross that bridge when you got to it."

"I see where you're coming from. There *are* opportunities out there and the world hasn't really ended, has it?"

"No. There are lots of opportunities as long as your attitude is positive. The only thing is, you should be cautious. A divorce is a pretty traumatic event, and you should move slowly. Also, it's going to take some time before everything gets sorted out. Even if *Tom* is rather optimistic that all the unpleasantness can be taken care of one-two-three."

"So, what should I do?"

"The first thing is find yourself a lawyer."

"I won't have any trouble doing that," Marlene interjected. "Half my friends have already been through this whole process. I'll just do a little phoning around. I'm sure a couple of my friends will be able to direct me to someone to whom I can relate."

"I'm sure that won't be a problem," I agreed. "The important thing though, is to negotiate some kind of interim agreement quickly so you can pay your bills."

"Interim agreement?"

"Yes, so many dollars a month so you can cover the household bills. And no matter what happens, *stay in the house.* I think if you leave and let Tom move in with his girlfriend, you'd be surrendering some major bargaining power."

"That sounds like good advice. I'll stay put and look at getting enough money to start with so I can cover the household bills, and buy food and things..."

"In the short run, you might have to make do with less, but remember, *you are woman and you've got friends!* You'll be okay."

"I guess now that I've talked to you, it seems pretty clear that, in the final analysis, I'll likely receive a lump sum and maybe some interim support. Will you help me manage my money?"

"I'll be happy to sit down with you to prepare a budget so you'll have some idea of what your living expenses are. It won't take us that long to do. When you do have some money, though, you should consult a qualified investment counsellor for advice. I'm afraid that's not my field, although if you need some recommendations, I can certainly help you."

"I guess I just *might* end up in a pretty good financial position, relatively speaking. What happens to women who aren't married to wealthy husbands?"

"Well, that's a problem, isn't it?" I said. "Marlene, not to be offensive, but I think I would have to describe you as being representative of a *transitional generation*. You are certainly more self-reliant than your mother and grandmother were before you, but you're nowhere near possessing the degree of self-reliance of women 10, 20 or 30 years younger than yourself...Not that you can't get there pretty quickly. In one afternoon, you've shown me you're a very quick study. In many ways, the most important lesson is: *women have to learn to put themselves first.* Our natural instinct to be a care-giver and looking after a spouse and children can undermine our well-being. In the long-run, if we, as women, learn to look after ourselves, we can teach our daughters to become self-reliant too, and the chain of male control will end.

"I read recently that women own over 50 per cent of all publicly traded stock, but that's because they either inherit it or receive it through the divorce courts. Only 12 per cent of women invest in anything other than bank accounts, and *that's the kind of thinking that has to change.* Maybe in the next generation, there won't be as many women out there who, when their marriages break up, get 'the lumps but no lump sum'."

"Do you really think it's an 'us' against 'them'?" asked Marlene.

"No, not at all. To paraphrase the old joke, some of my best friends are men. But I think what *we* need in our society is a level playing field. If the men aren't going to do the levelling, it's up to us to pick up the shovels."

Marlene nodded. "I only have one last question, and then I'll let you go back to work. It really was kind of you to see me on such short notice."

"No problem at all, really," I said. "What's your question?"

"Well," said Marlene, "between Tom and myself, who do you think should get custody of the dog?"

112

CHAPTER EIGHT
HER HOME IS A WOMAN'S CASTLE

SEVERAL MONTHS AFTER MY SOMEWHAT DRAINING EXPERIENCE with Marlene (more about her later), my phone rang and I picked it up to hear Francie on the other end.

"Guess what day it is?" she asked buoyantly.

I glanced quickly at my Daytimer and came up blank. "Haven't a clue," I said. "Is it your birthday?"

"Nope," she replied, "it's an anniversary."

"I don't get it," I said. "I didn't know you were married."

"I'm not, silly," she said. "It's been one full year now since I quit smoking. I feel a hundred times better, my credit card problems are far behind me and I owe it all to you. I don't know how to thank you enough."

"Well," I said, a bit flustered, "I'm sure anybody..."

"Nonsense," said Francie. "I needed that kick in the pants and I'm glad you gave it to me. So, how about lunch?"

For the second time in as many minutes I stared down at my Daytimer. "Today?" I asked. "I've got a meeting that should be over shortly before one o'clock so if you can wait..."

"No problem," said Francie. "Do you like Dim Sum?"

"Actually, I do, but I never know what to order."

She laughed. "Well, *I* do. How about meeting me shortly after one at the Silver Dragon? It's about a five minute cab ride from your office, and I can walk there."

"I'd be delighted," I replied.

"Mary," Francie continued hesitantly, "there's one more thing. Do you mind if I ask you a couple of questions over lunch?"

"Not at all," I said, "but I hope everything's okay."

"Oh yes, at least for the most part. I have some good news to share with you, and a little bit of upsetting stuff as well, but nothing I can't handle."

"Okay," I said, "we'll talk over lunch." I hung up thinking to myself it's always gratifying to be in a position to be able to help friends, but there's more than a little truth to the old adage, 'there's no such thing as a free lunch'.

♨

Francie and I both arrived at the Silver Dragon promptly at one o'clock. The restaurant was starting to empty out after the lunchtime rush, and we were shown to our table after a wait of only a few moments. It was my experience that Francie usually preferred to eat first and talk after. That afternoon, she surprised me, though, by jumping right into serious conversation.

"I have so much to tell you...and ask you...I don't even know where to start."

I shrugged my shoulders. "Start at the beginning. I've got the time, if you have."

"All right," she said, nodding her head to signal the waitress pushing a cart of Dim Sum delicacies past our table. She lapsed into rapid Chinese and suddenly three or four little plates appeared on our table.

"What's that?" I asked, pointing at a white gelatinous mass that seemed to encase some kind of fish or meat.

"You don't need to know," Francie said with a smile. "Just eat." She poured a bit of soya sauce over the food and motioned to me to help myself. I reached over and deftly speared whatever it was with my chopsticks. She was right. It was delicious. Maybe I didn't need to know what it was.

"So, what's on your mind?" I asked between mouthfuls.

"A couple of things. Nothing earth-shattering. Perhaps I'll give you the good news first. There's a company in Ontario that has written a software package designed for lawyers to help them handle real estate transactions."

"Oh, really?"

114

"Yes, it prepares mortgage documents based on the forms used by most banks and trust companies and also does things such as preparing the legal documentation and contracts covering the sale of property from one person to another. It can also be used to prepare lawyers' invoices."

"Really?" I interjected, not knowing where the conversation was headed.

"Well," Francie continued, "it seems this company wanted to get into the Quebec market. So they contacted a local notary who handles real estate transactions and he provided them with all the equivalent forms in both English and French."

"And?"

"And they needed somebody who could input all of this into their computer program. The notary, who's my cousin's husband, asked me if I'd be interested in doing it."

"And?"

"And I jumped at it. I don't only speak English and Cantonese; I'm also fluent in French, and it was really quite simple because the infrastructure for the software was already in place. But," she chuckled, "*they* didn't know how easy it really was. I just received my payment this morning."

She reached into her purse and pulled out a cheque. I looked at it. It was for $10,000. I whistled appreciatively.

"Not bad. How long did it take you?"

"About 200 hours spread over the last three months. I pretty well worked two nights a week, all day Saturday, and a half day Sunday each week. But I figure I still earned a little more than $50 an hour."

"Don't forget the government is going to take part of that away from you," I said.

"Yes, I know," Francie said, nodding her head ruefully. "I figure they're bound to take about a third, but that'll still leave me almost $6,500. And I've already got $1,000 saved up just from what I used to smoke, even after paying off all my credit cards!"

"It sounds to me like you're sitting on top of the world," I said as I helped myself to more from the array of small tidbits spread out in front of me. "What can I help you with?"

"I'd like your advice as to what I might do with my $7,500 nest-egg…By the way, I also had some rather unpleasant news this morning."

"What's that?" I asked.

"Well, it seems the building in which I live has changed hands, and the new landlords are bumping my rent by 15 per cent. I've been paying $510 a month for a two-bedroom apartment and now they want $585. My lease is up next month and I'm not really keen on going apartment hunting."

"You know, maybe it's a good thing you came into your windfall at the same time you're being forced to take a closer look at your cost of living."

"I'm not sure I understand what you're saying," said Francie.

"Did you know that the average family spends almost a third of its disposable income on housing?"

Francie whistled. "That's high, although, I suppose, if you stop to think about it, it's not that difficult to follow. Between my rent, utilities and the new increase…I'm not going to be paying much less than $650 a month which is…" She thought for a moment. "You're right, about a third of my take-home."

"Have you ever thought about buying a house?" I asked her. I could see the shock on her face.

"Me, buy a house? No, never. Should I have thought about it?"

I smiled in response to the puzzled look on Francie's face. "Just because you're single doesn't mean you shouldn't own a house. In fact, if you were to buy a house and pay for it over the next few years, that would take you a long way towards a comfortable retirement."

"How so?"

"Well, once your mortgage is paid, your only monthly costs would be taxes and utilities…"

"And I could live on a lot less than I'm spending now."

"That's right," I said. "A fully-paid home is one of the key factors in achieving financial security. Because once the house is paid, your cost of living becomes far more manageable."

"I can see that," said Francie. "With a fully-paid home, I

116

wouldn't have to worry about inflation and rent increases."

"And you also wouldn't have to worry about the possibility of a depression."

"A depression?"

"Well, what if you lost your job? Or were forced to take a big cutback in salary or early retirement? If you didn't have to pay rent, you could afford to live on a lot less."

"I see. But," suddenly her face clouded over, "we're dreaming. I've got $7,500 after taxes. How do you get from there to a fully-paid home?"

"Well, you certainly have enough money to make a downpayment, and I assume you already own the basic furniture."

She nodded. "So, it's a start. But can I really afford the payments?"

"We'll have to see," I said with a smile, "won't we? Now that I know a little bit about your new circumstances, let me do a little bit of checking and we'll talk about this some more. But I'll need a day or so. Let's see, today is Tuesday. What time do you finish work on Friday?"

"Well," said Francie, "if I take a short lunch I could be through by four o'clock. Why?"

"Do you mind coming up to my office at, say, 4:15 on Friday? I may be able to show you a thing or two that you'll find quite useful."

"No problem," Francie replied. "I sure appreciate your help. You will let me pay for this lunch, won't you?"

"Sure, if you insist," I said. (After all, I *am* an accountant.) "But I'll leave the tip. This has been a real treat."

৶

Francie arrived promptly at 4:15 that Friday afternoon. We exchanged pleasantries, and I told her we'd have to get right into what I wanted to show her.

"Jenny's in a play tonight. She's in a freshman drama group at the University," I said, "and she has one of the lead roles. I really must be home by 6:15 or she'll shoot me."

"What play is it?" asked Francie.

117

"Arthur Miller's *The Crucible*," I answered.

Francie rolled her eyes.

"What's the matter?" I asked.

"I'm afraid it's a bit heavy, lots of witch burning and other nasty goings-on."

I made a face. "Well, last year the group put on *The Sound of Music*..."

"Just make sure you drink a couple of cups of strong coffee with supper."

"You mean it's a real sleeper?"

"Afraid so," nodded Francie. "I wouldn't want to trade places with you tonight."

"It can't be that bad," I said as I reached for some papers on my desk. (Unfortunately, it was, but that's another story.)

"When I got back from lunch the other day," I said to Francie, "I called a friend of mine, Monique Lafleur, who sells real estate and is one of the top producers at Adanac Trust. I asked her to do me a favour and scout around for a good property in the $100,000 price range, not too far away from your office, which would also have a basement suite that could be rented out to offset some of the costs. She came up with a couple of properties, and this one here is her top recommendation. She faxed it over to me a few hours ago." I pulled out a listing sheet and waved it in front of Francie's face.

"Let's see," she said.

"By all means look at it," I replied, "but it isn't going to tell you very much. If you like the idea, we can look the place over tomorrow morning. I just love looking at houses...That's as long as you don't mind if I come along...No?...Great...We can look at some others also. More importantly, let's go over some of the numbers I've taken the liberty to put together. Even if you don't buy *this* property, I'm sure you'll get a couple of ideas that will help you make a decision on what to do."

"I should have known," Francie said with a mock groan, "confiding my problems to an accountant."

"Here, take a look at this. It's pretty easy to understand."

Projections for the Purchase of Francie's House

Purchase price			$ 93,800
Closing costs:	Legal, etc.	$ 715	
	Appraisal fees	235	
	CMHC ins. (2.5% x 90,000)	2,250	3,200
Total cost			97,000
Assumed downpayment			7,000
Mortgage financing @ 8%			$ 90,000
Monthly payment–15 year amortization			$ 853
Monthly taxes			82
Heating			100
Electricity			75
Insurance and miscellaneous			80
Subtotal			1,190
Less: Monthly rental income			450
Net occupancy cost			$ 740

"I'll run through this with you line by line," I said. "The asking price is $97,800, but Monique said they would probably accept an offer of about $4,000 less. So let's assume a purchase price of $93,800. To that we have to add closing costs."

Francie nodded.

"Oh," I said, "I actually expected I'd have to explain this to you, but since you're an expert on computerized real estate software, you probably know all of this already."

"Not really," said Francie. "By all means, go through this with me step by step. A lot of what I did on that computer program was really by rote—just entering forms into a computer and making sure various numbers added together properly and were carried over to the right places. It was really quite simple."

"Okay, then," I said, "closing costs include the legal fees, mortgage documentation, mortgage insurance costs and so on."

Francie motioned for me to continue.

"First, there are the legal fees, which cover the transfer of title, mortgage documentation and so on. I've budgeted $715. Then there's a CMHC appraisal fee of $235. CMHC stands for Canada Mortgage and Housing Corporation. Their job is to insure mortgages so lenders are protected if borrowers default on their obligations. CMHC charges a fee between 1¼ and 2½ per cent of the mortgage if the borrower's downpayment is less than 25 per cent of the total price. In your case, the fee is $2,250. By the way, the appraisal fee covers an evaluation report on the property to make sure it's worth at least the amount of the loan. Both CMHC costs only have to be paid once, which means you won't have to pay them again, even when you renew your mortgage down the road. I'll go through the mortgage with you soon, but do you follow me so far?"

Francie nodded.

"Okay," I continued, "so we'll assume a total cost of $97,000, and that you'd make a downpayment of $7,000."

"The money I've got after taxes from my moonlighting?"

I nodded.

"But I'll be broke!" Francie wailed.

"No, you won't," I replied. *"You'll simply be making an investment.* Instead of having all your $7,500 net worth in cash, in my scenario you'd have $7,000 of this invested as equity in your own home."

"But I'd have to spend almost everything I have."

"Sure," I said, "but you should be able to save a couple of hundred dollars a month..."

"Of course," said Francie. "I don't smoke anymore, and my credit card bills are gone."

"Exactly," I said. "I did some checking and the good news is this particular house comes with an almost new fridge and stove and washer/dryer."

"No more trips to the basement to do laundry, and no more ransacking the place for quarters to feed the machines! This is starting to look pretty good."

"That's right," I said, "and I guess you have all the basic furniture you'll need. Whether you buy this house or another one, you can probably make an offer that includes drapes and blinds. Usually the seller is prepared to leave them."

"Okay," said Francie, "let's look at the rest of your numbers. As I just said, this is starting to make sense."

"Right," I replied, turning my attention to the projections

sheet. "So, if you put down $7,000, you'd be left with a mortgage of $90,000. Based on your income and job history, I'm sure most lending institutions would be happy to let you have the cash you need with the property itself as collateral."

"Collateral?" Francie asked.

"Yes, the security. In other words, if you, as borrower, default on your payments, the lender can take the property away in settlement of the debt. So, if you didn't make your payments, you could lose your house and your equity investment could go up in smoke."

"I can tell you that's not going to happen!" Francie exclaimed.

"Certainly not," I said, again bending my head down towards the paper. "Now, you should be able to negotiate a five-year locked in mortgage at a rate of about 8 per cent."

· "Five years? Locked in?"

"Well," I continued, "there are all kinds of possibilities. Some mortgages have a six-month term only. That means they are renewed at whatever the prevailing rate is six months down the line; or there are one-year term, two-year term, three, four and five-year mortgages. And some institutions even give as many as seven and 10 years."

"Why do you recommend a five-year term?" she asked.

"The rate for a five-year term at this time is only about 1½ per cent, or 'points' as they're called, higher than the rate for a six-month term, and the trouble is, interest rates can fluctuate quite quickly and quite widely. In my opinion, many people make the mistake of going with the lower rate and shorter term and run the risk of getting caught if interest rates suddenly start to skyrocket. In my view, *the spread of 1½ per cent between the short-term rate and the long term rate isn't an interest cost; it's an insurance policy...*"

"So if rates go up," Francie said with apparent comprehension, "I'm protected."

"That's right," I answered. "Today, our economy is really very uncertain. And it's been that way for years now. I believe peace of mind is worth a lot, and knowing exactly where you stand for a five-year period is much more comfortable than having to panic every Tuesday when the Bank of Canada sets the interest rate for the next week."

"So," Francie said, "I should try to pay off my $90,000 mortgage over five years."

I laughed. "I wish it were that easy," I said. "Unfortunately, unless you start to make a great deal of money very quickly, it's not realistic for you to pay off your house over five years. Then again, if you can find some more lucrative software contracts, who knows? But, as you can see, I've actually targeted for a 15 year payout."

"I'm confused," Francie said. "First you talk five years; now you're talking 15."

"I'll explain," I replied. "What I suggest is that you lock into a fixed interest rate for a five-year period. This means that for the next five years, you'd know exactly what your monthly payment is. After five years, your mortgage would be renewed at the prevailing interest rate. If you're lucky, rates will stay down. If you're unlucky, rates will be higher."

Her face dropped at that last statement.

"But if rates are higher," I said, touching her reassuringly on the arm, "in all probability, this would mean we're having a bout of inflation. And if *interest rates go up in inflationary times, usually so do wages.* In any event, you can cross that bridge when you get to it. I'll tell you more about inflation and interest rates some other time. Anyway," I continued, "you should consider locking into a rate for five years, but you should *also* target, for now at least, to have your mortgage paid off over 15 years. If you start to make a lot of money, you may want to pay off your house that much more quickly. That's why it's also important that you look at various mortgage features offered by the banks and trust companies. Many allow you to increase your mortgage payment once a year by up to 10 per cent and/or also make lump sum payments of up to 10 or 20 per cent once a year. There are lots of special features, so look into them thoroughly."

"You can count on me being thorough," announced Francie. "This investment is important to me!"

"It would surprise me, Francie, if this house is your last one."

"What's the point then of paying it off quickly?" Francie asked.

"The point is, by establishing equity in *this* house, you'll be able to sell it eventually and use that equity to trade up to a nicer house if you wish."

"I see what you mean," she said, "but I just thought of something else."

"What's that?"

"I overheard my Mom and Dad talking recently about paying off *their* house over 25 years. In fact, they still have a few years left to go before their house is fully paid."

I shook my head. "That's where people get fouled up by following conventional wisdom."

"Why's that?"

"It's true," I said, "that if you arrange a 25-year payout, which is also referred to as a *'25-year amortization'* of your mortgage, your monthly payments will, in fact, be cheaper. *But you get killed by the amount of interest you have to pay because you're paying for a much longer time.*" I chuckled and pulled out another piece of paper. "Let's leave this first analysis on the projections of your house purchase for a moment and take a look at the alternatives of paying off a house over 15 years versus 25 years."

"I don't believe it!" said Francie. "You anticipated this whole discussion all along."

I simply shrugged and smiled.

COMPARISON OF FRANCIE'S TOTAL MORTGAGE PAYMENTS WITH 25- AND 15-YEAR AMORTIZATIONS

$90,000 AT 8 %	15-YR AMORTIZATION	25-YR AMORTIZATION
Monthly payment	$ 853	$ 686
Annual cost (monthly x 12)	10,236	8,232
Total cost		
($ 8,232 x 25)		205,800
($10,236 x 15)	153,540	
Total interest paid (total cost less $90,000 principal)	$ 63,540	$115,800
Differences:		
Monthly payment:	$ 853 minus $ 686	= $ 167
Total interest:	$115,800 minus $ 63,540	= $ 52,260

123

"Now," I said, "assuming you financed $90,000 at 8 per cent, if you go for a 25-year amortization your monthly payments are $686 against $853 over 15 years."

"Where am I going to find that kind of money each month?"

"We'll go back to the other analysis in just a moment or two," I said soothingly. "Remember, we have to factor in the assumption that you'll be renting out your basement. Also, consider part of your payments goes towards paying interest, which I suppose you might see as lost money, *but the rest of it goes towards paying off the debt itself.* Over time, you build up equity—in other words, your own wealth."

"I see," she said, "I won't panic yet. Please carry on."

"Okay," I said, "here are your monthly payments for both alternatives. Then what I've done is I've calculated the annual cost. It's simply the monthly payment multiplied by 12. The next calculation is the total cost. In the case of a 25-year term, it's $8,232 times 25 years. In the case of the 15-year term, it's $10,236 times only 15 years."

"Wow," she said, jumping ahead, "there's quite a difference in the total interest paid."

"That's right," I replied. "*For the sake of $167 more a month, by paying off over 15 years instead of 25 years, you'd save over $50,000.*"

"That's unbelievable," she said. "You know, I studied math all through school, after all, I am a systems analyst. But I never..."

"It's true," I interrupted. "Unfortunately, kids in school just don't learn how business math really works and how understanding it can save them so much over their lifetimes. It's really nothing more than the power of compound interest. You know. The concept of investing money and leaving it for a long term period."

Francie nodded.

"Well, in this case, *the power of compound interest works in reverse.* The power benefits the *lending institution* when people are foolish enough to extend their mortgages longer than they have to."

"Although it was unusual for older generation Chinese to

take out mortgages, my parents did, and like I told you a few minutes ago, they're still paying it off today. I've tried to tell them a couple of times they'd be better off paying it more quickly. But I was only acting from intuition. I didn't think about trying to show them specific calculations. To be truthful, I didn't get anywhere and I really didn't want to push. After all, I'm only their daughter, so how much could I know? Maybe you just can't teach old dogs new tricks," Francie added thoughtfully.

"Sometimes yes, sometimes no," I replied, "although I suppose it's easier to start learning when you're younger."

"Okay," she said, "you've convinced me that my intuition was sound. *I'd* certainly be in better shape paying off *my* house quickly rather than slowly."

"Now there is something else you need to know about buying a house," I said. "You need to *qualify* for a mortgage based on your own income and expenses and that *can't* include anticipated rental income."

"Tell me more," Francie said, leaning forward in concentration.

"This is one of the reasons you may want to shop around at various banks and trust companies before you find a house. They will help you determine what price of house you *qualify* for and even pre-approve a mortgage and interest rate for you. When you apply for a mortgage, it's good to have very little other debt. You may find out that in order to qualify for the amount of money you wish to spend on a house you need to initially agree to a 25-year amortization so the monthly payments fit within the bank's requirements. The bank has ratios they use for calculating, based on how much money you make, how much you can spend monthly. In order for them to initially loan you the money, you must fit within acceptable debt-equity ratios. If they force you to go the 25-year route, then make sure it's possible to immediately reduce the amortization to 15 years by increasing the payments shortly after you finalize the deal."

"I follow what you're telling me," said Francie with a smile. "It's really not that complicated."

"Good," I said. "You can pay off your mortgage even more

quickly by paying weekly or bi-weekly instead of monthly, or by using other acceleration programs that various lending institutions have in place. But for now, let's assume a monthly payment of $853." I turned back to my projection sheet. "We'll also have to take into account taxes, heating, electricity and insurance. I've taken the liberty of getting the numbers from Monique and then converting them from annual to monthly costs. You can see you're looking at just under $1,200 a month all inclusive. But if we subtract the monthly rent for the basement suite, your *net occupancy cost* is less than $750."

"Well," Francie said doubtfully, "that's still a heck of a lot of money. Even if we compare it to the increased rent that my new landlord wants if I renew my lease."

"True," I agreed, "but you should be able to afford it. If you were ever afraid of running short, you could also look at having a roommate for a while. That's one of the other benefits of owning your own home. If you have an apartment, there are usually restrictions against subletting. But when you own your home, a roommate can help with the yard work and help pay a percentage of the utilities, as can your basement tenant."

"I suppose you're right," said Francie. "Making those payments is going to be a good forced savings plan for me. As I pay down the mortgage, my equity in the house will grow. This is amazing stuff. I thought I was mathematically inclined, but I never took the time to really look at numbers for *myself*. So many people find numbers boring, but it isn't boring when you see your own figures in front of you."

"You're right, Francie," I replied. "*If people could just do away with their innate suspicion of numbers and confront their own financial situations the way you're doing, they'd be a lot better off. And the irony is, you don't need higher mathematics. The only thing you need is the ability to add, subtract, multiply and divide, and for that, a simple hand-held calculator will suffice.*"

"I guess I've spent too much time studying statistics, calculus and all that higher math and I've missed the basics. But it isn't complicated, is it? And to tell the truth, it's fun. Why do you think they always glamorize lawyers on T.V. and never accountants?"

"Just reactionary thinking," I said. "I guess accountants are really just the unsung heroes and heroines of our society."

Francie laughed. "Okay," she said, "I know you're in a bit of a rush. Let's look at this next set of numbers."

I passed her a piece of paper so she could read it.

FRANCIE'S NET OCCUPANCY COST PER MONTH OVER FIVE YEARS

Net occupancy cost per month		$ 740
		x12
Net occupancy cost per year		$ 8,880
Net occupancy cost over five years		$ 44,400
Mortgage outstanding at end of fifth year		
$90,000 x .786	$ 70,740	
Mortgage pay-down over five years:	$ 90,000 – $ 70,740	$ 19,260
"Real" net occupancy cost		$ 25,140
Average cost per month over five years:	$ 25,140 ÷ 60 months	$ 419

"Now," I continued, "at the top of this page we have your net occupancy cost per month multiplied by 12. That comes to just under $9,000 a year. Over the next five years you'll spend about $45,000..."

"On housing alone! That's almost two years' pay after taxes!" She started to go into shock.

"Hold on a second, Francie," I said. "Look at the rest of this. At the end of the fifth year, your mortgage balance will be just under $71,000. In other words, you will have paid down over $19,000 in principal by assuming these monthly costs of $740. The factor of .786 comes from a mortgage table in *The Money Manager* that tells you how much is owing at the end of each year. It's useful if you want to calculate your equity build-up."

"You mean, even if the house doesn't appreciate in value, my equity, instead of being $7,000, will be a whopping $26,000 after five years?"

"That's right," I said, "so your *real* net occupancy cost over five years is just over $25,000. That works out to a little more than $400 a month."

"I don't believe it," she said. "You mean over five years my final cost would be less than if I simply kept my apartment, even if my landlord wasn't asking for a raise?"

"Right again," I said. "This is the real benefit of home ownership. And to top it off," I continued, "what do you think would happen if your house appreciated by say 4½ per cent per year on average? Four-and-a-half per cent times five years, that's what, 22 per cent in total...ignoring the effect of compounding."

"You mean, *with* compounding, my $100,000 house would then be worth $125,000."

"And if you made a $25,000 profit by selling it, what would your net cost of living there be?"

"Zero," Francie said dumbfounded. "Between $25,000 of appreciation and $19,000 of mortgage principal payments, *I'd get back the entire $44,000 it cost me to live there over five years.* Mary, you're a genius."

"That may be true, Francie," I chuckled. "But remember *the appreciation isn't guaranteed.* I'd be rather surprised, though, if you didn't come out substantially ahead."

"You've certainly convinced me, Mary. Do you have some time tomorrow morning to go and look at that house?"

"I thought you'd never ask," I said. "In fact," I continued with a grin, "I've already made an appointment for 10 o'clock. If it's okay with you, I'd like to take Jenny along if I can get her up and going after her big night as a budding young actress. Frankly, I'd like her to take an interest in home ownership over the next few years. There's no law that says you have to be married and have two kids before you buy a house. Can you pick us up at a quarter to 10?"

Francie nodded.

"That should give us plenty of time. We'll also have a chance to look at two or three other houses so you can see what you like and make some comparisons."

"You know," said Francie, grinning thoughtfully, "I can't help thinking I'm being pushed a bit here, but I can sure see it's for my own good..."

CHAPTER NINE
WHERE THERE'S A WILL, THERE'S A WAY

THE NEXT TWO YEARS PASSED QUICKLY. We kept in touch and met as a group quite regularly, usually once or twice a month. Francie bought a house, although it wasn't the one we looked at first, and seemed quite content with her decision. Angie kept me posted on her progress in her quest to become mortgage-free and she confided that her little personal security fund was growing very nicely, thank you very much.

Marlene went through some tough times as her divorce from Tom proceeded at a snail's pace. He seemed very adept and quite creative at finding delaying tactics, designed to wear down her resistance so she wouldn't receive anything close to a reasonable settlement. Fortunately, our little group banded together and kept her spirits up with frequent pep talks and emotional support. But all this took its toll, and Marlene aged quite visibly during that time. She did, however, lose quite a bit of weight and was able to improve her tennis game dramatically, proving there is a silver lining behind each cloud.

As for myself, I watched Jenny bloom into a lovely young woman. And if truth be told, I could feel time starting to take just a small toll on me. I advanced from a size eight into a size 10 and doubled my budget for Clairol hair products.

For a while, I dated a rather interesting fellow—a lawyer of all people—but things didn't work out. He was too absorbed in his career to entertain any idea of a serious relationship, especially when his time commitments to his own two children from his previous marriage were factored in. I also found him too argumentative for my taste, and a bit too traditional in his view of a woman's 'proper place'. But life goes on, and all in all I didn't have too much to complain about. My practice was growing nicely and I still took plenty of time to smell the roses.

One Tuesday afternoon, my secretary buzzed and asked if I had time to see Angie. I was a bit surprised that she would call on me during the business day without an appointment, but I quickly shoved some papers into a drawer, cleaned off my desk and went out to greet her. I was even more surprised to find her dressed all in black.

"I'm sorry to barge in on you," she said, "but I guess I'm in a bit of a daze and wasn't thinking too clearly."

I ushered her into my office and brought her a cup of coffee.

"I guess you didn't know Joey's mother died the day before yesterday."

"I'm sorry to hear that," I said.

She shrugged her shoulders. "Actually, it was a bit of a blessing. She was 82 and her mind was starting to wander. But it was her heart that gave out...she died peacefully in her sleep. To be honest with you, she and I weren't really all that close. She didn't approve of my working full-time and we had our share of run-ins over the years. You know, the old-school Italian mentality."

I gave Angie an encouraging smile which prompted her to go on.

"The funeral was this morning and afterwards we went back to her house. She lived in a big old place in Notre Dame de Grace, not far from here."

I nodded.

"Anyway," Angie continued, "for the last, I-don't-know-how-many-years, Joey's sister and brother-in-law lived in the house with her and took care of her. It seems that Granny Larocca didn't have much money when she died, but the house was hers free and clear. Her will leaves it to Joey and his sister. This morning, after the funeral, Joey's brother-in-law, Stan, asked him if he'd be willing to sell his half for $65,000."

"Is that a fair deal?" I asked.

"I think so," said Angie. "Stan showed us a recent appraisal he had done for insurance purposes and the house is valued at $120,000. It's in a good location, but it can use a bit of work. Anyhow, Joey and I are inclined to accept the offer because Stan and Maria..."

"Maria?"

"Yes—Joey's sister—want to stay in the house and Joey told me he would find it awkward to ask his sister and brother-in-law for rent. Besides, and believe it or not, it was *Joey* who suggested this, we could use the $65,000 payment to get rid of our mortgage completely. We've been making all the payments you suggested and in the last couple of years, Joey's even thrown in an extra two thousand dollars out of his bonus money."

"Bonuses? I didn't think anybody was getting bonuses these days."

Angie laughed. "I guess I never told you last year, but Joey got a job working for Century Disposals. They're liquidators in bankruptcy and their business has been booming."

I chuckled. "I suppose you're right. Even in bad economic times, some people make money. In fact, the insolvency practitioners in the accountancy field are also doing extremely well. Although," I continued thoughtfully, "I wouldn't want to do that kind of work."

"Why not?" asked Angie.

"Well," I said, "it's pretty messy. When a business is going down the drain, its books aren't usually in great shape and it's pretty tough to figure out what they own and what they owe. But some of my colleagues seem to love that kind of work. More power to them." I shrugged my shoulders.

"So, Angie," I continued, "how can I help you, other than to agree with the analysis that you and Joey made yourselves?"

"Well," said Angie, "now that we won't have a mortgage anymore, I suppose we can use a bit of direction. After all, our payments were over $1,000 a month. I'm really overwhelmed because I had never, in my wildest dreams, figured on an inheritance."

"You know," I said with a small laugh, "inheritances are perhaps the most underrated aspect of a financial plan. For some reason, people tend to ignore them and yet they can have quite a substantial impact. A few years ago, I read that, in the U.S., the baby boomers stand to inherit over 5.3 *trillion* dollars."

"Wow," said Angie. "That means in Canada there must be *billions* of dollars of potential inheritances."

"You're right on that score," I said. "In fact, in the U.S., that same article calculated these inheritances to work out at an average of over $250,000 for each household headed by a person age 64 or older."

"Wow," repeated Angie.

"Well, obviously some people inherit more, some people inherit less and some inherit nothing. Maybe in a sense it's good that you didn't know *you'd* be inheriting any money because this gave you and Joey an incentive to start developing some good habits. But I think we should all face reality, and when it comes to financial planning, it makes sense for some people to take into account the *potential* of getting an inheritance."

"Grim kind of thinking, this realism. Don't you think?"

I shrugged. "Let me give you an example. A while back, I had a call from a former classmate who is a medical doctor affiliated with the Royal Victoria Hospital here in Montreal. His wife is a homemaker who doesn't bring in any income, although she's active in a lot of local charities. Anyway, he called and asked if they could come to see me. When they arrived, he began to complain about the fact that, as a salaried physician, he only earns about $75,000 a year."

"*Only* earning $75,000?" Angie said sarcastically. "Mary, that's a great deal of money!"

"It's all relative, Angie," I smiled. "I suppose the average medical practitioner earns double, but Doc told me he really loves his research and he and his wife live quite comfortably on his income. But they aren't able to save anything."

Angie shook her head in mock dismay.

"The problem is," I continued, "their friends tend to be professional people who make better livings and it's hard for Doc and his wife to 'keep up with the Joneses'. He said they weren't going into debt, but they were concerned about their inability to put aside money."

"I guess I can see the problem," Angie conceded. "Now that you mention it, between us, Joey and I earn almost $75,000 a year and until now, with our mortgage and all, we didn't have a whole lot left over."

I nodded. "While I listened to Doc, an idea hit me, and I asked him if he had any brothers or sisters. It turns out he has none, nor does Shelley, his wife. And it also turns out their parents have net worths of between $500,000 and $600,000 each, including their homes, and they are both on good terms with their families. It appears that Doc and Shelley will eventually inherit a bit more than a million dollars between them."

"Wow," said Angie.

"Believe it or not," I said, "I started to laugh, because it suddenly became clear to me that in *their* case, as long as they pay their bills including their mortgage, they really don't *have* to save money. Doc is a member of the University hospital pension plan anyway, and they have their inheritances to fall back on."

"So, what did you tell them?"

"I explained to Doc that it makes no sense for anyone to sit back and do nothing in anticipation of inheriting money. Take your situation. Joey's inheritance, a small one, came when he is what, 41?"

"43."

"Right. It could have happened at age 55 or even 65. So sitting back and doing nothing is not a smart way to go. Nevertheless, it is nice to know there's an inheritance somewhere in the future. It takes a bit of pressure off daily living and is something prudent planners should take into account when they're shaping an investment strategy."

"But we never considered it in any of our plans," Angie objected.

"Frankly, I guess it's my fault for not asking the right questions. If I had thought Joey's Mom would leave a substantial amount of money, I wouldn't have pushed you as hard as I did to pay off your mortgage. But since we're talking about this subject, what are your prospects?"

"I'm afraid that's all she wrote," said Angie. "I haven't seen my father since I was 10 years old, and Mom has been remarried for many years now, living in Florida. Her husband had some money, but with lower interest rates..."

"I get the picture," I said. "Anyway, people should consider inheritances if they are likely to come into play at some point. Obviously, an inheritance is found money because it's uncertain. In a way, it can also be a nuisance because it has to be dealt with."

"So, what you're saying," said Angie, "is that when people do their financial planning, one of the important things they should consider is any *expectation* of receiving an inheritance *without being dependent on the possibility.*"

"I couldn't have said it better myself," I replied. "You can't plan on relatives dying young so you'll get your inheritance early, and it doesn't make sense to help them along and accelerate the process. An inheritance won't do anybody any good if they're behind bars," I laughed. "But the possibility of an inheritance is something I think financial planners should consider in dealing with their clients. As a matter of fact," I continued, "in some cases, it wouldn't hurt wealthy people to pass some of their wealth on to their children while they're still alive. I think those who have money to spare might as well have it do some good, and it helps the heirs become used to the idea of handling money. Kind of like a safety net."

"I see what you mean," said Angie. "If I were someone who would ultimately inherit $2,000,000 and my parents gave me $100,000 while I was still in my mid-thirties, I would have already learned how to manage money better."

"Exactly," I said, nodding my head for emphasis. "Also, if you blew the first $100,000, you would be more careful with the remaining $1,900,000 when you got it."

"It's a great idea," smiled Angie.

"Ah. Maybe now we can talk about *your* will," I continued, "and we'll still have time to discuss some financial planning in a few minutes." I paused for a moment, then looked closely at her. "You and Joey do have wills, don't you?" I asked slowly.

Angie hung her head sheepishly in reply.

I shook my head. "Right, first order of business is for you two to see your lawyer in the next week or so to prepare a will. Give Joey a few days to get over the shock of his mother's death, and I think it won't be too tough for you to convince him to move in the right direction. It won't cost you too much money because your situation is pretty straightforward.

"You might disagree with me, but, as I see it, the proper way for most people to make a will is simply to leave all assets to a spouse—preferably their own." I paused to let this sink in. "The tax rules in Canada actually encourage this approach because all the property can pass from husband to wife or wife to husband tax-free. It's only when the second spouse dies that Canadian capital gains provisions kick in if there is property outside of a principal residence that has appreciated in value."

"Property? As in...?" Angie asked.

"Oh, stocks, corporate bonds, real estate, business interests and so on. In your case, there isn't much to worry about. In fact, if you leave a Registered Retirement Savings Plan to a spouse, there are no taxes when the first of you dies. The survivor gets to put the deceased's RRSP into his or her own plan and draw the income from it as would have been the case before."

"I'm sorry," said Angie with a puzzled look, "you've lost me. I don't know a lot about RRSPs and besides, we don't have any to speak of."

"You will shortly, Angie," I said. "That's next on the agenda."

Angie sighed. "You accountants..." She shook her head thoughtfully from side to side. "But before we get to RRSPs," she continued, "what you're saying then is that, in most cases, it's perfectly acceptable for husbands to leave their estates to their wives and vice versa."

"Who else should a spouse worry about?" I asked.

She shrugged.

"Well, I'll tell you," I volunteered. "There are a couple of exceptions. The major one would be when there is more than enough in an estate to provide for a surviving spouse. Let's assume for a moment you had $5,000,000 in assets and your annual income was $400,000."

"I wish."

"Give it time. Who knows?" I suggested. "Look, this is just a 'what if'. It's part of my *common sense approach* to estate planning."

"No more interruptions," Angie promised.

"So, assuming your assets were sufficient to generate an income of $400,000," I continued, "what if you felt that Joey could easily live on $300,000, even taking potential inflation into account?"

"Then I could leave say, $4,000,000 to Joey and $1,000,000 to Marcie," Angie suggested. "This way, she wouldn't have to wait until she's old and grey to benefit from the money."

"That's right," I said, pleased with Angie's intuitive grasp of the situation. "If you consider life expectancy, the average male might live to age 72 or 73 and the average female might live to 78. But if you look at a husband and wife together, especially if you're both non-smokers, have inherited good genes and don't drink too much, there's a good chance at least one of you will live well into his or her 80s."

"And Marcie would already be a senior citizen herself before she inherited anything."

"Exactly," I said. "If there's more than enough to go around, it makes sense not to force adult children to wait until both father and mother are dead before they inherit. Also, it doesn't hurt to make gifts to them in one's lifetime and if the gift is cash, there's no gift tax in Canada because cash represents income on which taxes have already been paid."

"I see," said Angie. "That makes sense, too."

"Now, the only time you might run into a tax problem is if you gift property that has appreciated in value. The appreciation will be treated as a capital gain. But let's not get too technical. Let's assume you had this $5,000,000 that I was talking about. What would be wrong with giving Marcie $100,000 at the age of 25 so she could buy a house? It wouldn't hurt your lifestyle at all, and the gift would make her life considerably easier." I paused to sip my coffee.

"Okay, so you wouldn't will an entire estate to a spouse if

there's more than enough to go around," Angie said. "Is there any other situation when you wouldn't give an entire estate to a spouse?"

I nodded. "It's a little more complicated and it doesn't really apply to you, but I'll explain briefly. It's when there's a second marriage later in life and both parties have children by previous marriages. If you give everything to your spouse, there's no guarantee your assets will eventually be passed on to *your* children and not to your spouse's children. The only way you can protect your kids is through something called a trust will. But, if you have what I can just simply describe as 'complex family circumstances', my suggestion is you should seek professional advice from a lawyer who makes his or her living out of helping people in those kinds of circumstances."

"Well, that's one thing Joey and I don't have to worry about," Angie said thankfully.

"Great. Now, let me recap this so we're clear," I insisted. "For most people like yourself, a standard will is all you need. You and Joey should both leave your respective assets to each other. Then, when both of you are gone, whatever is left should pass to Marcie. If you were wealthy people, I would strongly suggest that you consider some kind of a gifting program to her while you are both still alive, or perhaps at least a significant bequest when the first of you does eventually die."

Angie nodded as I spoke and took careful note of each item as I said it.

"Anyway, your first concern is getting wills drawn up," I continued. "Oh, and you should talk with Joey about this some time in the next couple of days to make sure he goes with you. If he does delay because he's still upset over his Mom's death, give him a bit of time, but don't be afraid to push. It's really important."

"Don't worry, Mary, I'll look after it. But what about these RRSPs?" Angie glanced down at her watch. "Do you have time to talk? I mean I know I barged in on you uninvited. I took the whole day off from work for the funeral, but I'm sure you have work to do."

I sure did, but I wasn't about to let Angie get away. I mean, it's hard enough to get most of my clients to be enthusiastic about planning for the future, and it was a real treat to have someone come to me in as receptive a state of mind as she was.

"I'll tell you what," I said. "Let's just go and freshen our coffees and then we can talk some more. I can spare an hour or so." I rose from behind my desk and began walking towards the door, coffee cup in hand.

CHAPTER TEN

THE RRSP—YOUR TICKET TO A CAREFREE RETIREMENT

I POURED US BOTH FRESH CUPS OF COFFEE and managed to find two Granny Smith apples in the fridge. I tossed one to Angie and we headed back to my office.

"That's a nice dress you're wearing," said Angie, munching thoughtfully on her apple. "Where did you get it?"

"Holt Renfrew, on sale," I said.

"Really?" asked Angie, arching her eyebrows. "Don't tell me you, a successful accountant, watch for the sales like the rest of us!"

"Of course I do," I replied a bit taken aback. And then I noticed the grin on Angie's face. "Financial planning," I said, "doesn't only involve saving money. After all, it's important that we live too—one day at a time. And proper planning also means spending wisely. In fact, saving money without some rewards along the way just doesn't make any sense. You know that yourself. If I remember correctly, you're the one who saves for five months then skips a month, and then repeats the process."

"You have a good memory," said Angie approvingly. "I'm a sucker for nice lingerie. Any time I feel down, I run over to Chez Yvette on my lunch hour and look around. It's amazing how therapeutic buying a silk teddy and panties can be."

"At least you've got someone you can model for," I said, a bit ruefully.

"Just be patient," Angie said, grinning again. "Someone with your looks and brains won't be alone forever."

"Thank you," I said. "I'm sure my day will come, and if it doesn't, I like my life the way it is. Anyway," I continued, "what do you know about Registered Retirement Savings Plans? Do you know how RRSPs work? You know, they're a very important corner-stone to your financial security."

"I know something about them," Angie said slowly, "but not a whole lot. I know there are all these ads about RRSPs in January and February. Then, after the tax deadline on them is over, I hear nothing about them. I know they offer some tax benefits, but I've never paid much attention because Joey and I never really had a plan. At least, none that he discussed with me. I told you when you and I first got to know each other how he had put some money into an RRSP and had only told me about it after he had already decided..."

I nodded as I remembered.

"That's before we started to focus on paying off our mortgage. But now that that's done..."

I nodded again for encouragement.

"I suppose we should be looking at RRSPs. That's what everybody seems to say. But Mary, do you mind telling me how they work? I don't want to seem stupid..."

"Now, just one minute, Angie," I said interrupting. "If you don't know something, that doesn't make you stupid. There's a big difference between being uninformed and being stupid. One of the big problems is that a lot of women, and men too, are afraid to confront their lack of knowledge and overcome the accompanying embarrassment. Unless you're willing to ask questions, you aren't going to learn. There's nothing wrong with asking questions, especially when it's for your own benefit."

"Okay, so I won't be afraid," said Angie. "Tell me about RRSPs. I'm all ears."

"All right," I said, nodding my head and switching into lecture mode. "I won't bore you with all the gruesome details, but basically here's the deal," I began. "The government encourages Canadians to save for their own retirements by offering a formula for saving."

"Sort of like a pension plan?"

I nodded. "Are either you or Joey members of pension plans at work?"

"No," Angie said. "Joey just changed jobs and he told me his company doesn't bring new employees in until they've completed two years of service. And at the agency where I work, there's such a tremendous staff turnover I was told there's no point in having a pension plan."

"That's probably true," I said. "Anyway, I'm not all that keen on pension plans."

"Why?"

"Because the way economics and business have gone, I wouldn't put my faith in a workplace, or for that matter, government pension plan. Most people just sign the pension papers when they begin their jobs and never read the fine print until it's too late."

"I know what you mean. I've got a friend whose husband died and she received widow's benefits from his pension."

"And?"

"She gave the money to her son to help him through university. And then when she remarried, she suddenly found she was cut off."

"An excellent example," I said, nodding emphatically. "There are pensions where widows' benefits are eliminated on remarriage. Also, consider all the companies who have moved their head offices to other countries with different pension regulations and have forced their Canadian employees to take early retirement."

"Gee, I remember a few years ago reading about some big corporate boss in Toronto who took the excess earnings from a pension fund and put them into his own company's operating funds," Angie said. "There was quite a scandal."

"There are lots of these stories," I said. "The key is, I wouldn't get emotionally or psychologically attached to any security-from-a-workplace pension. I've got friends in Alberta who participated in a teachers' pension plan that was technically bankrupt in the '80s because the provincial government which ran the plan mismanaged it. I'm much happier with RRSPs."

"You can concentrate on your own efforts," Angie said.

"Exactly," I nodded. "Each year, you can put up to 18 per cent of your *previous year's earned income* into an RRSP program. Whatever you contribute is tax-deductible. Now, what did you and Joey earn last year?"

"Well," said Angie, "I earned about $25,000 and Joey made $45,000. That's $70,000 between us."

"Okay," I said, multiplying the numbers, "18 per cent of $70,000 means you could put in a total of $12,600 between you. That's a little over $1,000 a month."

"Where are we going to find that?...Oh my goodness...It'll be *easy* now that our mortgage is paid off. The money that we were putting into our mortgage..."

"You've got it. And remember, while your mortgage was paid with *after-tax dollars,* your contributions to an RRSP are *tax-deductible.*"

"That's what confuses me most about RRSPs, Mary. I'm not completely sure what tax-deductible is. I mean, is it something that reduces the amount on which we pay taxes each year? I read somewhere that all we get is tax credits."

"Most of what used to be deductions are now tax credits," I said. "But RRSP contributions are still deductions. They are actually more like tax deferrals."

"I'm afraid you've lost me, Mary," Angie said, shaking her head.

"Hang on and it'll all come clear. The combined federal and provincial tax rate in this country on incomes greater than $30,000 averages around 40 per cent. On the first $30,000, you only pay 25 per cent and then if your income is over $60,000, the top rate goes to about 50 per cent." I could see the puzzled look on Angie's face. "Here," I said. "I keep forgetting you're not an accountant. Let me write it out for you. It'll only take a second."

Approximate Income Tax Brackets
Federal and Provincial Tax

INCOME	TAX BRACKET
$0–$30,000	25%
$30,000–$60,000	40%–45%
$60,000–??	45%–55%

"That seems pretty straightforward," said Angie. "So, let's get back to 'tax-deductible'."

"All right," I said. "Let's assume an individual earns $45,000, like Joey, and then contributes $8,000 to an RRSP. For tax purposes, it's as if he only earned $37,000 instead of $45,000. That means that the government will give him a tax refund of 40 per cent of $8,000 or $3,200."

"You mean," said Angie, reaching for my calculator, "if Joey and I together put in $12,000 into RRSPs, we can save 40 per cent of that, which is $4,800? That means that our cost drops to only...let's see...$12,000 minus $4,800 is $7,200."

"Exactly. In this way, when the smoke clears, the government absorbs 40 per cent of your $12,000 contribution in the form of a tax refund."

"You mean it only costs us $7,200 to have $12,000 working for us in our RRSPs."

"Right again," I said, nodding emphatically.

"Wait a minute," said Angie. I could see she was deep in thought. "When we were paying off our mortgage," she said slowly, "we were using after-tax money. It was costing us $12,000 a year from our paycheques. Couldn't we contribute $20,000 to our RRSPs and our net out-of-pocket costs would only be 60 per cent, which is that same $12,000?"

I laughed. "You're a quick study, Angie. Technically, you could contribute considerably more than $12,000, except there are a couple of key points. First, remember you're limited to 18 per cent of each previous year's earned income."

"Oh, that's right," said Angie, "our maximum is only $12,600 as you said."

I nodded. "Except there is one other point."

"What's that?"

"Well, ever since 1991, the government has had carry-forward legislation in place."

"What's that?" Angie echoed.

"It means, if you don't contribute up to your maximum in any given year, you can carry that amount forward for up to seven years and play catch-up."

"So, that means Joey and I really *could* put in more than $12,000."

"I guess you can. But there is one big question you should think about."

"Shoot."

"Do you really *want* to put in more than $12,000? Remember, a few minutes ago I said there's more to life than saving money. If you put in $12,000, you'll get a refund of $4,800, and that'll give you some extra money to spend."

"Spend?"

"Sure, why not? $400 a month. You can upgrade your car, buy nicer clothes, put money away for Marcie's education or even take a nice holiday once or twice a year."

"But if we spend $4,800, what about our old age? You just said that you wouldn't trust government to look after us."

"True, but do you have any idea what $12,000 a year really is?"

"I don't understand."

"Well," I said. "How old is Joey? I know you told me, but I forgot."

"43."

"And you?"

"41."

I nodded, getting up from my desk. I walked over to my bookcase and returned with *The Money Manager for Canadians*. "Let's see. Let's assume you put aside $12,000 a year for the next 20 years with a 10 per cent rate of return."

"Ten per cent? Where do we get..."

I held up my hand to stop Angie in mid-sentence. "I'll get to that soon. For now though, let's figure 10 per cent on $12,000 a year for 20 years."

"Let's see, that takes us to Joey's age 63. I don't know, what does it amount to?"

I checked the calculations. "One dollar a year invested at 10 per cent amounts to $57.28. That means," I said crunching the numbers on my calculator, "at the end of 20 years, you'd have $687,360." Angie whistled in surprise. "And, if you put aside $12,000 a year for 25 years, that'll give you..." I couldn't help a small whistle of my own, "$1,180,200."

"Wow," said Angie, "we'd be rich."

"Well, you'd certainly be comfortable, even if we had a bit more inflation in this country. After all, by that time not only is your house paid for, but you wouldn't have Marcie as a dependent. I'm sure you and Joey would live very comfortably. Of course, if your incomes increase over time, then you can always put in more than $12,000 a year without any reduction in your ongoing lifestyle."

"I see," said Angie. "If there is inflation, as you say, our wages would go up..."

"And you could contribute more."

"We'd be rich," said Angie. "If we can save for the next 25 years in RRSPs, that's all we'd really need...But why isn't *everybody* rich?"

"I wouldn't say you'd be rich, dear," I said, "but you'd certainly be comfortable. The problem with most people, though, is *they don't have a focus*. In your case, you've paid off your mortgage. That gives you a tremendous amount of security. If either of you lost your jobs, you'd be able to live on a lot less, although, of course, saving money would become more difficult."

"I see," said Angie. "You say most people don't have a focus. You mean they don't *make a plan,* or they go off in too many different directions at the same time."

"Right. In fact, one of the key points is timing. Remember how a couple of minutes ago you mentioned RRSP advertising in January and February? Most people wait until the last minute to make their contributions for the previous year, because the government lets you have until March 1st each year to contribute for the previous year ended December 31st."

"What's wrong with waiting?" asked Angie.

"Two things. First, most people find they don't have the money in one lump sum at the end, so they miss out on making their contributions. Also, even if someone had the discipline to save, they'd be better off contributing throughout the year rather than waiting for the end."

"Is that because they'd be earning compound interest starting earlier?"

"Bang on, Angie," I said. *"Now, in order to make sure you and Joey don't go off the rails, you've got to treat your RRSP the same way you did your mortgage."*

"What do you mean?"

"You've got to make *monthly contributions,* preferably on the same day each month that you deposit your paycheques."

"I see," said Angie. "That way we won't fall behind...or be tempted to spend the extra money."

"And there's one other thing that you can consider doing if you want to, in order to help your cash flow."

"What's that?"

"You and Joey could arrange to have your tax deductions from your paycheques reduced to take into account the fact that you're contributing to RRSPs."

"You mean, this way we'd get an extra $400 a month in our pockets rather than as a tax refund at the end?"

"Yes, that's it. That's exactly what I'm driving at. Most accountants will tell you that you're much better off getting the government's money monthly rather than waiting for a tax refund at the end."

"That's not hard to understand," said Angie. "We'd have more money faster to spend as we saw fit."

"On the other hand," I interrupted, "getting a *lump-sum* tax refund isn't a bad thing if *you want to ensure you've got money coming in for a relatively short-term but larger spending goal."*

"Such as?"

"Say you want to take a nice vacation. You may be better off with a lump sum tax refund of $4,800 rather than $400 a month."

"But if we have the *discipline* to save the $400 a month..."

"Of course, then you'd be further ahead. But some people don't. They're better off with the lump sum even if it costs them a few dollars in lost income."

"I'll have to think about that one," Angie said, "and discuss it with Joey."

"Well, that's not a decision you have to make immediately."

"The main thing, though," said Angie, "is that I see your point about having a focus."

"Right. Let me tell you a little story. A few months ago, I was approached by a church group to present a financial planning seminar one evening. After I finished, a young couple came up to me and asked what I would recommend as a method of saving money for their children's education. They told me they had a five-year-old and a three-year-old. I asked them if they had a mortgage on their home and they said they did. I told them that, if I were them, I would just concentrate on paying off my mortgage. 'Once you're debt free,' I said, 'then, you'll have ample disposable income to pay for your children's education when the money is actually needed.'"

"I see what you're saying," said Angie. "When my daughter goes off to university, and I hope she does, we'll be able to use our tax refunds from our RRSPs to subsidize her costs. And it all wouldn't have been possible..."

"If you hadn't paid off your mortgage first," I concluded for her.

"I suppose one other thing I may have to do in a few years is use my RRSP tax refund to help out Mom and my Stepdad. They're finding it a bit difficult to carry on with interest rates being as low as they are. They don't have RRSPs or pensions, but thank goodness their house down in Florida is paid for. My brother Tommy suggested that each of the four of us kick in $100 a month. My other brother, Larry, isn't all that happy, but my sister Katherine is in agreement."

"Yes," I said with a sigh, "you've just brought up one of the biggest problems facing women today—it's double parenting."

"Double parenting?"

"Yes, it's usually women who are responsible not only for caring for their own children, but frequently for their aging parents as well."

"I see what you mean. Even Joey's Mom was cared for by his sister, and not by him."

"I think you're going to have to talk to Joey about this so that, if you do feel you should help contribute, he won't object when part of the tax savings from your RRSPs goes to your Mom and Stepdad."

"Is there anything else we should know about RRSPs?"

"Yes, there are a few more important points you should consider. It's good to know, for instance, that you can draw out up to $7,000 per year from your RRSP without having to pay income tax on the money—as long as you have no other income. Suppose your circumstances change—so Joey plans to leave his job and start his own business. If it takes awhile before he starts making a profit, he can draw out $7,000 from his RRSP tax free, and use the money for whatever you need. But with RRSPs, the most important thing to consider is that in the final analysis, you and Joey should try to equalize your incomes."

"Why's that?" Angie asked.

"Well, look at the tax schedule I gave you a few minutes ago." I pointed at the paper. "One of the key rules in Canadian tax planning is to *always do what you can to use the low tax bracket twice.*"

"You mean the first $30,000, taxed at only 25 per cent?"

"Right. The taxes on two incomes of $30,000 each are substantially less than the taxes on one income of $60,000."

"So, how do we equalize our RRSPs? Joey earns more and can obviously contribute more than I can if the limit is, as you say, 18 per cent."

"Good point, but I haven't yet brought up the concept of a *spousal* RRSP."

"Spousal RRSP? How does that work?"

"Well, actually, any individual can contribute up to 18 per cent of the previous year's income into *either* a plan for *himself* or *herself or* a plan in the name of a spouse. By the way, this includes a common-law relationship. So, if Joey contributes say, $7,500 a year and you contribute $4,500, you might contribute all of your $4,500 into a plan for yourself, while Joey contributes $6,000 into a plan for himself and $1,500 to your plan."

"So we each get $6,000 working in our respective plans?"

"Exactly," I said. "The concept of the spousal RRSP does not mean that any individual can double up and contribute more than his or her limit. But it *does* mean that all, or part, of an RRSP can be earmarked into a personal plan or a spousal plan."

"I see what you mean about equalizing. Are there any exceptions?"

"Only one exception comes readily to mind," I said. "The RRSP rules require you to start drawing money from your plans by the time you each reach age 71. Starting at that point, whatever you get becomes taxable income."

"I knew there was a catch," said Angie.

"No, there's no catch. Remember, the government is subsidizing your contributions in the first place, and all the income that you earn in your RRSP—in your case over the next 20 or 25 years—is not taxed on an ongoing basis. So, I suppose the government deserves to be compensated at the end. Besides, when you start drawing money from your RRSPs down the road, you'll need a cash flow to meet your living requirements. So the RRSPs are simply going to replace your earned incomes at that time."

"I see what you mean. I guess it really isn't unfair if you put it that way. But what's your point about equalizing incomes between husband and wife?"

"Ah, I'm glad you reminded me," I said. "Remember that you have to start drawing money from an RRSP no later than age 71. You can start drawing earlier if you need it, but 71 is the outside age."

"So?" prompted Angie.

"Well, what about those circumstances where one spouse is considerably older than the other and is likely to retire much earlier?"

"I see," said Angie, "you mean if Joey were 15 years older

than me instead of two years..."

"You would probably be well-advised," I said, "to load up heavily into *his* RRSP so that *he* could start drawing from it when he retires."

"And if we could afford it, I could still contribute to *mine* while he was drawing from *his*."

"If you could afford it," I echoed.

"But there's one problem," Angie said with a puzzled look on her face. "If Joey were much older than I and we did what you said by having him contribute to his own plan and having me put my money into a spousal plan also for him, what happens if, God forbid, we got..."

"Divorced?" I finished her sentence. Angie nodded tentatively. "Fortunately, the rules in Canada are such that, in a divorce, an RRSP is considered a family asset, which means the value is split between the parties irrespective of whether the money was originally invested in the husband's or the wife's plan."

"You mean, it really doesn't matter where it goes?"

"True. The only thing you might have to worry about, though, is that it's technically possible for someone to deregister his or her RRSP before asking a spouse for a divorce."

"You mean and hide the money instead."

"Right. But if you have a good lawyer, he or she will figure that out pretty quickly. After all, RRSP withdrawals are taxable and there are records."

"But what if the money has been squandered?"

"Well...I suppose there is that risk."

"But, then again," said Angie with a laugh, "marriage is a big risk in the first place."

We both paused for a moment's silence.

"I can't believe financial planning is as easy as all that," Angie said. "Pay off our mortgage and sock away money in an RRSP! You really think we can have as much as $1,000,000 or more by the time we retire?"

I nodded.

"I still can't believe," Angie continued, "that *everyone* doesn't retire rich."

"Again, it's because they don't have a focus," I said. "Actually, in *my* opinion, one of the big problems is that RRSP limits are, would you believe, *excessive* and therefore *intimidating*."

"I don't understand."

"Well, the maximum amount that any individual can put in is, as I said, 18 per cent of the previous year's earned income and the maximum dollar amount at the present time is around $15,000 a year. Most people think they *have* to put in $15,000 a year in order to accumulate a meaningful sum. And since they don't feel they can even come close, *they don't even try.* If a 25-year-old person puts *only $2,000* a year away at say 10 per cent for 40 years till age 65, he or she would have almost $900,000 at the end—$885,186 to be exact."

"Wow," said Angie.

"If *I* were running the show," I said, "I would *lower* RRSP limits. But I would also do my damnedest to make them *compulsory*. It's all part of a proper education and a great deal of the fault is not the government's. It's the financial institutions. They're so interested in getting your money, they don't even try to give you a focus on where you're going to end up. If only people could see how easy it is..."

"But where are we going to get a 10 per cent return?" Angie asked. "I mean, the prevailing interest rate isn't even half that."

"Right," I said, "that's the last part of the exercise. Essentially, if today was a couple of years ago, I would simply suggest that you and Joey put your RRSP investments into term deposits at the prevailing rate of interest. When interest rates were 9, 10 or 11 per cent, there wasn't much point in doing anything different in a situation where the gross yield and net yield were the same."

"Gross and net yield?"

"Yes, because you don't pay tax on your accumulating income in an RRSP."

"Oh, right."

"You see, outside an RRSP, even a 9 or 10 per cent rate isn't all that great when you consider the government will take away almost half. But when the yield is tax-sheltered..."

"You get the whole thing. So, what do we do because we

can't get these interest rates anymore?"

"I think you pretty well have no choice but to invest in growth mutual funds."

Angie groaned. "How do those things work?"

"Well, maybe we should defer a detailed discussion on this to a later date," I said. "We've certainly covered enough for one day, so I'll just give you a brief overview. In a mutual fund, money contributed by many different people is pooled together and administered by professionals. Each investor receives units in exchange for the money invested. In a *growth fund,* the money is invested in publicly-traded stocks that will hopefully appreciate over time. Professional money managers usually do far better than private individuals in selecting appropriate investments. They have the proper training, research facilities and so on. Over the long term, these professionals will generate average annual returns that will probably well exceed 10 per cent a year, even without going into speculative investments."

"But what if the market drops?"

"Oh, it certainly does from time to time. There was the crash of '87 for example, and yet, in the four or five years following, the market rebounded enormously. Once you recognize that there are bound to be some bad years, and you get relaxed about this fact..."

"How can anyone become comfortable with losing money?"

"I know it's difficult, but you tend to benefit, in part, from the fact that if you make ongoing contributions, *you'll also be buying into the market in years when the market is down.* This means you buy more units for the same monthly contribution when the stock market is low, and there is a proportionately larger gain on these units in the end."

"So, in the long run..."

"It's called 'dollar cost averaging'. And the bottom line is you should do reasonably well when you take a 20 or 25 year period into account."

"Are there other alternatives besides growth mutual funds?"

"Oh, there are lots of alternatives, although there are some restrictions. For example, you can't buy real estate or gold and other precious metals and only up to 20 per cent of your money can be invested in foreign securities. You can invest in gold or real estate *stocks,* though, and there are some mutual funds that concentrate in these areas. In general, I'd suggest you look at investing in several different growth funds and take advantage of the opportunity to invest up to 20 per cent in foreign content."

"Diversify?"

"Yes. If you and Joey are going to invest $1,000 a month, why not put $333 a month into three different mutual funds?"

"What do we have to look for?"

"I strongly suggest that the major criterion is medium-term track record."

"Which means?"

"You should try to determine how the various funds have performed on average over the last five years."

"What about longer than five years?"

"I don't think longer than five years makes a lot of sense. Think about it. The performance of any fund is only as good as the individuals who are managing it. Often, or at least periodically, there's some turnover and I think a five-year track record is a pretty good indication."

"Who should we go to?"

"I suggest you visit a financial planner who has access to mutual fund investments. The key point is that no reputable financial planner would want to steer you in the wrong direction. Remember, he or she receives a commission no matter what you buy. So the planner may as well recommend what's appropriate. You can also buy your RRSP through a bank, trust company, insurance company or brokerage house. Just make sure that you're buying into well-established portfolio managers and that the planner has a clear understanding of your objectives in the first place."

"Is there anything else to look at?"

"Yes. You'll want to make sure that, as long as you don't draw out any money over the next five or six years, there are no fees for pulling the money out afterwards. In order to cut administrative costs, many mutual funds impose a deregistration fee, often called a 'loading charge'. However, in most cases, if you're committed to leaving your money with them for extended periods, the loading charge decreases over time and disappears completely after five, six or as many as eight years. This means if you withdraw money afterwards, your withdrawals are free. Also, you should try to invest in a family of mutual funds that will allow you to switch from, say, equity funds to interest funds if circumstances change."

"You mean, if interest rates start to go up?"

I nodded. "And you'll want to switch from growth funds to interest-earning investments."

"What you're saying is, Joey and I should be allowed to do this without any charge."

"Exactly. Most of the larger mutual fund companies operate several funds to accommodate clients with different financial requirements and also because they recognize that general economic circumstances change from time to time."

"Whew," said Angie. "You've certainly given me a lot to think about. I'm going to give all this a week or two to gel and I'll give Joey a bit of time to get over his Mom's death. I think, though, that he'll catch on pretty quickly to your suggestions, and we'll go see his cousin Marty, who's with one of the big brokerage firms downtown."

"I'm sure any one of the many reputable and well-established brokers can help you. Again, whether you buy mutual fund A or B or C doesn't really make any difference to them."

"Right, their commission is the same, so why would they recommend something that we wouldn't be happy with?"

"Just be careful not to put all your eggs into one basket, and don't panic if, at any given time, the value of your investments drops. In the long run, equity markets have always outperformed interest markets and even if you earn an average rate of return of one or two points less over the next 20 or 25 years..."

"We certainly won't starve to death," finished Angie. "I'll also have the $2,000 a year I've been saving on my own," she continued with a chuckle. "You never know. If Joey's a good boy, some day I'll let him know how much my 'little' account has

CHAPTER ELEVEN
NEW BEGINNINGS

I WAS HARD AT WORK AT MY DESK in the growing dusk of a late fall afternoon, when suddenly my office door burst open to reveal a smiling Marlene, clutching an official-looking document in her hand. Louise, my secretary, was hot on her heels wearing a most indignant look at this rude, unheralded interruption. Marlene was grinning from ear to ear and once I got over the initial shock of her grand entrance, I quickly signalled to Louise that everything was okay and I would handle the situation.

"I know I didn't make an appointment," said Marlene, slapping the paper down on my desk, "but I wanted you to be the first to know. I am now officially a free woman...on the move!"

I looked down at the paper and I read the first words, 'In the matter of the divorce petition'...

"You mean..." I said, looking up.

"Yes, the divorce is through, and I can now get on with other things."

I motioned Marlene into a chair. "Congratulations," I said dryly. "But seriously, you must have known for weeks now that everything was going to happen. Why are you suddenly so 'up'? There must be more to it."

"Well, actually, there is," said Marlene with a wicked laugh. "Tom's girlfriend has left the company and she's moving to Vancouver. The poor boy is devastated."

"Do you think there's any chance...for a reconciliation?"

"Never. It may have taken a while, but I now realize I'm far better off alone, even if I never meet anyone else. All those

155

years married to a weekday workaholic and would-be golf pro on the weekends. I mean, who needs it? I came over to share my good news and ask you to have dinner with me. There's an early-bird lobster special at Monsieur Neptune, and it's only five blocks away." Suddenly she paused. "Oh my goodness. I forgot about Jennifer!"

I laughed. "You're in luck," I said. "Jennifer's in Toronto. She gets her degree next June and she's busy checking out graduate schools. I kind of hope she'll stay in Montreal and go to my old alma mater, McGill, but if she wants to go out of town..."

"They grow up quickly, don't they?" said Marlene, wistfully. "Anyway," she added, brightening considerably, "it looks like we're on for dinner. Do you think you can tear yourself away from your desk a little bit early? I know how you accountants love routine, but *I'm* in the mood for a celebration."

"I'd love to," I exclaimed. "Can you give me five minutes to clean up?"

"No problem. I'll wait outside," she said. "I'm sure I can always find some interesting reading in your CA Magazine." She laughed.

"I think you'll find I have a more varied selection of reading material," I said, "but you never know. You just might find you can learn a thing or two..."

"Oh for sure," said Marlene, as she left my office closing the door behind her.

🦆

We walked the five blocks to Monsieur Neptune without saying too much, huddled in our coats against the strong autumn wind. It was depressing. Another Montreal winter just around the corner. Where did the summer go?

But a great dinner and a bottle of wine revived our spirits quite nicely. We declined desserts and Marlene ordered tea while I ordered a decaf.

"So, if I may ask," I said, "how did you make out?"

"You mean financially?"

"Uh-huh."

156

"Well, as you expected, it took a lot longer than it should have, but I wound up with the house and Tom's agreement to give me $1,000 a month for two years until I get back on my feet. I did get an extra bonus on top, though. In exchange for letting him keep all his pension rights and the cottage in the Laurentians, I'm going to get a $100,000 lump sum. He's agreed to put a mortgage against the cottage and my lawyer said she'd have a cheque by next week."

"Do you have any plans?"

"Well, I'm going to take the advice you gave me and spend some of that money by investing in myself. I'm also going to go away for a month's holiday in Hawaii before the winter rains set in. Then, starting January, I've enrolled in a two-year diploma course at the École des Beaux-Arts. If all goes well, I'll follow through on that business idea I told you about when I graduate."

"You mean the art rental business?"

"Yes, that's the one. I went to a couple of seminars on preparing a business plan. So far, mine is very rough, but even in this preliminary stage, it looks like the business has excellent potential. I figure that I'm likely to spend about $30,000 or $40,000 out of the money Tom's giving me over the next two years, just to upgrade myself. But, thanks to you, I'm looking at that as an investment. Otherwise, depleting almost half my capital would be awfully depressing. I should be okay, though. The house is paid for and Tom's $1,000 a month will cover my car expenses, taxes and utilities quite nicely. I suppose," she continued, a bit ruefully, "I won't be able to buy a lot of clothes, but I shouldn't have too much trouble putting food on the table."

"What are you going to do with the rest of your money?"

"Well," said Marlene, "I was hoping you could give me some direction."

"Ah ha," I said to myself, "which all goes to show, not only is there no such thing as a free lunch, but there's no free dinner either!" My eyebrows went up of their own volition.

"You don't really think I had an ulterior motive for inviting you tonight?" asked a perceptive Marlene in mock horror.

I simply laughed in reply. "Okay," I said, "let's assume you have $40,000 to invest. Your first and most obvious alternative is to put your money in the bank to earn interest."

"But the rates are so low."

"I know," I said. "Also, earning interest income on top of the $12,000 a year that Tom is going to pay you for support means the government would take away 25 per cent of what you earn."

"Terrific. Instead of getting 4 per cent, I'll only keep 3 per cent."

"Well, there are other alternatives. The good news, of course, is that the lump sum itself isn't taxable, and you won't pay a whole lot of tax on that first $12,000 that you get because of your standard personal tax credit. In fact, you'll also be permitted to claim a tax credit for your tuition fees."

"So, what other alternatives are there?"

"I guess there are several. One possibility is that you could buy a real estate rental property with the money."

"Really?" asked Marlene.

"Well, you obviously couldn't buy an entire property, but $40,000 would give you the downpayment. Then, your tenant or tenants could subsidize the rest of your costs through their rents."

"You mean I should become a landlord?"

"I'm not saying 'should', but I thought I'd raise the possibility. To be honest, it may be difficult to qualify for a mortgage because you have no work history."

"It doesn't matter. I don't think that's for me anyway," said Marlene. "I wouldn't want to get calls at two o'clock in the morning because a toilet is overflowing, and I'm not a particularly handy person. No, I don't think I'm cut out to be a landlord."

"I agree, it's kind of tough to run a property if you're not there. Francie's got it a lot easier with her property because she lives there all the time, so she's on hand if anything goes wrong. Also, her basement tenant is pretty careful not to do any damage with Francie watching out for her own investment. I wasn't really recommending real estate to *you*, but I thought

158

we should at least explore that idea. Marlene, have you ever thought you might like to have a student or two staying with you from time to time?" I queried carefully. "A friend of mine is in the same situation as you with a large house and her kids off at school. She really enjoys providing room and board to these young adults and it covers all her utilities and repairs, and brings in a profit."

"Gee, that's an interesting idea. I might really enjoy the company. But where do you find the students?" quizzed Marlene.

"Well, my friend is fortunate. She takes advantage of a program for foreign students wanting to learn French. They stay for specific periods, while attending school. The program finds the students and usually pays well over $600 a month." I added, "I'll give you her number if you call me tomorrow and you can ask her about it. Apart from that, you could talk to the student housing offices at McGill or Concordia." I paused to catch my breath before continuing.

"Whether or not you decide to supplement your resources with income from providing room and board, there is another alternative you might like to look at. What do you know about mutual funds?"

"I hate to admit this," said Marlene, "but I know absolutely nothing about them."

"What do you know about the stock market?" I asked.

"Not a lot," she confessed. "I know there's something about shares, that they trade and go up and down, but to be truthful, I don't even know exactly what a share is."

"Well," I said, "let me start with the basics. In fact, I've recently discussed this same topic with Angie, although in a different context. When a business is set up, whether it's big or small, the owners invest some of their money. Usually they *incorporate*, which means they set up a separate legal entity. What they get back in exchange for their investment is shares. *Shares are simply pieces of paper that bear evidence of each owner's share of the business.* In a simple example, let's assume a particular business is formed and there are going to be five equal owners." I looked at Marlene to see if she was following and she nodded her head. "So, each investor puts up $200 for a total of $1,000. In exchange for these investments, the corporation, which again is a separate legal entity, issues 1,000 shares—200 to each investor." Marlene nodded again to indicate she was still with me. "Okay," I continued, "let's now look at one investor out of the five. He or she owns 200 shares out of a total of 1,000 shares. What does that mean?"

"I guess," said Marlene, "it means that this person owns 20 per cent of the company."

"Exactly," I replied. "This person has invested $200 out of a total of $1,000 and therefore owns 20 per cent of the company."

"So," Marlene interjected, "let's see if I've got this straight. If you have a share certificate, this means that you own a certain percentage of a company."

"That's right," I said. "If you take your number of shares and divide that by the *total* number of shares that the business has issued, you would then be able to calculate your percentage."

"But how do shares change in value? Like when they're traded on a stock exchange?" asked Marlene.

"I'll explain," I replied. "Let's go back to the same example. Five people have each invested $200 for a total of $1,000. At that moment in time when the company is just formed, what is each share worth?"

Marlene shrugged her shoulders. "I suppose it's worth what these people put in—200 shares at $200 per person—$1 for each."

"That's right. But now, what if the company starts to make money?"

"I get it," she said, as the light bulb went on. "If the company starts to make money, the shares become worth more."

"Right," I said. And if the business loses money?"

"The shares will drop in value. They go down," said Marlene.

"Exactly," I continued. "Now, in the case of a public company, such as one that is traded on the New York or Toronto Stock Exchange, all we have is the same example I just gave you, but it involves thousands of investors and companies that haven't issued 1,000 shares, but have issued perhaps millions of shares. So each individual share represents a very, very minute percentage interest in a big company."

"And if these companies make money," said Marlene, "their shares go up; if they lose, their shares go down."

"That's part of it, although the stock market is a more complex animal than an institution that simply reflects whether businesses are or are not profitable. In a lot of cases, share prices will go up if it's *expected* in the foreseeable future that a business will start to make profits or bigger profits than before. Conversely, if a company releases some bad news, like they've lost a big contract and they've had to let a lot of employees go, the stock value will drop in *anticipation* of reduced earnings. There are several other factors that come into play as well."

"Such as?" Marlene asked.

"For example, what if interest rates suddenly skyrocketed upwards? A lot of people who are investing in stocks might be inclined to sell these investments in order to put their money back into the banks, especially those people who borrowed some of the money to buy stocks."

"And when a lot of people sell," said Marlene, "the market would drop."

"Exactly!" I exclaimed. "On the other hand," I continued, "when interest rates are low, even novice investors such as yourself would be more inclined to put money into the stock market than into a bank."

"And with more people looking to buy stocks, the price goes up," she interjected.

"Yes," I replied. "The stock market is like an auction sale. What you've just 'discovered' is a very basic law of economics called the law of supply and demand. If there's a high demand, price goes up. If supply out-strips demand, sellers have to lower their prices in order to make sales."

"But how does all this relate to mutual funds, Mary?" asked Marlene.

"I can see you're ready for lesson two. There are literally thousands of stocks traded on stock exchanges in North America, and that doesn't even include the overseas market. Stockbrokers are the people who actually do the buying and selling on behalf of their clients—whether the client is a rich individual, or the administrators of a pension fund, or even a small investor like yourself. Stockbrokers make their money by charging fees or commissions on transactions they handle for clients." I paused to see if she was still following. Marlene nodded her head enthusiastically. "The problem is that, in general, to get a decent price for some shares, one has to buy at least 100 shares at a time.

"This may not be a particular problem if you're speculating in an inexpensive mining stock that sells for just pennies a share. But if you want to buy a 'blue chip security' such as Bell Canada or General Motors, you might be looking at a single investment that costs anywhere between say $1,000 and $10,000. So, to buy individual stocks, you have to have a large amount of investment capital at your disposal."

"Makes sense to me, Mary," said Marlene, urging me to carry on.

I took a sip of my coffee and then continued. "Moreover, you've no doubt heard the expression 'don't put all your eggs in one basket'."

"Sure," said Marlene. "I guess what you're telling me is that even if I had many thousands of dollars to invest, which I don't, it wouldn't be wise to put all that money into any one stock."

"Right again," I said. "It's best to diversify—so here's where mutual funds come in. Mutual funds are administered by professional investment analysts. Their job is to study the various publicly traded companies to try to determine in advance which companies are likely to do better than others. What these fund managers do, is they take a pool of money that they receive from many different people and then invest it in many different stocks. This spreads the risk around. In other words, instead of owning 100 per cent of an investment in *one* company, you, as an individual, own a very, very small percentage in literally *hundreds* of companies. If most of the investments held by a mutual fund go up in value, the value of *your* investment in the mutual fund *itself* goes up. Also, when you invest in a mutual fund, you have the buying power of many investors rolled together. Your commission—that is the fee brokers charge for buying stock—is lower and you also are buying professional advice. You wouldn't run the risk of dealing with a broker who might try to churn your portfolio..." I stopped at Marlene's look of confusion.

"Churn?"

"That's turning your holdings over and over. The broker buys and sells your shares more often than necessary to make more commissions. This is not really honest, but there are a few unscrupulous brokers who walk a fine line. The important point is to interview a number of different people and companies who might handle your investment and not blindly trust anyone. Most people spend more time researching which car to buy than investigating someone to handle their money. Make sure you're comfortable with your advisor and that they have a good reputation and track record."

"So how do these guys who run the mutual funds make their money?" Marlene asked.

"Good question," I said. "First of all, almost all the mutual fund managers charge an ongoing administration fee, often around 2 per cent of the value of your investment on an annual basis. It's in their interest for you to be successful because the more your investments are worth, the higher their fee. Also, in most cases, there is what is called a front-end load."

"What's that?" asked Marlene.

"It's a commission charged on your initial investment every time you put money in. For example, if you invest $100, the mutual fund sales people and sales managers might take, say, 5 per cent. So you'd initially only have $95 working for you."

"You mean they take away my nest egg?" Marlene asked in dismay.

"They're providing a service," I replied, "and they have to be paid for it. The thing is, if the mutual fund goes up in value—say 15 per cent in one year—it doesn't take long for you to recover this commission. Sometimes there's a back-end load which applies if you want to sell and liquidate investments into cash. In a lot of cases though, there is no back-end charge as long as you're willing to leave your money with that particular fund company for at least six or seven years."

"Are all mutual funds set up to buy stocks that are supposed to go up in value?" Marlene asked.

"No," I replied, "there's a wide variety. Up till now, the type of fund I've been describing to you is what's commonly called a *'growth fund'.* The object of the exercise is to invest money and hope that, on balance, the portfolio of company stocks held by the mutual fund will grow in value. The more valuable it becomes, the more each mutual fund share, or unit, is worth. There are other mutual funds that also invest in the stock market, but the fund managers invest more in stocks that pay an ongoing *income.* In these cases, growth in value is of secondary interest."

"How do stocks pay income?" asked Marlene. "I thought they were only supposed to get more valuable over time if you've invested in the right funds."

"Okay," I said, "I'll explain how that works as well. Let's go back to the example I used before where five investors get together and put up $200 each to start a business. Let's assume the business makes a $2,000 profit in the first year, and, just for illustration, let's assume the government takes 50 per cent of that away for income taxes."

"Boy, that's highway robbery!" exclaimed Marlene.

"I'm just giving you an example, Marlene. In real life, corporate taxes aren't necessarily all that high, especially for small business. I'm sure the time will come when we'll get into a more detailed discussion of how the business tax system works, but for now, just please bear with me."

"Okay, Mary, the company has earned $2,000 and has paid $1,000 in taxes."

"Right, so what's it got left?"

"That's easy," said Marlene, "$1,000."

"Correct again," I said. "What do they do with that $1,000?"

"I suppose," said Marlene, "the owners could use the $1,000 to help the business get bigger." Marlene shrugged her shoulders.

"Bang on," I said. "That's what a lot of businesses do. They use their after-tax profits for expansion. They buy equipment or inventory or sometimes they use the profits to even buy up other businesses. And there are other things the owners of a business can do with its profits."

"Like take the money out and spend it?"

"Good point," I replied. "Although if the owners take money for themselves out of the profits of the company, they have to pay personal income taxes on the withdrawals."

"So the same profits are taxed twice?" asked Marlene.

"I think maybe you should consider going into accounting school instead of art school," I said. "You're pretty good with these tax consequences."

"No thanks," said Marlene dryly. "The idea of having an art business really appeals to me and that's what I'm going to do."

"I predict you'll be pretty good at running your own business," I said with a smile. "Now, when the owners of a corporation take after-tax profits out of a business, these distributions are called *dividends...*"

"So that's what a dividend is," Marlene interrupted. "I've often wondered. You know, one of the cards in Monopoly even talks about getting a dividend, and I never knew exactly what it was."

"That's right. *A dividend is a distribution out of a corporation's after-tax profits.* When the owners take this money, they have to report it as part of their personal incomes when they file their own income tax returns, but, as you yourself said just a minute ago, since dividends are distributions of profits that have already been taxed once, the owners are given what's called a 'dividend tax credit'. Now I don't mean to make this too complicated for you. Suffice to say, dividends from Canadian companies are taxed more favourably than most other kinds of income. To put this in perspective, if a high income investor is in the 50 per cent tax bracket, his or her tax on a Canadian dividend will only be about 37½ per cent. It's like getting a discount."

"I understand what you're saying, Mary," she said, "but how does all this relate back to mutual funds?"

"I'll explain," I responded. "When companies make money and have paid the tax on their profits, they basically have the two choices that you yourself figured out. The profits can either be used for business expansion or they can be distributed to shareholders as dividends. Some companies, at one extreme, reinvest all their profits in expanding their businesses, and at the other extreme, other companies distribute the vast majority of their profits as dividends to shareholders. Most businesses fall somewhere in the middle. So, if you were to select a single stock, you could, on the one hand, choose a company that reinvests all its profits. If management makes good business decisions, you'll profit in the long run from that company's growth. On the other hand, you could take your same investment and put your dollars into the shares of a second company that takes most of its profits and distributes them back to you as dividends. If the company is paying big dividends they probably won't grow as quickly, but you'll receive an ongoing income."

"So," said Marlene, "the choices are growth or income."

"Exactly," I said. "Often retired people require ongoing income to meet their living expenses, while younger people might be more interested in growth. Now, the mutual fund industry has recognized this and therefore some mutual funds which are equity-based..."

"Equity-based?" she interrupted.

"Yes, that means they invest in stocks."

"Oh," she said.

I continued, "Some mutual funds that are equity-based invest with an emphasis on growth stocks, while others invest to build income."

"In my case, I'd be looking for some combination, wouldn't I, Mary?" Marlene asked.

"That's right. I'll just add one or two more points to complete the picture. Once you make a choice between growth and income or some combination of both you can also select mutual funds based on geographical considerations."

"Which means?"

"Some funds sold in Canada invest only in Canadian securities. Some invest in the U.S. Some invest in the Pacific Rim countries, Japan, the Hong Kong market, etc., and some invest in Latin America or overseas in Europe. Some mutual funds are blended and have diverse portfolios from all over the world. Some concentrate their investments in specific industries such as natural resources. There are also mutual funds that invest in bonds and mortgages."

"I know what a mortgage is, Mary, but what's a bond?"

"A bond relates to a corporation or government body or even a municipality or school board that borrows money and agrees to pay it back at a later time. The people who lend the money get a piece of paper that summarizes their rights to receive interest and the return of the original principal. When you invest in shares, you own a piece of a company. When you invest in a bond, you are lending money in exchange for interest. The rate of interest depends, in part, on the risk of the loan and also the prevailing rates of interest that other loans bear, such as when you lend money to the bank."

"So how does *this* relate to mutual funds?" Marlene asked.

"Ah," I replied. "In the same way that most people don't have enough investment capital to buy a single stock, they also can't invest in individual bonds or mortgages. How would you feel, for example, if you were asked to lend your entire $40,000 to one particular person to buy a house?"

"Not great," she replied. "I suppose the borrower could lose his or her job and wouldn't be able to make the payments, or the house might burn down. No," she shook her head, "I really wouldn't want to invest in something like that."

"Well, this is the problem that a mutual fund is designed to solve. In a mortgage-based mutual fund, for example, the fund managers take a pool of money they receive from many different people and spread the risk around. So, instead of owning 100 per cent of one mortgage, you might own a very, very small percentage of literally thousands of mortgages."

"So I share the risk and the reward," Marlene said slowly.

I nodded. "I don't want to give you the impression that you're always going to win. There's some element of risk in *any* mutual fund. For example, the whole stock market can collapse overnight, and it's been known to happen. Also, even a mortgage fund could suffer a substantial loss if all the mortgages are secured by property in one province and its economy falls apart. But the point is, mutual funds are designed to spread out risk."

"I see," she responded. "Let's go over this again. For me, investing in a fund geared toward paying out interest or dividends doesn't necessarily make sense at this time. On $40,000, even 6 or 7 per cent isn't all that attractive. After all, in a couple of years I'll be on my feet earning a decent living, I hope."

"True. What you need right now is a growth fund in which your money is invested in a balanced portfolio of stocks, probably some Canadian and some foreign, that is geared toward giving you capital appreciation. *I don't think you should concentrate in any one industry or country.* Many of the funds that have good track records over the last three to five years have averaged better than a 12 or 14 per cent annual rate of return. And as long as your capital investment and growth in value remain in the fund—in other words, you don't cash out—the tax collectors don't see what's called a *disposition.* As far as they're concerned, as long as you're not pocketing your earnings, the earnings don't count. It's only when you cash in all, or part, of your fund that you pay taxes. Money invested over a long-term period at 10 per cent or more can really result in quite a substantial sum. And this kind of annual growth is pretty darn good when inflation is around 2 to 3 per cent. Also, when one earns interest or dividends, one has to pay tax. But if you can get your growth on a tax-deferred basis, as long as you don't sell, you're going to get quite a benefit. Once you're in business and you start to make some money, there's something else you should consider."

Marlene looked at me expectantly.

"Let's assume your business prospers and you can free up an extra $1,000 a month for investment. This shouldn't be too difficult given that your house is paid for. You'll then benefit from something called *'dollar cost averaging'.*"

"Mary, I thought I told you I don't want to become an accountant," moaned Marlene with more than a hint of exasperation. "What's dollar cost averaging?"

"Well, as I started to say, if you invest $1,000 a month," I retorted, "if the market drops at any point in time, you'll be able to buy more shares in your mutual funds for the same money. So, when the market goes back up again, you'll be in a position to make bigger profits. By having money going into an investment program on a regular and recurring basis, in the long run you'll do a lot better than just by trusting luck, which is what you have to do when you make a single investment only. If you're lucky, you may make a one-time investment at the bottom of the market when prices are really low. But if you're unlucky, you could be investing at the top when prices are over-inflated. So, an ongoing program makes a lot of sense. It'll give you the best return and it's great for building up discipline.

"A lot of women get into investment clubs for that reason. It gives them more knowledge to use when interviewing prospective investment advisors or when actually selecting specific investments. Each of the participants invests, say, $100 a month, and by being a member of the club, each has the benefit of learning more and more as time goes on about how the market works. Members can be assigned responsibilities to investigate specific stocks or funds and often a group of people can attract some pretty good guest speakers."

"So, how do I pick a suitable fund?" Marlene asked. "Do I get a list and just throw darts?"

"By track record, Marlene." I laughed. "I've already said that there's a number of growth funds out there which have consistently averaged 12 to 14 per cent or better over the last three to five years."

"What about longer than five years?"

I shook my head. "It seems to me anything longer than five years doesn't really mean anything. You see, any fund is only as good as its managers, and you have to expect some turnover in personnel, especially if you go longer than five years. Of course, there are some exceptions, especially where the managers of the mutual fund management company are also the owners."

"I see," she nodded. "Overall, I really shouldn't concern myself with long track records, but I should pay particular attention to three and five-year performances."

It was my turn to nod. "You might want to get into two or three different funds with different managers to hedge your bets."

"You've got me all excited," said Marlene happily. "It's nice to have some direction. But there is one other thing."

"What's that?"

"My lawyer suggested I might want to borrow against my house to increase my investment portfolio. She wasn't very specific, though, and she suggested I talk to my accountant. I suppose you're really my friend first, but I guess you're my accountant too, because I don't have another one."

"Gee, thanks," I said with a wry smile. "What your lawyer was referring to was the concept of leverage. If you wanted to, you might be able to borrow another $50,000 or $100,000 against the value of your house."

"What would that do?"

"Well, let's assume you could borrow at 7 per cent. Now, the interesting thing is that, if you borrow for investments, your interest expense becomes tax-deductible. If you were in a high tax bracket—say 40 or 50 per cent—borrowing at 7 per cent really means you'd be out-of-pocket only 3 or 4 per cent after tax."

"I understand," said Marlene, "and if I took that money and invested in growth funds that produced 12 or 13 per cent..."

"You'd be way ahead of the game. That's called leverage, and it's a technique usually adopted by high-income people in order to generate more investment holdings. But in your case, it's not something I'd recommend for a couple of reasons."

"Why not?" asked Marlene.

"Well, to start with, you're not in a high tax bracket. At least not yet. And consequently there wouldn't be much benefit for you to have interest expense at 7 per cent to write off against your income."

"You have a point there."

"A second thing is that for you to take advantage of leverage, you need cash flow from a job, business or profession to *pay* the interest expense in the first place—especially if you're going to invest in growth investments that don't yield an ongoing income."

"I'm not sure I understand."

"Well, let's assume you were an executive, professional or business owner, earning $100,000 a year."

"Okay."

"Let's assume you only needed a pre-tax income of $70,000 a year to live."

"Right."

"So, what if you borrowed $400,000 at 7½ per cent against the value of your house?"

"$400,000?"

"Well, this is just an example. Bear with me. Let's assume you were living in a million dollar home that was fully paid. If you borrowed $400,000 at 7½ per cent, your interest expense would be $30,000 a year. You could use your income from your job, business or profession to cover the interest. Then, if you took the $400,000 and invested in growth mutual funds, what if the investment appreciated by 15 per cent a year? Your after-tax interest expense would only be, say, 55 per cent of the $30,000 that you're paying, which is $16,500 while your appreciation at, say, 15 per cent could be as much as $60,000."

"Why doesn't everybody do this? It sounds pretty good to me."

"The problem is risk. Your investments could *decline* by 15 per cent in one year and where would you be then? Or, what would happen if suddenly you lost your job, or your business fell on hard times? Leverage is a way to become extremely wealthy, but it also could mean a lifetime of poverty."

"So, it really isn't the way for me to go."

"No, not at all," I said. "If I were you, the last thing I would do is jeopardize the fully-paid status of my house."

Marlene glanced at her watch. "Wow, it's getting late," she said. "Do you have time for one more cup of coffee? I have one other question to ask."

"Sure," I said, signalling for the waiter and pointing at our cups. "What's your question?"

"Well," said Marlene, "how do you go about picking an

investment advisor? I mean, who do you trust?"

"That's a good one," I said, nodding. "I remember going through that discussion with Angie a few months ago, although in her case, we didn't go into great detail because there's someone in her husband's family that she and Joey can rely on. I'll tell you what. Let me make a brief trip to the the ladies' room, and we'll talk about investment advisors when I get back."

WHO LOVES YOU?
PICKING AN INVESTMENT ADVISOR

WHEN I RETURNED TO THE TABLE, Marlene looked up at me hopefully.

"Mary, I never asked you...Would *you* like to manage my finances for me? I mean, after all..."

"Yes, I know," I interrupted, "I'm a Chartered Accountant and a Chartered Financial Planner, as well. But, in my practice, even I don't follow the markets from day to day. There's a common misconception that Chartered Accountants are knowledgeable when it comes to investment selection. Unfortunately, that's not the case. Our training doesn't have anything at all to do with the operations of various investment markets. We're trained to do accounting, audits and the like. Most of us are pretty adept these days with computers and some of us specialize in taxation or insolvency. I suppose some accountants who work extensively in the real estate area might be pretty knowledgeable when it comes to evaluating real estate as an investment, but when it comes to most stocks and bonds, uh uh, we're not the right people. Again, there are some exceptions—I mean, professional accountants who have chosen to work with some of the large investment houses."

"So, should I look for a CA who's with one of the big brokerage firms?" asked Marlene.

"Not necessarily. You see, the problem with stockbrokers is that, in general, they're just sales people and they're only as good as the research done by their firms' analysts. In fact, it may surprise you to know that some of the representatives with certain large firms will make recommendations in areas where their company does little or no independent research whatsoever. One of my friends gave her investment portfolio over to a broker with a large firm. He invested the money on her behalf in U.S. defence stocks at the worst possible time. It was when Bush lost the election and Clinton became President. The perception in the marketplace was that, with Clinton's budget cutting and medicare platform, he would put pressure on the defence industry to reduce its prices and profits would drop. In spite of the fact that the stock market as a whole advanced, the defence industry stocks dropped like a stone."

"So what happened?"

"My friend sued, and when they came to discoveries it was determined that this large respected firm didn't even do its own research. All it relied on was reporting services that were available to anybody at the public library. That same broker invested some of my friend's money in Trizec. She didn't follow the market and had no idea the company was in trouble."

"Did your friend win her case?"

"Not so far. The wheels of justice seem to grind very slowly."

"So, are you saying that you can't trust brokers either?"

"I'm not suggesting that most brokers don't mean well. But, like I say, some of them don't do their own independent research. And this doesn't apply only to brokers. As I mentioned earlier, the key point to remember is that whether it's banks, financial planners, brokers or for that matter, other professions such as doctors, lawyers, accountants and psychologists, we have to keep our minds in gear and listen to our intuition and stay within our comfort levels."

"I always thought banks were a safe place to get advice."

I started to laugh.

"What's so funny?" Marlene asked.

"I read a survey recently," I said. "It says that over 75 per cent of Canadians ask for financial advice from their bank tellers, especially when it comes to registered retirement savings plans. Unfortunately, most bank personnel are not trained to dispense investment advice. And even if you go to your bank *manager*, he or she is expected to know about their particular bank's products, but is not likely to be knowledgeable when it comes to comparisons."

"So, who can I go to?" asked Marlene. I could see she was getting frustrated.

"Well, if you don't have a whole lot of money, as I told you earlier, my suggestion is that you look at mutual fund investments, and for those you *can* go to a brokerage firm. Interview a number of different brokers and firms. And then, as I suggested, you would ask the broker you've chosen to simply select two or three funds of the type which suits you that have good three and five-year track records."

"But how do I know what suits me, unless I happen to have talked to someone like you first?"

"You've got a point there," I said. "I suppose there are, now that I think about it, a couple of choices. The first thing that someone can do is seek independent advice from a financial planner who has no vested interest in selling you *anything*, but simply charges on a fee-for-service basis."

"There are planners who operate that way?"

"Yes, except they usually handle clients with larger portfolios. If I were going to a fee based planner, I would look first at his or her professional accreditation."

"Which means?"

"Well, most professional planners are members of the Canadian Association of Financial Planners and they carry the designation RFP which stands for 'Registered Financial Planner'. A lot of them have also completed both the Canadian Securities Course and the courses offered by the Canadian Institute of Financial Planning which awards the designation CFP—'Chartered Financial Planner'."

"So, you're saying I should look for…What is it again?"

"An RFP and a CFP. You also may want to ask some questions about the advisor's prior training. For example, did he or she major in finance at university? How long has he or she been in practice?

"When a qualified financial planner sits down and reviews your position, he or she can usually figure out what approach to take within an hour or two. Obviously, the approach that is suggested has to fit your outlook and comfort level. If you prepare yourself adequately before your meeting, the cost is certainly not going to be prohibitive."

"How does one prepare oneself?"

"By simply putting together a statement of what your assets and liabilities are. In other words, what you own, and what you owe. You should also have a list that shows your projected income from all sources, a calculation of your taxes and a budget of your personal expenses. From all this, the planner can tell how much disposable income you have each month or year to invest, or alternatively, how much income you'll need from your investments each year to make ends meet properly."

"Sounds like a lot of work."

"Not really. One's income and tax information can usually be extracted easily from tax returns, and preparing a budget of expenses isn't difficult. In fact, the next time I see you I can give you a blank form. You'll see it really isn't too tough to complete."

"What happens next?"

"Well, the financial planner can look at your situation and lead you through a discussion geared towards crystalizing a clear understanding of your goals and objectives."

"Goals and objectives?"

"Yes. For example, whether you're interested in having your portfolio grow for the long-term or whether you want investments that yield ongoing income. The planner also has to have a handle on your tolerance for risk."

"Ugh."

"Well, *you* might be 'risk averse' as they say, but there are other people who are not opposed to taking some percentage of their portfolio, generally between 10 and 20 per cent, and investing in more speculative areas."

"Such as?"

"Oh, precious metals for example, or mutual funds that invest in precious metals. Most of the big advances that have been made in markets in recent years come from the Far East. There are special mutual funds that only invest in what's called 'emerging markets', and they've had a spectacular run-up for the most part. But if you're looking at that kind of investment, you can't ask for a five-year track record because very few, if any, of these funds have been operating for that long. I didn't mention them to you sooner because I didn't think they were particularly relevant."

"So what happens at the end?"

"Well, by the time you're finished this fact-finding mission, your planner is usually in a position to recommend specific investments for you, and I think most of them would probably hedge their bets the way I would by recommending that you diversify into at least two or three different funds. If you have a large portfolio..."

"What's 'large'?"

"I guess at least $100,000, or more likely $250,000 or even a half a million. If you have a large portfolio, the planner might recommend specific investments."

"You mean individual stocks and bonds?"

"That's right. And he or she would then arrange for you to buy these securities through a brokerage firm."

"So you still have to deal with a brokerage firm?"

I nodded. "But in this case, the role of the brokerage firm is simply to fill orders—to buy and sell."

"But then you're paying double, aren't you?"

"That's a very good point, Marlene. I suppose, to some extent, you might say that, because you're paying a fee to the planner and you're still paying a commission to have the securities bought and sold for you. The only thing is, if you go to a brokerage house solely for the purpose of buying and selling, you can use one of the many *discount brokerages* out there who make it very clear they are there simply to *execute orders* and *not* to provide advice. Their commissions are often less than what the so-called 'full service brokers' charge."

"So you suggest that one should go to a fee-based planner for advice."

"For the most part," I said, shrugging my shoulders, "although, I suppose now that I think about it a little more, *if you have a good handle on your own goals and objectives, you could go directly to a broker for advice, especially in the mutual funds area.*"

"I'm confused. First you said I shouldn't go to a broker, now you say I could."

"Well, let me try to make that a little clearer. If you really don't know what you want from your investments, like I said, I think you should go to a fee-based planner and invest a few hundred dollars for some independent advice. But if you have a pretty good idea of what your needs are, especially if you're looking at mutual fund investments, you could bypass that step and go directly to a commission-based broker."

"Can you give me a concrete example?"

"Sure," I said, "I have a friend who recently sold her dental practice for about $250,000. She decided the stress of being in practice was too much for her and she's taken a teaching job at McGill. Obviously, her teaching salary is significantly less than what she had been earning from her practice."

"Then what?"

"She went to her broker and told him she wanted to invest her money to provide ongoing income. She was clear that she wasn't looking for any significant capital growth."

"But aren't interest rates very low?"

"That's the point. The broker recommended that she put her $250,000 into an international bond fund where she could count on a yield somewhere between 8 and 11 per cent."

"That's not bad in today's market."

I nodded my head. "I can see you're learning the language. She asked him which bond fund would be most appropriate and he recommended three. All of them have been around for a while. They have top-grade managers and excellent reputations. When she pressed him for a decision on which one of the three to invest in, he simply shrugged his shoulders and told her to split her investment into three equal components. That's what she did and this allowed her to hedge her bets."

"So how does she get paid? I mean, you said she needs the

income."

"Well, one of the things you can do when you invest in mutual funds is set up a systematic withdrawal program where the mutual fund sends you a monthly cheque."

"But don't you eat into your capital?"

"Not as long as your withdrawals aren't any greater than the income or growth that is earned by the fund."

"I'm sorry?"

"Well, let me give you an example. Let's assume my dentist friend invested $100,000 in Mutual Fund A and arranged to draw $800 a month—$9,600 over the course of the year."

"Okay."

"What if that same fund earns 10 per cent? Perhaps a bit simplistically, at the end of one year her $100,000 would have grown in value to $110,000, but she would have taken $9,600 out, which means..."

"I see what you're saying. The value of her investment would be almost the same at the end of one year as it was when she started."

"Right, that's what I meant when I said you can withdraw money from a mutual fund for living expenses or for whatever other purposes you have in mind, and the value of your portfolio won't decline as long as the fund earns at least as much as you've taken out."

"That seems fairly simple. But how did your friend know that the salesman wasn't going to steer her into something where he gets a better commission?"

"Ah, that's a very key point! In general, a person selling mutual funds, or for that matter even individual stocks and bonds, doesn't care what you buy because his or her commission is likely to be the same. So the sales person has no vested interest in steering you into something that isn't suitable. In some cases, mutual funds companies offer perks such as free trips to sales people who push their products. You should ask outright whether the person you're dealing with is looking for such a benefit. One of the major advantages, though, of dealing with an individual who has an RFP designation is that he or she is bound by the ethics of the Canadian Association of Financial Planners, and one of the cardinal rules of the Association is that no one is allowed to market any product where he or she has a vested interest, without full disclosure."

"Oh, what's that called? Conflict of something..."

"You're right. There can be no conflict of interest."

"I see. Two other questions."

"Okay."

"Does the person you're dealing with have to be rich?"

"You know, that's another really good point. Rich, of course, is a relative term, but I certainly think that the person you're dealing with has to be at least comfortable financially—maybe even more than comfortable."

"That's what I thought."

"Frankly, I'm glad you raised that point."

"Actually, I have to admit, I might have learned one or two things over the years from my ex. He always maintained that he'd rather deal with successful people than losers."

"Well, maybe that's a bit crude, but in general I can see what he meant. Within the investment community, the problem is that there are a lot of people who drift into it after having failed in other fields. It's like real estate or life insurance. You get the opportunity to put on a business suit and you're not necessarily chained to a desk eight hours a day. The firms hire these people in the hope that some of them will become successful and generate lots of income. But there's big turnover in these industries as people come and go. It doesn't cost the firms a whole lot because their employees get paid on commission. If they don't generate sales, out they go! In fact, in the insurance industry I read that about 80 per cent of the business is written by 20 per cent of the underwriters. I suppose, the same holds true for real estate and investment brokerage, as well. So, I guess I would agree with you that you're better off dealing with a successful person rather than someone who hasn't done so well."

"Another question. Do you think I should pick a man or a woman as an advisor?"

"Now there's a real tough one! Many women today are ardent feminists who tend to support other women wherever possible, sometimes going to even ridiculous extremes. Then there are other women who go off in just the opposite direction and will only deal with males. Perhaps they want to show everybody they can compete on the same playing fields as their male counterparts. My own view is somewhat more moderate. *The key point is to ask yourself: to whom can you relate the best?* Gender should not be an issue. Look for someone who has been a broker and a financial planner for at least several years and has a good reputation. This person should have survived market fluctuations and should understand how they work.

"If you're more comfortable dealing with a female, go to a female. If you're more comfortable going to a male, go to a male. Personally, I would be really uncomfortable going to a male gynecologist. On the other hand, and I really can't explain why, I've always gone to male dentists. Friends of mine were recently divorced. His lawyer was female while hers was male.

"I suppose, what you might try doing is closing your eyes and picturing the person from whom you wish to ask advice, whether it's a lawyer, doctor, dentist, architect, what have you. Once you picture a person of a particular sex, then go out and try to find someone. If that doesn't work, interview a couple of men and women and choose the one you feel you can trust the most with your money. Don't be afraid to interview; after all, it's your money. If you find that your personalities aren't suited to each other, walk away. There's lots of choice out there.

"The important thing for *you* is to be cautious. I recently reread a book called *Women and Money* by Anita Jones-Lee. She says that one should be ultra-cautious after a divorce or becoming a widow. Her recommendation is that one wait at least six months before making *any* investment decisions with the money one gets. Fortunately, in general, women tend to be more strategic risk-takers because they're more likely to surround themselves with good people. Women believe in consensus and they tend to seek a great deal of advice before making decisions. So, in your case, even if it means taking your money and putting it into low-yield term deposits or treasury bills with the government for a few months until you have a better focus, it's not the end of the world. I mean, if you earn only 3 or 4 per cent for this period instead of 8 or 10 per cent, what's the big deal?"

"You're right there, Mary," Marlene said, reaching for the bill. "I don't know how I'll ever repay you for your help."

"Well," I said, looking down at the paper in her hand. "I suppose *that's* a good start."

We shared a laugh.

CHAPTER THIRTEEN
TAKING CARE OF BUSINESS

"HELLO, IS THAT MS. POOLE?"

"Speaking."

"My name is Neena Gill. I work with Francie Chow and she suggested that I call you."

The voice was lightly accented—Indian or Pakistani—with a hint of a British accent thrown in for good measure.

"How can I help you?" I asked.

"Well, my husband and I would like to start or buy a business and we could use some advice. Francie referred me to you."

"When would you and your husband like to see me?" I asked, reaching for my Daytimer.

"My husband is actually out of the country for two weeks. Would it be all right if I saw you by myself?"

"Certainly," I replied. "If you work with Francie, your office is only a short distance from here. What time do you finish work?"

"Four o'clock. If it's all right, I could come to your office at about a quarter past."

"Let's see," I said, picking up my pen, "today is Monday the 9th. Um, my daughter and I have tickets for the Ice Capades... Tomorrow I've got an early dinner with my investment club...How about this Wednesday the 11th, at 4:15?"

"That sounds perfect to me," she said. "I'll see you then."

◆

That Wednesday at about 4:25, Louise buzzed to tell me I had a visitor. I rose from my desk and greeted Neena at the door.

"I'm sorry I'm late," she said. "I forgot these and I had to go back and get them from my locker." She reached out and handed me a small parcel.

"What's this?" I asked with a surprised smile.

"Just some pastries I baked last night. You mentioned you had a daughter. I didn't ask her age, but I thought the two of you might enjoy these. They're an old family recipe."

I opened the bag and took a peek. My nose was immediately assailed by the wonderfully sweet aroma of fresh pastry.

"Smells heavenly," I said, "but actually, Jenny's away on a three-day ski trip. It's the mid-winter University break and it's her last chance to party before her finals."

"That's too bad."

"Not really," I said eyeing the treats with a wicked grin. "Why don't you join me right now for a cup of tea or coffee and a bite to eat? We wouldn't want these to go to waste."

Without waiting for a response, I walked quickly into my combination storage room/kitchenette and proceeded to pull out three small plates. I placed a pastry on each and carried one of them over to Louise's desk.

"Coffee or tea?" I asked Neena.

"Tea would be nice," she replied. "Black with one lump of sugar if you have it."

I nodded and went back into the storage room. "Why don't you take a seat in my office?" I suggested. "I'll be there in a second."

"Can I help you?"

"Well, if you'd like to take these two plates, sure," I replied, coming out with pastry in hand.

Several minutes later, I settled in behind my desk and took a sip from my cup. I bit into the pastry and experienced pure heaven.

"What's that flavour?" I asked. "I can't quite place it."

"Nutmeg," replied Neena with a smile. "It's an old family recipe."

"Um, delicious," I said. "You should go into business."

She laughed. "Actually, that's why I'm here. My husband and I want to start or buy a business and I thought we could use some advice."

"Do you have any idea of what you want to do?"

"We're thinking of a gourmet coffee and pastry shop. Actually, I've only been working at the power company for a short time and, to be honest, I'm not all that happy there. We live over on the South Shore and it's a long commute. Also, I'd like the chance to be closer to the children when they come home from school. I have a son who's 14 and a daughter who's 11. We also look after my husband's mother. I thought if we had our own business..."

"Unfortunately," I interrupted, "most people who own their own businesses tend to work longer hours than people who are employed by others."

"That's true, but with what I have in mind, my mother-in-law can help us and the children can work after school and weekends. I think it would be good for them, especially for Saleem."

"Saleem?"

"Yes, my son. I don't mean to be uncharitable because Canada has been very good to us, but many of the young people in Saleem's class don't seem to have much of a work ethic. A lot of them smoke and hang out at those video parlours. My husband is an engineer with Insight Construction and he travels quite a bit. He's usually not away, though, for more than three or four days at a time and he's certainly willing to help me on the weekends. But during the week..."

"That's a novel approach to parenting you're suggesting," I said with a laugh. "Instead of Mom staying home with the kids, why not *bring the kids to mom's business after school?*"

"I think if I can get Saleem working with me, he'll adopt a more mature approach regarding his studies. I mean, he has no idea of what it costs to live. Last month I took him to the orthodontist and it's going to cost over $3,000..."

"Welcome to the 'braces stage of life'," I said with a smile. "I know, I've been there with Jennifer. Fortunately, when those horrible things come off, it's worth it in the smile! So, tell me more about your coffee shop idea."

185

"Well, there's a shopping centre about three blocks from the house. It's actually a strip mall with about seven or eight stores. There's some vacant space, about 800 square feet, and I think it's an ideal location. There are five or six office buildings within a two block radius and a larger shopping centre across the street that has an Italian and a Chinese restaurant. But there really isn't any place for people to go for a light, healthy lunch or for a mid-morning or mid-afternoon coffee; or even to get out on the weekend and read the paper.

"I know a few of the merchants in the mall and they've told me they've set up their own little support network if someone's children are sick or if someone has to go out of town on holidays or family emergency or whatever. There's a real sense of community and my mother-in-law, in addition to helping me out, would be willing to babysit for some of the other merchants."

"Sounds interesting," I said.

"Of course," Neena continued, "I would do quite a bit of the baking at home and there are a few specialty coffees and teas I think most people would like. I have a brother-in-law who's in the import/export business in Toronto and he has some good sources of supply."

"It sounds like you've thought of just about everything," I said. "It's kind of interesting how you seem to have come up with a solution to your two problems—the children and your mother-in-law. *If you can't be with them, let them come to you.* Women are so often caught in a bind when it comes to double parenting."

"I suppose that's true. As we get older, so many of us become parents to our own parents."

"That's exactly what I'm getting at. And it's usually us women who end up looking after the elderly."

"I guess that's because we're naturally care-givers by inclination."

I nodded my head, pleased that we were both on the same wave length.

"I also think it's extremely important for us to instill a good work ethic in our children," I said "One of the other problems that baby-boomers are confronting today is the problem of boomerang kids."

"Boomerang kids? Is that an Australian phenomenon?"

"Hardly. It's very much a North American problem. It's when the children go out on their own, then lose their jobs or get divorced, and come back home to Mom and Dad. In so many cases, people in their late 40s or early 50s breathe a sigh of relief when the last child is gone, only to find within a short time that the empty nest is full again."

"I think the focus of education has to change," said Neena. "There really aren't a whole lot of good jobs out there and today's children have to be taught entrepreneurism."

"You're right," I said, getting up from my desk and walking over to my bookcase. "There's a really good book," I said, "that, as far as I'm concerned, is a must read for Canadian teens. Here it is. It's called *The Wealthy Paper Carriers.*"

"Oh really?" said Neena. "I've heard of it. What's it about?"

"It follows the story of two teenagers from age 15 to age 35. They have a mentor who happens to be a Chartered Accountant like myself who gives them guidance as they grow into adulthood. The book takes them through their first jobs and then leads them into home ownership, saving for the future, buying RRSPs and so on. In fact, there's even a chapter on starting a small business. It's all easy reading and it's geared towards teenagers and young adults in their 20s or 30s who need to know more about financial matters. Does Saleem like to read?"

"Actually, he does, but he'll never admit it to his friends. Reading just isn't cool."

"The author uses a neat expression when he encourages teens to do well for themselves financially. He says that the key to financial success is *giving up sleep or sitcoms.*"

Neena laughed. "I suppose that's appropriate. I suspect if I go through with the coffee shop idea, Saleem might have to give up a little bit of both."

"It's important that you pay him a fair wage, though," I cautioned.

"Oh, I have every intention," said Neena, "but why did you..."

"Well, I've found in a lot of cases, people who own businesses expect their kids to work for them without a monetary reward. They take the position that, after all they're supporting the kids, so why shouldn't the children give back? The problem is, young people don't always see it that way and I think if you can see fit to actually pay—I don't know, $6 or $7 a hour—you'd be helping them immensely. Your children will then get a sense of the value of money and they'll learn how to manage it." I pointed to the book. "This author, Cimmer, suggests an interesting formula for youngsters."

"What's that?"

"He says that if teens can earn a few hundred dollars a month while still in high school, they should first be encouraged to spend a third. Adults have to recognize that their children are only young once, and they should have the opportunity to enjoy the fruits of their efforts."

"Makes sense to me," said Neena.

"With respect to the next third," I continued, "Cimmer suggests that teens be encouraged to save that money for relatively short-term goals. In other words, saving $50 or $60 a month towards the purchase of a mountain bike or ski equipment—something that is readily attainable within a relatively short time-frame."

Neena nodded. "And the last third?"

"The last third, he suggests, should be put away into a long-term savings program. It's quite astounding what compounding income or growth can do if you start very young."

"I'll definitely buy the book," said Neena. "You've sure sold me."

"Speaking of income and all that, how much capital is this venture going to take? Do you have any idea?"

"My husband and I have done some preliminary costing and we figure we'll need about $75,000. We actually have $50,000 now and I don't think with that kind of investment it will be too difficult to borrow the rest."

"Whose money is it?"

"Actually, most of it is mine from an inheritance, but Rajeeb—that's my husband—will contribute about $10,000 from his savings."

"You're going to manage the business, then, are you?"

"Yes, for the most part, although, as I said before, he's promised to help evenings and weekends when he's in town. And I'm sure he will. He's a very hard worker." She paused for a moment. "Why do you ask?"

"A book I like to refer to is *Women and Money* by Anita Jones-Lee. I have a copy here. This is another one you might want to buy—not for Saleem, but for yourself. What the author says is 'Don't put your money where your brain is not welcome'. In other words, she advises women against investing in their husbands' businesses unless they have a say in what's going on. She also cautions that if you co-sign or guarantee, you should make sure you receive some financial benefit and have some control over the income that is going to be used to repay the loan. It's pretty good advice, especially since so many marriages don't last."

Neena smiled. "Well, fortunately, my husband and I have a very good relationship. Maybe it's a bit surprising because we hardly knew each other when we were married, but I suppose the similarity of cultural backgrounds helped and I think we communicate very well."

"You seem to have everything well in hand then. What can I do for you?"

"Well, to start with," Neena said, "I would like some independent input. What do you think of the idea? It doesn't hurt to have feedback. Also, if we do get going, we'll need an accountant to set up a proper set of books. Once we're underway, I think I'll be able to keep the books if you show me how. So what do you think of our prospects?"

I thought for a moment. "The way I see it," I said thoughtfully, "there are several criteria for business success and I think your idea basically meets all of them."

"And they are?"

"I've believed for years there are four things a person should consider before starting or buying a business," I said. "In no particular order they are," I ticked them off on my fingers as I spoke, *"one, you don't want a business in which you have to maintain a significant inventory, especially any inventory subject to obsolescence; two, you don't want a business that is capital intensive and requires a significant investment in machinery and equipment; three, the product or service you furnish should be, if at all possible, recession proof, and four, in general, you should provide products, not personal services, to your customers."*

"Nice list," Neena said. "Could you possibly go through them one by one with some more detail?"

"Of course," I responded. "Would you like another cup of tea and some more of your wonderful pastry?"

"No thanks," Neena said, patting her stomach. "One of the big problems with baking pastry is..."

"I know, the inclination to eat what you've made. All right then," I said, leaning back in my chair, "first, some background. The biggest problem that has always faced new business operators is under-capitalization. Many people have had good ideas over the years, but they haven't had enough money to carry through. Fortunately, some lenders are willing to lend money if they think there's a decent chance of success. In your case, given that you're coming up with two-thirds of the capital and your husband will keep his job..." Neena nodded, "...financing shouldn't be a problem."

"Yes," she said, "our house is also completely paid."

"Great," I smiled, "you obviously have a good track record. Rajeeb has his profession and I assume you've got no bad history with credit cards." Neena shook her head emphatically. "I'm sure the bank will take a risk with you. Now, remember the first criterion. You don't want any business that has to carry a significant amount of inventory because, even with low interest rates, your financing costs can kill you if your inventory doesn't turn over fast enough. Part of the problem is that inventory purchases are usually covered with borrowed money. And with floating interest rates businesses can't effectively budget for

190

interest costs because they never know what they'll actually be. Unfortunately, most politicians are lawyers, not businesspeople and what they don't realize is that this country needs a *stable interest rate policy* where the rates are *not* allowed to fluctuate every week."

"It's too bad governments don't realize that. Have you tried to tell them?"

"I've written a letter or two to the Prime Minister and the Finance Minister and various senior cabinet people, but they won't listen. Anyway," I shrugged my shoulders, "unless business owners can count on a stable interest rate for anywhere from two to five years, it's almost impossible for them to budget for the cost of borrowed money. Let's assume a business borrows $100,000. If the interest rate over a five-year period averages 7 per cent, the total cost over that time is $35,000. If the average interest rate is 12 per cent, the interest cost becomes $60,000—almost double. The $25,000 spread could be the difference between being profitable and going broke. You can budget for rent, you can budget for salaries, you can set a limit for advertising and promotion, but the one area that small business has no control over is financing costs." I couldn't help becoming agitated so I took a deep breath and paused to regain my composure. Neena was with me all the way.

"I see what you mean," she said. "Even if it means that our dollar falls relative to the U.S. dollar or other currencies, we need a stable interest rate. It makes sense to me."

I nodded. "Until we have interest rate stability," I continued, "my first criterion stands. You don't want a business in which you must tie up a lot of money—especially borrowed money—in inventory. In your case, the inventory will turn over rapidly. I suppose if you have goods that haven't sold on a given day, you can always unload them at a discount the following morning and coffee and tea will keep for a while, won't they?"

"That's true," said Neena. "In fact, I'm pretty sure I could sell all of the day-old stuff to the other merchants in the mall when they open for business each day. When it comes to coffees and teas, my brother-in-law told me he can provide three-day turnaround. I've already done some figuring and I don't think we'll need more than about $5,000 for inventory."

"Good, that's one problem solved," I grinned. "Whatever you do, stay away from any business that requires you to carry a lot of inventory. This is especially true if products are seasonal or subject to obsolescence."

"I know what you mean by that," Neena said. "I once tried to figure out the logic behind a Christmas ornament shop that went broke. The owners had a whopping good selling season in October, November and December, but whatever they didn't sell before Christmas, they had to hold onto for at least eight or nine slow months."

I nodded. "I know the store. They couldn't win. The owners were stuck with inventory that wasn't moving."

"It's funny, though," Neena said. "Last summer, we took a two-week vacation camping near Banff, Alberta. There's a similar shop on the main street there that's been in business for over 10 years."

"But it's in a tourist location where people buy things just for having been there, so it really isn't just a Christmas decoration store. Think of it as a shop that deals in the novelty of selling Christmas goods to tourists. Remember, business is marketing: positioning, positioning, positioning."

"I see your point. The inventory issue is a big one for anybody starting a business."

I nodded again. "In what year did you come to Canada?" I asked.

"1986. Why?"

"I suppose you remember how so many of the giant retail chains collapsed or were seriously downsized in the early '90s. Sears gave up its catalogue business, Woodward's in the West was taken over and the name disappeared, Birks Jewellers went bankrupt, then found a buyer who saved the company, and so on."

"Those weren't good times for the retail industry," Neena agreed. "I have no doubt about your first point. Fortunately, my specialty coffee shop business is one where inventory carrying costs won't harm me. Now what's the second criterion?"

"You don't want anything that is too heavily capital intensive," I said.

Neena nodded. "You mean a business where the owner has to buy a lot of machinery and equipment. It sounds a lot like the problem with inventory."

"Exactly," I exclaimed. "If you have to spend hundreds of thousands of dollars buying equipment, then again your carrying costs can kill you. When it comes to equipment, you not only have to pay interest charges, but over a period of time you have to pay for the capital cost of the equipment as well. At least you can sell inventory at a profit—you hope—and buy more, but with equipment you generally keep it and it depreciates over time."

"But doesn't the tax system help out by letting people claim depreciation on the equipment which somehow offsets income?" Neena objected. "Even I know that much."

"Yes, but most equipment really *does* depreciate over time and eventually it has to be replaced. A major investment in machinery and equipment can cripple even big companies and that's something a fledgling entrepreneur should avoid."

"Well, I don't have a serious problem there, even though a coffee shop does require a fair investment in equipment."

"How much?"

"I've done some checking and there is a reputable supply house that will provide what they call a 'turnkey operation'. They'll install all the equipment I would need for about $50,000. That would include ovens for baking, coffeemakers, cappucino maker, countertops, tables, chairs, refrigeration and so on. Alternatively, they have offered to lease everything to me with a seven-year payout for $875 a month."

"Have you calculated the interest rate?"

"Well, actually I haven't, but Rajeeb has. In some ways," she chuckled, "engineers are like accountants. They have these little calculators that do all kinds of magic."

"So, what's the rate?"

"14 per cent."

I whistled.

"I know," Neena said, "it's high."

"Especially in today's market, but I imagine they have to take into account the fact that so many restaurants go out of business and then they're faced with repossessing used equipment."

"I suppose," said Neena. "If they can get that rate, more power to them, but in our case we feel that we'd rather invest our own money and not be saddled with a big debt. Paying off the bank for the balance will cost us a lot less. The money we borrow will also cover our opening inventory and give us a budget for some advertising. We'll also need a small line of credit for any emergencies and contingencies. Realistically, we know it can take months for any new business to build a reputation, gain repeat customers, and turn a profit. Fortunately, with Rajeeb working it doesn't matter if it takes six months or more before I start seeing a profit. The other good news is that the equipment will probably last at least 10 years or so before it becomes obsolete and we don't need a lot of space."

"Space? What do you mean?" It was my turn to ask. "And, by the way, please call me Mary."

"Well, okay, Mary. If we had a business with a lot of inventory and a great deal of equipment, we would need a lot more space and that would clearly increase our overhead—rent, utilities and the like. Low inventory means less space. The equipment is expensive but it doesn't take up a lot of room. We'll have the space for about 10 tables, half of which will seat four people, the other half, two. We'll also have a counter near the window where people can sit more privately, drink their coffee and read the paper. So, what's your third criterion, Mary?" She paused for a moment. "And please, call me Neena."

I nodded. "Anyway, Neena, the third criterion is that you want a recession-proof business—one where people need you or want you whether times are good or bad. Remember the Birks' bankruptcy of the early '90s I referred to? Birks wasn't the only jewellery company to hit on hard times."

"Of course not," Neena said. "That was during one of the

worst depressions Canada has had since the end of World War II. People just weren't buying jewellery."

"Exactly," I replied. "No matter how good your product, if people don't consider it necessary in bad times, they just aren't going to buy. But you've never heard of a pharmacy chain going bankrupt, have you?"

"No, can't say that I have."

"Know why?"

"I guess it's because people get sick in good and bad times. Probably more in the bad because of the stress," she suggested. "And things like shampoo and toilet paper are staples and the sales volumes don't vary much whether the economy is up or down."

"I think you know more about business and economics than you give yourself credit for, Neena," I said. "Mind you, becoming an economics expert probably doesn't require zillions of years of training. Anyone who can think clearly can profit from getting a feel for basic economics."

"Maybe I'll set up an economic consulting division to our business," Neena suggested brightly.

"Ha," I growled, "too many amateurs and witch doctors muddying up the field. But seriously, stick to what you know best—baking. I think you've come up with a pretty good idea, especially if you don't have a lot of competition in your neck of the woods. People need to eat regularly and it's nice to have a place where one can go, have a bite to eat or a cup of coffee, socialize a bit and get out of the house or away from the office for a few minutes, without it costing an arm and a leg. I think you've picked a field that's recession-proof. You're a lot better off than many of the high-class restaurateurs who are really suffering."

"Yes," said Neena, "it's really become pretty bad, especially with the new tax rule that allows businesses to deduct only half of their entertainment and meal costs."

I nodded again. "That's true. Coupled with the GST and provincial sales taxes, going out to eat even when you have a legitimate business motive is a pretty expensive proposition."

"I think our coffee shop can do quite well under these circumstances," Neena said happily. "And the last criterion?"

"I think the best businesses are those that provide *products* and *not personal services*. Now, here the idea of a coffee shop doesn't quite fit, but one does have to make compromises."

"You've just confused the issue, Mary."

"Sorry, Neena, let me explain. If you provide products for resale, you profit from marking up these goods above your cost. Obviously the mark-up must factor in your overhead costs such as rent, supplies and so on. The problem with being in a business that provides personal services is that you must always work or you aren't earning money. Now in your case, a lot of the goodwill will depend on repeat business and that means prompt, courteous service coupled with good food and coffee. I'm afraid that you'll be spending a lot of hours running your own show."

Neena shrugged. "I expected that and I'm not afraid of hard work."

"Actually, your situation isn't that terrible. You wouldn't be all alone, would you?"

"No, I'd have a part-time person to help me during lunch periods as well as my mother-in-law, probably about 20 hours a week. Then there are my children..."

"Now, what happens when you take holidays?"

"I hadn't really given that too much thought. I suppose for a couple of years, we may just have to shut down, but by the time the children are in university it would be nice if they can take over and operate the business while Rajeeb and I are away. If we're doing well enough so we can take holidays sooner, I suppose we'll just have to pick a time when business is slowest. I guess it's not that uncommon for a business like ours to close down for a week or two in the summer."

"After you've been in business for a while," I cautioned, "I predict you'll come up with other alternatives. Customers—even regulars — can be quite fickle. If they are forced to change their pattern for even a day or two they may find a new place and take their business elsewhere.

"You can cross that bridge when you get to it. But for now,

let's get back to the key point. I suppose, to a large extent, your business would really be a combination of products and services. Have you actually prepared a budget to figure out what you think you could make?"

"We've done some preliminary figuring, Mary, but I'd like you to help me refine our calculations over the next few weeks."

"I'll be happy to go through your business plan with you, and I'm glad you got a start on your own."

"I think, if all goes well, we can earn $70,000 a year even after paying my mother-in-law and the children for their services. That's more than double what I'm earning at Quebec Power."

"That's not bad," I said, "but of course, you're going to be working a lot more hours."

"I suppose you're right. My income per hour may not initially be as much as before, but it'll be nice to be my own boss. Self-employment has its advantages."

I nodded emphatically in agreement.

"Do we need to incorporate or anything like that?" Neena asked.

"Quite possibly," I said. "Do you mind telling me how much your husband earns?"

"He makes about $60,000 a year. After taxes and his RRSP contribution, he brings home a little bit more than $30,000."

"That little? On $60,000?"

"Well, he is putting $10,000 a year away in RRSPs. Half of that is going into my name as a spousal plan."

"Great," I said. "So how much more do you need to meet living expenses?"

"I think we'll do pretty well if I draw a salary of $30,000 before tax. I figure that would leave us $21,000 or $22,000...almost $2,000 a month of extra disposable income."

I did some fast mental arithmetic. "You're about right there. So, if your business can earn $70,000 and you only need to draw $30,000, there is probably a big advantage to incorporating."

"Does it have to do with liability?"

"No, not at all. When you borrow money, the lending institution is going to require your personal guarantee anyhow, so the limited liability protection afforded by setting up a corporation, which is a separate legal entity, really isn't going to matter. The big advantage actually comes from the fact that you'll be earning more than you need to live."

"How so?"

"Well," I said, "since the early '70s, Canada has had a tax structure that favours incorporation for profitable businesses. You see, even at relatively modest income levels, an individual is soon paying tax at 40 to 50 per cent on each dollar of income. But a small incorporated business, which is an entity that is separate from its owners, can earn up to $200,000 a year in business profits and pay only about 20 per cent tax. The $200,000 annual limit has been around for quite a number of years now."

"What does that mean to us?"

"Let's make up a simple example," I said. "Let's assume your business grows to a point where, within a few years, your profit before you take any salary is $130,000. You've paid your employees including your children and covered all your overhead. Okay so far?"

"Yes," she said, "all the bills are paid, the employees are paid, I haven't been paid, but my profit is $130,000."

"Now assume you personally need a pre-tax income of $30,000 which leaves you after taxes enough money to pay all the household bills when your take-home is added to your husband's income. Hopefully, you might also be able to put away a few dollars for yourself in RRSPs or other investments."

"What you're basically saying is the take-home on my $30,000 income should cover all my *living and saving expenses.*"

"Correct," I nodded. "So, you take out $30,000 and have $100,000 left in the business. If you're unincorporated, this $100,000 gets taxed at your top personal rate, which would be anywhere from 40 up to 55 per cent. Actually, taxes in Quebec are higher than they are in most other jurisdictions."

"That's between $40,000 and $55,000," Neena calculated.

"I don't know which is the bigger crime," I responded, "the way we're taxed or the way the tax dollars are being spent."

"Do tell!" Neena commented. Then she realized something.

"But you said the corporate rate was only about 20 per cent. So, if this $100,000 stays in the business, the taxes would only be $20,000. The corporation would be ahead by about $30,000 on the tax side and because my husband and I control the corporation..."

"You would control the 80,000 after-tax dollars."

"Wonderful," Neena said, clapping her hands. "Why does the government allow this? It's not out of any love for us or concern for our success or financial well-being, I'm sure."

"The government wants small businesses to use cheaply taxed profits, which I sometimes call 80¢ dollars—the after-20-per-cent-tax dollars—for business expansion," I said. "In other words, it provides a way that a small business can finance its growth from within without borrowing. That means machinery, inventory, staff..."

I could see Neena was confused.

"Mary, you just got through telling me we're better off without a lot of machinery or inventory."

"Exactly," I said, "and here's the key point. *If you have a profitable small business that qualifies for the low rate of corporate tax, you can use those 80¢ after-tax dollars to create* **investment capital** *for yourself.* Even though you wouldn't be permitted to draw out the money into your own hands without paying personal tax, the corporation could make investments on your behalf. And where do you think the corporation would invest its money?"

"I don't know," said Neena. "What do you think?"

I continued. "Well, you yourself have already figured out that a small business is nothing more than an extension of its owners and you recognize that you and your husband can own all the shares of this corporation. So, if you like term deposits, your company would invest in term deposits. Obviously this would make sense only if interest rates were considerably higher than they are today. Or if you like stocks, your company could play the stock market. If you wanted mutual funds, real estate, gold, silver, even paintings and antiques, your company could buy all this on your behalf. The point is *you* would control the wealth even if you don't own it directly."

"I see," she said as the light went on. "Instead of only having 50¢ dollars after personal taxes to control directly, we would control and be able to indirectly spend or invest our company's 80¢ dollars," she summarized, "which means we can invest it any way we want. So, if we wanted to buy growth mutual funds, the company could buy a lot more than we could." She savoured that thought for a moment. "We could use the system instead of the system using us. Why didn't we go into business years ago?"

I didn't bother answering.

"I know," she said, "we just had to be ready and now the time has come. It would've been a lot harder when our children were younger."

"You're not doing too badly, Neena," I said. "You're still in your 30s. It's the perfect time for you. Now there's a lot more to owning your own business than what we can cover in just one evening. After you have your game plan together, I can help you get started and assist you in setting up your bookkeeping."

"I'm glad you'll be here to be our accountant," Neena said. "I suppose you could also help us with our taxes. Rajeeb likes to do the returns on the computer, but perhaps you can check them before we file."

"I'll be happy to do that. In fact, it makes a lot of sense for people to take a stab at doing their own taxes first and then have an accountant review their returns instead of preparing them from scratch. It's a lot cheaper and people will usually pick up quite a bit of financial awareness when they are personally involved."

"One question, Mary, if I may. What if you weren't here? How would I go about finding an accountant?"

"It's like trying to find any other kind of professional," I said. "If you don't know where to go, you ask around, speak to your friends and then go to someone who comes to you with a high recommendation. It's also important that you feel comfortable...feel some compatibility with this person and that you can communicate openly and effectively."

"Sounds no different than general principles for shopping around for a doctor or dentist," Neena said.

I nodded. "One concrete bit of advice I can give you, though, is you need to know the type of accountant you're dealing with."

"Type of accountant?"

"Well, broadly speaking," I continued, "accountants in public practice come in two types."

"You sound like you're describing gerbils," Neena laughed.

"No, they don't use quite as much paper these days," I shot back, and we both had a good laugh before I continued. "Some accountants prefer dealing with big business. Like here in Montreal, they'd rather work with companies like your employer, Quebec Power or Bell Canada. Then there are accountants who prefer working with small businesses."

"Well that simplifies the search," Neena said. "I suppose small business owners could always look towards one of the larger firms that has a small business unit in its practice."

"It's possible," I nodded. "But I think you're better off dealing with a smaller firm that's a sole proprietorship or has, say, three or four partners at most. Chances are you'd receive better treatment from a firm accustomed to dealing with small business clients that is itself a small business. Small firms would likely value your business more than large firms and definitely would tend to charge lower fees."

"Basically, you're saying that the average small business owner is better off as a small fish in a small pond rather than a small fish in a big pond."

"That's one way to put it," I said.

"Mary, I feel a lot more comfortable now than I did when I first arrived. I'll work on perfecting our business plan and maybe we can meet next week before we sign the lease with the landlord and commit to buying the equipment."

"You'll probably have to work harder than you ever did in your life for at least a few years," I said, "but the rewards will be there for you. Take your time. A month more or less isn't going to make a lot of difference."

"We'll need to find a lawyer who can handle the legal work."

201

"If you have any trouble, call me. I can probably recommend someone to you. Be sure you find a lawyer whose specialty is small business and contract work. Have you thought of a name for the shop yet?"

"Not really. Our family has a little border collie named Bessie and my daughter wants to call it Bessie's Bistro, but somehow I don't think that'll do."

"I don't know," I laughed, "I've heard worse."

CHAPTER FOURTEEN
TIPS FOR TEENS

"MS. POOLE, THIS IS MARCIE LAROCCA SPEAKING."

I settled back into my chair at the sound of this very young female voice on the other end of my phone. "Another charitable appeal," I said to myself, sighing. "If I keep on eating all of those cookies and chocolate bars..."

"Yes, Marcie, what can I do for you?"

"I'm your friend Angie's daughter," she said hesitantly.

I bolted upright, suddenly all ears. "Is everything all right?"

"Oh sure, everything's fine. But actually, my Mom asked me to call you."

"Oh?"

"Yes. I'm going into my last year of high school and I'm kind of, like...up in the air about where I'm going. I mean, Mom's trying to encourage me to take a business course next year, but I don't know if I'd like that kind of thing. I know it's tough for young people to find jobs and..." Her voice trailed off.

I looked at the clock on my desk. It was about ten past noon. "Marcie," I said, "you must be calling me on your lunch break...Marcie?"

"Oh, yes, I'm sorry."

"That's okay, dear. Hm," I said, scanning my Daytimer quickly, "do you think you can get downtown after school one day this week, or maybe next?"

"Well, actually we finish at 2:00 on Thursdays and there's a bus right outside school that'll take me to the Metro Station."

"Great. I'm only three blocks from the Peel Street Station."

"Yes, I know where your office is. Mom gave me one of your cards."

"Well, then," I said, while scribbling the appointment down in my Daytimer, "how about this Thursday, around 3:00 or 3:15? Don't worry if you're a few minutes late. I have plenty to do. And Marcie..."

"Yeah?"

"Don't be nervous. I promise not to bite."

I was rewarded by a giggle on the other end of the line.

"Oh, I'm not worried, Ms. Poole. Mom said you were really nice."

Thursday afternoon found Marcie sitting across from me at my desk, a cup of hot chocolate in hand, at about 3:30. She had her Mom's dark Italian looks, although she was considerably taller and thinner.

"Do you play sports?" I asked.

"Actually, I'm on the school volleyball team," she said. "They wanted me to play basketball. I'm 5'9", you know. But I just don't enjoy it. Last year, our team went all the way to the provincials, but we were beaten in the semi-finals by a team of Amazons from Trois Rivières. But *they* were mainly seniors, while four of the girls on our team were only in Grade 10. I think we'll do a lot better this year."

Marcie's gym bag was open by my desk and I couldn't help noticing a package of cigarettes. "Just like Francie when we met," I thought. Aloud, I said, "I don't mean to pry, dear, but I couldn't help noticing." I pointed at her purse. "I thought athletes didn't smoke."

"Well, I don't *really*. Usually not more than two or three a day."

She had turned beet red.

"I'm sorry," I said, "I'm not here to lecture you. I'm sure you hear a lot of that from your teachers."

"Yeah, I know smoking's bad. Did you see that goofy ad on T.V. where the government's trying to get teenagers to quit?" She laughed.

"I think the government could have done a lot better by putting together a campaign that talks about the high *cost* of smoking. You mentioned you were thinking about taking a business course when you finished high school."

She nodded.

"Well, one of the big problems in many high schools is that you learn stuff like algebra and geometry, but they don't teach you business math."

"What do you mean?"

"Well, let's assume you smoke a pack a day for the next 20 years."

"I'd never..."

"I know, I know. But I'm just giving you an illustration."

"Okay."

"Well, over the next 20 years, the average cost would probably be $6 or $7 a pack, right?"

Marcie shrugged. "Sure. Makes sense."

"Well, $7 a day times 30 days is about $200 a month, times 12 months per year for 20 years – do you know what that comes to?"

"I don't know without a calculator," Marcie said.

"Even if I gave you a calculator, I don't think you'd come close to figuring it out. You see, if you took $200 a month and invested the money instead at 10 per cent, after 20 years you'd have over $150,000 with compound income."

"You're kidding! I know what compounding is. That's when you earn income on top of income. Mom explained that to me a couple of months ago."

"Do you know what $200 a month at 10 per cent comes to after 35 years?"

She shook her head.

"Over three quarters of a million dollars! You know, at your age, if you had a little over $8,000 saved and *you never put aside another penny but invested this money instead, you'd probably have over a million dollars by the time you retire.*"

Marcie emitted a low whistle. "Wow."

"That's the kind of practical math I think every student

should learn, whether they choose to go into business or anything else. It's a great motivator."

"That's amazing."

I sighed. "Another problem in the school system is that, for the most part, your teachers don't reinforce the idea that it's really no sin to become wealthy."

"Yeah, rich people!"

"Well, there you go. I mean, sure, often the rich are stereotyped as being stuffy, heartless people who step on the little guy but it doesn't have to be that way. You can be quite well off financially without being a bad person. Unfortunately, most of your teachers are not wealthy themselves. They're part of a vanishing breed."

"What do you mean?"

"They're people who have relatively secure jobs for their entire working lives with a pension at the end. The whole focus of education has to change, and quickly, too!"

"I'm not sure I follow."

"Well, if you read the papers..."

"I do...once in a while..."

"You've read about all those layoffs then, haven't you?"

Marcie nodded.

"Unfortunately, there are just not a whole lot of good jobs out there."

"Why's that?"

"Well, not only has the government mismanaged the economy, but your generation has been sold down the river by big business."

"How?"

"Because North American labour costs grew so quickly during the 1970s and the early '80s. So, big business found it much cheaper to close their manufacturing plants in North America and open up in third world countries where they could hire cheaper labour. Now, the traditional manufacturing jobs don't exist as much any more, and, with more and more people losing their jobs, people in general have less money to spend and that hurts other industries as well, such as retail."

"You're not painting a very nice picture."

"I wish I could be more positive," I said with a sigh, "but there are a lot of traditional occupations and careers that may not be as promising down the road as they once were. It's also generally tougher for women than it is for men. After all, we're the ones who have families and usually take primary responsibility for raising children. It becomes hard, for example, for a woman to do well in a law firm or accounting firm. If she wants to spend a couple of years at home looking after her young children, she often loses opportunities for advancement."

"But *you* did okay. You're an accountant, aren't you?"

"True, but I did it outside the framework of the large firm. I'm much more of an entrepreneurial accountant." I could see the questioning look in Marcie's furrowed brow. "I mean I look after small business clients and I try to help people with their finances and their taxes."

"Oh, I see."

"Entrepreneurship is the way of the future, and if you're a bright person and eager to get ahead, that's something you might look at."

"You're kidding. You mean, owning my own business someday?"

"Possibly. Most of the new businesses started these days are run by women. For a lot of us, it's better than trying to fight our way up the corporate ladder in institutions that are predominantly run by males."

"Don't you like men?" Marcie asked.

"I sure do. Some of my best friends...But the truth is, even today, in spite of all the advances that women have made in the last 20 years or so, many of our traditional industries are male dominated. Also, there are certain careers where men still seem to have an advantage. As I said before, accounting and law are good examples. There are many women lawyers, but relatively few of them are partners in large firms. A lot of them go off to work for corporations as in-house counsel, meaning they work for one company only, while many others form smaller firms and specialize in family law – you know, divorce, child abuse cases and so on. On the other hand, the concept of gender association, where men tend to do certain things and women to do others, has a *positive* side, too."

"Oh, yeah?"

I got up from my chair and walked over to my bookcase, returning a moment later with a paperback book that I handed to Marcie. "You see this? It's called *Megatrends for Women* and the authors suggest that two of the major concerns of the last part of this century, which will certainly carry on into the next, are health care and the environment. These are growing fields, and women tend to do better than men because, as a rule, *we* are more inclined to be care-givers by nature than they are."

"Care-givers?"

"Yes. Our natural instinct is to look after other people. So it's usually the woman who will look after children, or elderly parents, the way your Dad's sister looked after your Grandmother before she died."

"I see what you mean."

"Recognizing trends is extremely important in order to make a decision on what to do with your life. If you're interested in health care or the environment, you may want to consider one of these as a career. On the other hand, if you think you'd like to be your own boss and run your own business some day, you might be better off with a business education."

"How do I know what's best for me?"

"That's a difficult question, Marcie. I suppose you can take some aptitude and career tests and I know there are books that your guidance counsellor can give you to read that discuss different careers. Perhaps the best suggestion I can give you is to find something you might be interested in and talk to someone who is already in that field."

"You mean someone who can tell me all the ins and outs?"

"Right. It's called finding a mentor. I've read that most women who are successful in their careers have had someone who has guided them along the way. Women tend to be better communicators than men and are also more used to sharing. In fact, over the years I've probably spoken to dozens of young women who were thinking about careers in accountancy."

"But don't you need to be a math whiz?"

"Not really," I said. "For the most part, I don't need to know a lot more than how to add, subtract, multiply and divide. Granted, I understand numeric *concepts* probably better than most people...And that leads to something else. Don't you find in school that it's okay for a *boy* to be a math whiz, as you put it, *but not for a girl?*"

Marcie thought for a moment. "Well, some of the math whiz guys are really kind of nerdy, but I suppose you're right. There's this girl, Patricia, in my class who's really pretty. I remember back in Grade 8 and 9 she was one of the most popular kids around and then last year we had a math teacher who really encouraged class participation. Pat really knew her stuff. For a while, she was answering all the questions and then she suddenly noticed the guys were avoiding her. As soon as she stopped answering, she became popular again."

I sighed. "Unfortunately, that's not an uncommon occurrence. Bright young women tend to be intimidating to their male counterparts, and sometimes try to hide their intelligence because they want approval from the young men in their lives."

"It's not only the guys," said Marcie. "Some of the girls, too..."

"That's true," I said sorrowfully. "Often women can be their own worst enemies. I don't know what it is. Sometimes, I suppose, it's nothing more than jealousy that causes certain women to get upset when others have gotten ahead."

"So what's the answer?"

"I suppose if you're really bright and determined, you've got to develop self-confidence to go after what you yourself want. And then you've got to be selective in choosing your close friends. If someone isn't going to be supportive, you have no choice but to look for someone else. To get ahead, I think to a large extent, you have to be an individualist." I pointed at Marcie's gym bag. "One of the key factors in achieving financial success is to avoid smoking, excessive drinking, bingeing and visits to the video arcades. And it's not only the health hazards. It's the financial considerations. You're probably still too young to appreciate this, but all too often you'll find that the people who congregate in the bars after work are the self-defeatists. They get together just to complain about how badly the world is treating them."

"You know, I think I like your idea about owning my own business someday, but I don't know where to start."

"Well, nothing happens overnight. I can share a few ideas with you, though. First, I think you should get a part-time job. Get used to the idea of earning a few dollars. Here, I bought you a present." I reached over and handed Marcie a book.

"*The Wealthy Paper Carriers* by Henry B. Cimmer. What's this?" she asked.

I could tell she was quite surprised and at least a bit pleased.

"It's a book written by a colleague of mine, another accountant, about financial planning for teenagers. It's written as a novel and it takes a brother and sister all the way from ages 15 to 35. They have an uncle who guides them along the way as they get their first jobs, start little part-time businesses, graduate from high school, go on to college or university, buy their first homes, and so on. Cimmer phrases it very nicely. He says for a teenager to start working means '*giving up either sleep or sitcoms*'."

"Sleep or sitcoms?"

"Yes, you either get up early in the morning to work as these kids did for a while as paper carriers, or you work after school or evenings, which means..."

"You don't get to see the sitcoms. I get it. What else does he suggest?"

"He suggests that you try to turn a hobby into a money-making proposition. In the book, for example, young Andrea is a computer whiz and she sets herself up in business teaching software programs to people while she's still in high school. Her brother, on the other hand, has a pet parrot and he starts a little business cleaning bird cages."

"Yuk."

"Well, obviously not every hobby is suited to every person, but think about what you like to do and how it might just make you some money."

"You know," said Marcie, "I really like photography."

"There you go," I replied. "Maybe there's some way you can turn photography into a little business venture."

"I don't know. I'll have to think about it. I'm not all that good..."

"But if you practise and maybe take some courses, you'll get better. Just have confidence. Believe me, having your own business someday is going to be a lot better than taking a McJob somewhere."

"McJob? What's that?"

"A fellow by the name of Douglas Coupland wrote a book called *Generation X*. He talks about how so many young people today are stuck with low-income, low-prestige, and no-future jobs in the service industry."

"Yuk, I sure don't want that."

"Tell me, have you given any thought to where you're going to go next year when you finish high school?"

"Well, my parents want me to go to university, but..."

"Ah, it's a big but. I'm certainly not suggesting you shouldn't go on with your education. But you might also consider a community college rather than a traditional university. Unfortunately, a general arts or science degree, which was popular in my day, just doesn't mean a lot now, at least not without post-graduate training. Today, half the waiters and waitresses at the better restaurants have degrees in languages or biology."

"What other choices are there?"

"Maybe you can start off by going to a community college and taking some courses that are practical and of interest to you. You might be better off with a directed study, say in photography, rather than with a bunch of general, eclectic courses in the arts or sciences. One thing I do recommend, though—"

"What's that?"

"It wouldn't hurt for you to take a basic accounting course and learn a bit about the fundamentals of the income tax system."

"But Ms. Poole, that sounds b-o-r-i-n-g!"

"It isn't necessarily boring, Marcie. I'm not suggesting you should become an accountant if that's not where you're coming

211

from, but it's nice to be able to read financial figures so you can understand how a small business runs. Also, too many people bury their heads in the sand and they're victimized by the tax system. Did you know by the time you earn $30,000 a year, the government takes over 40 per cent of any additional money?"

"You're kidding. What can I do about that?"

"Well, unfortunately, there aren't a whole lot of loopholes, but there are some pretty good tax breaks available for people who own their own businesses. You never know. You might find that once you start, you'll actually grow to like some of this stuff. Eventually, you'll want to learn about investing money. In fact, if you do get a part-time job now, you may want to start learning right away. Read this book." I pointed at *The Wealthy Paper Carriers.* "I think you might find it'll provide some motivation."

I could see Marcie was skeptical.

I continued, unperturbed. "What Cimmer recommends is a few simple steps for young people like yourself. For example, if you can earn, say $210 a month, he suggests that you spend a third of your earnings as you earn the money. He recognizes, as I do, that it's important for you to reward yourself along the way. After all, over-saving isn't a lot of fun and you're only young once. He then suggests you take the second third of your earnings and invest that towards relatively short-term goals. In other words, if you want to buy ski equipment, or, in your case, a new camera, it might take six or seven months at $70 a month for you to accumulate enough money..."

"What about the last third?" Marcie asked.

I could see she was becoming intrigued – in spite of herself. "Ah, that becomes your long-term savings program. Cimmer suggests that you learn a bit about the stock market and something called mutual funds. In fact, I expect your Mom and Dad can tell you a thing or two about these. You see, my dear," I continued, "there are a few sad realities in life."

"Such as?"

"You know how in the movies people get married and live happily ever after. Now, sometimes married couples are lucky like your Mom and Dad and it works. But unfortunately, 50 per cent of the time, it doesn't and you won't necessarily have a husband who will look after your finances later on. You're also going to have to make a decision at some point, if you do get married, whether you want to concentrate on a career or raising a family. Now, sure you can do both, but if your marriage does break down..."

"I'll be the one with the kids."

"That's probably true. *It's important to learn to pay yourself first while you're earning money.* If you have your *own* savings, you won't be accountable to anyone. What if you want to take a trip or need to attend a funeral in a different city, or better yet, a wedding? You want to be able to afford to go and you don't want to have to ask someone else for permission, so *learning how to* **invest** *money is as important as making it.* Do you get along well with your Mom and Dad?"

"Reasonably," Marcie shrugged. "They're okay."

"Another thing Cimmer recommends, and I agree, is that you should live at home as long as possible. Take advantage of free room and board, although maybe if you're earning more than a few dollars, you could pitch in. But the longer you can save and invest money, the better off you are. Eventually, without having to spend it on living expenses, you'll be in the same position as the paper carriers in the book and you'll be able to afford to buy your own home, if that's what you choose to do. It's important to develop proper *attitudes* towards money. You know, a lot of people have more difficulty in hanging on to what they get than in making it in the first place."

"Huh?"

"Well, for example, you've heard about people who've won the lottery but are broke again a year or two later?"

"Yeah, and I can't believe the turkeys..."

"The same often holds true for people who inherit money, or in some very unfortunate cases, when a woman receives a lump sum settlement in a divorce. If you don't have a healthy respect for and understanding about money, you tend never to accumulate it in the first place and you never attain the security you need, or else you blow it. I guess, to sum it all up, in the final analysis, *we're all responsible for ourselves* and we have to assume that responsibility. One of the reasons our country is in such trouble is because too many people grew used to relying on the government to provide for their support and the times, they are a-changing. The government, meaning us taxpayers, can't afford it anymore and perhaps never could."

"Do I have to become a workaholic to get ahead?"

"Not at all, Marcie. The key to success is *to work smart, not hard.* And to know what your priorities are. You know, if you walk into some of the larger accounting firms in places like Place du Canada or Place Ville Marie, you'll see they have incredibly lavish offices with fancy carpeting, original artwork on the walls and so on. In fact, I've been in offices where the furniture in the reception area costs more than everything I've got in three rooms.

"The point is, the people in these firms work incredibly long hours partially in order to finance their image. Now, maybe that's okay for them, but that's not what I want to do with my life. Other than during the tax season, March and April, I'm rarely here after 5:30 at night and I usually don't get in before 9:15 in the morning. I have a daughter who's just a little bit older than you are and I'm a single parent and I take that responsibility seriously. I also enjoy theatre, dining out with my friends and the odd hockey game. I love hiking in the summer and cross-country skiing in the winter. One night a week, I get together with some friends. We have an investment club. I love to read. There's much more to life than work and again *the secret is to work smart, not hard.*"

"Work smart, not hard?"

"Yes, find something you genuinely enjoy doing. Find a niche, a new trend and go for it with enthusiasm and a well-thought-out plan. Learn everything you can about it and then do it. And try to be the best you can. Above all, always make sure to maintain a sense of balance between work and your personal life. Take up hobbies, but never let them become obsessions. Your tastes will change over the years. Hopefully, you'll make a few long-term, permanent friendships. On the other hand, as you grow you'll become attracted to all kinds of different people."

I could see Marcie was lost in thought. I looked at my clock and I couldn't believe it was a quarter to six.

"Anyway," I said, "I think you've got enough to think about for the next little while."

Marcie nodded emphatically, after also checking her watch. "I'd better call Mom and let her know I'll be a bit late for dinner."

"Can I drive you home?"

"Isn't it out of your way?"

"Well, it shouldn't be too bad. The rush hour is almost over, and I'll still be able to make it to my investment club meeting at seven o'clock. My daughter's involved with an amateur theatre group and she's gone to rehearsal."

"Well, if you're sure it's not too much trouble," Marcie said, reaching for the phone.

"Nope. Just make your call and we're out of here."

CHAPTER FIFTEEN
A BETTER FUTURE FOR US ALL

WELL, JENNIFER, CONGRATULATIONS on your 21st birthday. I suppose if nothing else, this book is a rather unique present, to say the least. I hope it'll be worth something to you in the years to come.

I guess I could've spent more time in the past lecturing you on financial planning, and maybe even on life in general. But would you have really paid any attention? After all, I'm 'only' your Mom. I don't know whether sharing my own experiences with you would've been enough. It's probably better that you learn from a variety of different people in different circumstances.

When my friend Henry Cimmer wrote his book, *The Wealthy Paper Carriers,* he sent a copy, shortly after publication, to his son and daughter who were in university at the time. He told me they both read it and thoroughly enjoyed it. His daughter asked him why he hadn't told her all these things about planning when she was 15, like Andrea in the book. He said, "I smiled and told her, 'Cheryl, you weren't ready to listen. After all, I'm only your Dad.'"

Several weeks ago my friends and I got together at Neena's cafe (sure enough, they named it Bessie's Bistro) to celebrate her first anniversary in business. And a wonderful party it was, although a bit more fattening than I would have liked. It took her about eight months to turn the corner and begin showing a profit, but she is already so confident that she's starting to talk about franchising. She told me that the key to success, especially in the service industry, is prompt, courteous service with a view towards encouraging repeat business. It looks like Rajeeb might take early retirement next year, as his employer "downsizes", and if he does, I'm quite sure they'll open a second outlet modelled on the first.

Angie brought Marcie with her and after a bit of coaxing, she showed me a few photographs that she had recently taken. Believe it or not, she's done a whole series of portraits of unemployed people taken in and around the unemployment office. The facial expressions she's been able to capture are quite startling and reminiscent of some of the old, somewhat haunted-looking portraits from the "Dirty Thirties". Marlene was quite impressed, to say the least. She encouraged Marcie to let her blow up and frame several of the studies for an exhibit that she's putting together for the museum. By the way, her art business is also doing well and she's just about paid off the money she borrowed against her house to get started in the first place.

Francie, believe it or not, is becoming a "real" landlord. She's managed to save quite a bit of money by moonlighting and developing software products and she's bought a fourplex two blocks from her home. I think she's working too hard, though, and the rest of us lectured her gently about the need to slow down and smell the flowers.

Angie has left the agency and is starting up a full-time advertising/design business out of her home. You remember how she had her own special savings fund? Well, it turns out Joey had also been saving up money on his own for quite a number of years. When she finally decided to strike out on her own, she came home one day and found that he had bought her a spanking new $12,000 computer system. I guess he can afford it. He was just made vice-president of the liquidation firm he works for.

I told them all about my idea of writing this book for you and I was touched by their enthusiasm and encouragement. In fact, they made me promise to give them all copies.

There's a great quote I'd like to share with you from a book by Jeannette Scollard called *Risk to Win*. She says that "getting married and having children is life's biggest risk, if you ignore hang-gliding and sky-diving". I suppose she's right. If there's one thing that parents should teach their daughters, it's to be self-reliant. Our natural instinct to be care-givers can, in many ways, be harmful. Too many of us don't leave enough time for ourselves. *It's not sinful to put ourselves first.* Taking care of ourselves first can mean a better life for those around us. If *we* are happy and feel personally and financially secure and satisfied, we make better people, employers, entrepreneurs, partners, wives and mothers. Maybe if we do this for a generation or two, the chain will be broken. Of course, if we all teach our daughters to look after themselves, who's going to look after *us* when *we* reach old age? I suppose it may not matter if *we* attain sufficient means that we don't have to turn to *our* children for financial help.

Quite possibly, someday in the next few years, you'll get married. Earlier on, I described how the authors of the book, *Women's Work,* characterize men as traditional, transitional and non-traditional. I suppose it may be too much to hope that you find a man who is non-traditional enough to completely share household as well as financial responsibilities. Frankly, I'm not that optimistic. I recently read a newspaper article that quotes a Statistics Canada report which says teenage girls work considerably harder than boys because they're expected to do more in the way of household chores. I suppose if *you* have sons, the best thing you can do is teach them to cook and clean. You'll be doing your *own* daughters-in-law a tremendous service.

If there's one bit of concrete advice I can give you on selecting a mate, it's to find a *good communicator.* It's so important that you be able to communicate openly on many things—including saving, spending and investing which are the major topics of this book. But, for goodness sake, protect yourself at all times. Maybe you should re-read the section where I talked with my friend Angie about pooling money for joint expenses on the one hand, while still keeping a separate account for herself.

Take advantage of women's study groups and consider joining an investment club. *Learn, learn, learn, because that's what life's all about.*

When you choose a career, consider doing something that you truly enjoy. Make sure you always have something to look forward to and *always love someone*—if not a human, at least a pet. Don't worry too much. Keep up your self-esteem.

I hope you consider starting your own business someday. I think self-employment is far more rewarding than working for someone else. Self-employed people are task-oriented. They're not bound by a time clock. Often you can do a full-time job in five or six hours if you cut out extraneous conversation with co-workers, unproductive meetings and commuting. Cutting down on breaks and lunch hours also helps. One major advantage of focusing intensely is that when your day's work is done, you'll have more time for family, recreation and fitness.

If you do decide to work as an employee and you take some time off to have children or whatever, when you return to the work force, consider going to a small business where the managerial skills you will have learned in running a household can be appreciated and put to good use.

Never take too many big risks simultaneously. For example, if you ever get divorced, don't rush off to relocate or start a new business immediately. Wait and get reacquainted with yourself. Take it slowly, one day at a time.

Continue to volunteer as you did from time to time through high school and university. In addition to contributing to the well-being of the community, it may present wonderful opportunities to broaden your skills, take on new challenges, and create a truly richer quality of life than you might otherwise have experienced. Life is full of opportunities and possibilities. May you always be open to recognizing them.

Between the ages of 25 and 35, make sure you put your career on a solid foundation. Learn to invest aggressively. At these ages, you can afford to take chances. Try to maximize capital gains and growth. Most importantly, *invest consistently even if you do so in small increments*. Consider buying a house even if you're not married. Otherwise, set up a registered retirement savings plan.

Between ages 36 and 50, you'll hit your peak earning years. Unfortunately, you'll probably find that with increased earnings come higher expenses. Make sure you continue investing but consider moving to a more balanced portfolio. If you have children and you're worried about looking after their education, *your best plan is a fully-paid home*. If you're not making mortgage payments, there's ample money left over for educational costs and much, much more. I've tried to ensure you'll never have to look after me, financially, but being mortgage-free is also the key towards being able to support elderly parents without undue hardship.

I know it's hard for you to visualize this now, but someday you'll hit the big 5-0. I'm not that many years away from it myself. Long before then, make sure your will is in order, that you have an estate plan and consider moving more heavily into fixed income investments. Remember the power of compound income. *No one who sets aside even a small amount of money each month for 20 to 35 years should ever find themselves living below the poverty line, dependent on government or charitable support at the end.* I'm not suggesting that all of us women will become rich. In reality, though, *wealth means more than having money in the bank*. Sure, having money is empowering and people with money tend to be admired, respected and—yes—envied too. But attaining wealth is more than that. *If you can eliminate the need to worry about money you'll be free to enjoy the finer things that life has to offer—free time to enjoy your family, friends, hobbies, concerts, holidays, dining out or whatever else turns you on.*

None of my friends whom you've met in this book are wealthy in the traditional sense of the word—although they are all on the right track. There's an old commercial—I don't exactly remember what it's about—where the punchline is "getting there is half the fun". That's what this book is all about: getting there— setting goals, making a plan and following through. If you've gotten this far, Jennifer, I hope you've enjoyed my story of *becoming* the wealthy woman.

MARY POOLE'S
MONEY MANAGEMENT TIPS FOR WOMEN

ONE

Always maintain a separate savings account from your spouse's account or any joint accounts. It's important to establish your own credit rating and a relationship with your bank manager. Try to accumulate sufficient funds for six months' expenses.

TWO

Never invest in a loved one's business unless you take an active role. *"Don't Put Your Money Where Your Brain's Not Welcome."*

THREE

Decide early on whether you want to break the 'Glass Ceiling' or go around it by going into your own business.

FOUR

Buy a home even if you're single and pay for it as quickly as possible. If you're married, make sure your name is on title.

FIVE

Save money regularly—but reward yourself along the way by skipping one month twice a year.

SIX

Learn business mathematics—The Power of Compound Interest. Becoming financially secure isn't really difficult.

SEVEN

Don't place your trust blindly in lawyers, accountants brokers and financial planners. Research, network and learn to interview advisors before making a choice. Read the financial news, keep up on today's trends and join an investment club. Learn about mutual funds. Remember the old adage: Buyer beware!

EIGHT

Foster your entrepreneurial instincts with a positive attitude. Turn a hobby or ethnic advantage into a business opportunity.

NINE

Volunteer and encourage volunteerism within your family. In addition to contributing to the community, helping others will provide you with a network of contacts, develop your skills and interests, and open your eyes to new possibilities.

TEN

Learn basic tax concepts and how to read a financial statement.

ELEVEN

Avoid smoking, excessive drinking, junk food and credit card addiction.

TWELVE

Think carefully about whether or not you want to have children. Balance the rewards and costs. Children demand an investment in time and money and while they are a source of continuous joy and learning, they are reputed to cause wrinkles!

MARY POOLE'S
REFERENCE LIBRARY

The Canadian Tax and Investment Guide	Henry B. Zimmer McClelland & Stewart 1993
Hardball for Women	Pat Heim, Ph.D. Plume 1993
Megatrends for Women	Patricia Aburdene & John Naisbitt Fawcett Columbine 1992
Men, Women & Relationships	John Gray, Ph.D. Beyond Words 1990
The Money Manager	Henry B. Cimmer Springbank 1993
Risk to Win	Jeanette R. Scollard MacMillan 1989
The Richest Man in Babylon	George S. Clason Penguin 1955
The Wealthy Barber	David Chilton Stoddart 1989
The Wealthy Paper Carriers	Henry B. Cimmer Springbank 1993
The Wealthy Procrastinator	Henry B. Cimmer Springbank 1993
Women and Money	Anita Jones-Lee Barron's 1991
Women's Work	Nancy Johnson Smith & Sylva K. Leduc Detselig 1992
Your Canadian Guide to Planning for Financial Security	Henry B. Zimmer C.C.H. 1989

The Springbank Wealthy Series Order Now!

How do people with no greater advantages than you manage to achieve so much more success? In his highly-readable books on personal financial planning, Henry Zimmer gives the answers, outlining simple techniques for making your income work harder and helping your investments grow.

THE WEALTHY PROCRASTINATOR
Financial planning for those over forty!

Unlike David Chilton's The Wealthy Barber, Zimmer's new book, The Wealthy Procrastinator is aimed at men and women over forty. This intriguing story spans a twenty-year period from 1995 to 2015, anticipating the kind of political, social and economic restructuring that might occur and its effect on the ordinary Canadian. Using Zimmer's commonsense principles, the book's fictional heroes progress from mid-life financial chaos to a successful retirement . The Wealthy Procrastinator goes beyond the basics of mortgage prepayment, mutual fund programs and life insurance protection to cover such issues as the wise use of severance payments, inheritances, wills, and specific criteria for buying or starting a business.

"For people over forty who have neglected their financial planning, The Wealthy Procrastinator takes the mystery out of money management. If you want to spend less time worrying about your financial future and more time enjoying life, I strongly recommend it."

Dian Cohen, former Financial Editor,
CTV News

Quantity_____   **$15.95**

THE MONEY MANAGER FOR CANADIANS
Henry Zimmer's 70,000 best-seller - updated and revised!

Already a stand-by for investment-minded Canadians, The Money Manager is a useful companion book to the Springbank Wealthy Series. In this new edition, Henry Zimmer has updated his popular guide to show that you don't need to be a mathematical genius to survive in an uncertain economy. This complete and easy-to-understand reference book includes simple tables for calculating investment yields, the costs of borrowing money and leasing, life insurance costs and benefits, current mortgage rates and terms, and other financial arrangements.

Quantity_____   **$15.95**

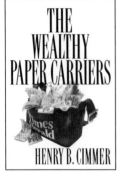

THE WEALTHY PAPER CARRIERS

For the first time—a motivational story on wealth accumulation for young adults!

The Wealthy Paper Carriers is an entertaining and motivational story that shows young adults how to gain more from life than low-paying, low-prestige jobs with no future. Written in the novel form, it tells the story of a brother and sister faced with various life choices over a twenty-year period. Henry Zimmer demonstrates how success is a matter of working intelligently rather than excessively. He shows how to set goals and priorities and suggests a step by step plan to achieve them. For young people—and anyone intimidated by the world of financial planning—The Wealthy Paper Carriers is easy to read and easy to understand. Written in collaboration with students and teachers, it is particularly recommended for educators.

Quantity_____   **$15.95**

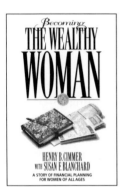

BECOMING THE WEALTHY WOMAN

A story of financial planning for women of all ages.

Destined to be a sure-fire best seller, this intriguing financial planning novel is aimed specifically at Canadian women of all ages and circumstances. Written with extensive input from women in various fields, Becoming The Wealthy Woman reviews the standing of women in our changing society, spotlights exciting opportunities, and suggests practical ways of setting goals and achieving personal success.

Quantity_____   **$15.95**

TOTAL NUMBER OF COPIES OF ALL BOOKS

Quantity_____ x $17.07 (GST Included) = $ _____

Name _____

Firm IF APPLICABLE _____

Title IF APPLICABLE _____

Address _____

City _____ Province _____ Postal Code _____

Telephone (   ) _____ Fax (   ) _____

Charge to VISA: CARD NO | | | | | – | | | | – | | | | – | | | |

Expiry Date | | | / | | |

Please mail or Fax your order to:

Springbank Publishing

5425 Elbow Drive S.W. Calgary, Alberta T2V 1H7
Fax: (403) 640-9138
Telephone (403) 640-9137 for information only

For bulk orders and to arrange Mr. Zimmer's speaking engagements, please contact: Susan Blanchard: (403) 242-9769
Fax: (403) 686-0889

Springbank Publishing–Responding to the Challenges of the Nineties!

BECOMING
THE WEALTHY WOMAN   Henry Cimmer & Susan Blanchard
A story of financial planning for women of different circumstances and ages.
ISBN 1-895653-11-8   **$15.95**

BUILD BRIDGES, NOT WALLS   Janet Andersen
A lighthearted book of advice, ideas and anecdotes for today's business person from Janet Andersen—selected from 23,000 employees as Air Canada's ideal service representative.
ISBN 1-895653-17-7   **$12.95**

HUSTLING FOR A BUCK   Dave Greber
A survival guide for the self-employed! Written by award-winning writer and instructor Dave Greber, Hustling for a Buck is a must-read for fledgling entrepreneurs and people contemplating self-employment.
ISBN 1-895653-18-5   **$15.95**

Springbank Publishing 'Bestsellers'!

THE WEALTHY PROCRASTINATOR   Henry B. Cimmer
A story of financial planning for those who thought it was too late! Aimed at Canadians over forty, Cimmer guides his heroes from mid-life chaos to a successful retirement over the period 1995 to 2015—anticipating the kind of political, social and economic restructuring that may occur in Canada.
ISBN 1-895653-08-8   **$15.95**

THE MONEY MANAGER FOR CANADIANS   Henry B. Cimmer
75,000 top Bestseller and companion to the Wealthy Series. Cimmer shows 'you don't need to be a mathematical genius to survive in today's uncertain economy'! It includes easy-to-use tables for calculating investment yields, costs of borrowing money and leasing, life insurance costs and benefits, current mortgage rates and terms and other financial arrangements.
ISBN 1-895653-10-X   **$15.95**

THE WEALTHY PAPER CARRIERS   Henry B. Cimmer
Shows young adults that they can more confidently determine their own futures! Ideal for young adults (12 to 25) and anyone intimidated by the world of financial planning.
ISBN 1-895653-09-6   **$15.95**

THE WEALTHY PAPER CARRIERS TEACHER RESOURCE GUIDE   Prepared by educators Drs. Sharon Gibb and Lynell Korella
*Created by teachers for teachers! "Students now believe they can actually have some control over their own futures" was the overwhelming response of teachers who piloted **The Wealthy Paper Carriers** in their classes.*
     $15.95

(Order Form on Next Page)

Order *Now* from Springbank

QTY		PRICE	TOTAL
_____	*BECOMING* THE WEALTHY WOMAN	$15.95	_____
_____	BUILD BRIDGES, NOT WALLS	$12.95	_____
_____	HUSTLING FOR A BUCK	$15.95	_____
_____	THE WEALTHY PROCRASTINATOR	$15.95	_____
_____	THE MONEY MANAGER FOR CANADIANS	$15.95	_____
_____	THE WEALTHY PAPER CARRIERS	$15.95	_____
_____	THE WEALTHY PAPER CARRIERS *TEACHER RESOURCE GUIDE*	$15.95	_____
	SUBTOTAL		_____
	7% GST		_____
	TOTAL		_____

Name

Firm IF APPLICABLE

Title IF APPLICABLE

Address

City   Province   Postal Code

Telephone (   )   Fax (   )

Charge to VISA: CARD NO | | | | | |–| | | | |–| | | | |–| | | |

Expiry Date | | | | / | | | |

Please mail or Fax your order to:
Springbank Publishing
5425 Elbow Drive S.W. Calgary, Alberta T2V 1H7
Fax: (403) 640-9138
Telephone (403) 640-9137 for information only

For bulk orders and to arrange Mr. Zimmer's speaking engagements, please contact: Susan Blanchard: (403) 242-9769
Fax: (403) 686-0889